The Life of
Lazarillo de Tormes

Also by Alfonso J. García Osuna

The Cuban Filmography: 1897 through 2001
(McFarland, 2003)

The Life of Lazarillo de Tormes

A Critical Edition Including the Original Spanish Text

Edited and Translated by
Alfonso J. García Osuna

McFarland & Company, Inc., Publishers
Jefferson, North Carolina, and London

Library of Congress Cataloguing-in-Publication Data

Lazarillo de Tormes. English
The life of Lazarillo de Tormes : a critical edition including the original Spanish text / edited and translated by Alfonso J. García Osuna.
p. cm.
Includes bibliographical references and index.

ISBN 0-7864-2134-7 (softcover : 50# alkaline paper) 

1. García Osuna, Alfonso J., 1953– II. Title.
PQ6408.E5 2005b
863'.3—dc22 2005010592

British Library cataloguing data are available

©2005 Alfonso J. García Osuna. All rights reserved

No part of this book may be reproduced or transmitted in any form or by any means, electronic or mechanical, including photocopying or recording, or by any information storage and retrieval system, without permission in writing from the publisher.

Cover art *Lazarillo de Tormes* by Janiel Corona.

Manufactured in the United States of America

McFarland & Company, Inc., Publishers
Box 611, Jefferson, North Carolina 28640
www.mcfarlandpub.com

Para Elvira y Xavier

Contents

Contents

La vida de Lazarillo de Tormes

Preface

Few things so deter students and researchers from achieving an accurate comprehension of classic masterpieces as translations into an English idiom that is not fresh and alive, an idiom by means of which the translator attempts, with artifices and long-forgotten phrases, to produce in the reader the feeling that he or she is being enlightened by a timeless, venerated text. Timelessness and veneration are subjective concepts of the translator's own making; if transferred to the text through his choice of words and style, they impose a vast and misleading value system on the text's original and unique syntax. A truer translation will show a feeling for the English language as it is spoken and written in the translator's own time.

Translation is never uncomplicated, and the *Lazarillo* is a case in point. In this short novel the reader often has the impression that this poor, uneducated, cuckolded town crier is "talking up," as it were, to the level of that enigmatic "Vuesa Merced" whom he is addressing, using a language that he feels appropriate for approaching a person of prominence and distinction. A language, in short, artificially inflated and not natural to a man with, as far as we know, very limited schooling. Capturing the essence of Lázaro's speech without introducing one's own artificial structures is a daunting task for the translator, as the protagonist himself may be using artifices that distort or adulterate the language.

My aim in translating the *Lazarillo de Tormes* has been to capture in modern English not only the meaning of this exceptional text, but also the breathing, genuine qualities of its style. I have purposely chosen to preserve as many as possible of the idiosyncrasies that portray Lázaro as he is: the word play, the short, open-ended sentences, the meandering associative order often contemptuous of logical connectives, the desolate expediency of the macabre scenes. I have smoothed over the irregular spots only when the claims of reasonable English usage seemed to prevail over those of rigorous conformity to the original text. In a word, I've attempted to express Lázaro as I suppose he would have expressed himself had he been speaking in English in our day.

The basic text of the *Lazarillo* followed here is that of Francisco Caso (*BRAE*, Anejo XVII, Madrid, 1967), the same one to which Alberto Blecua (Madrid: Castalia, 1972) adheres in his excellent edition. The earliest extant editions of the *Lazarillo de Tormes* are four, all from 1554 and it has been compellingly demonstrated that they are independent of each other.[1] In other words, it would be reasonable to suppose that none of the texts is the source of the other three. Perhaps because of the perplexity caused by its innovation, the novel had limited success in its time: to the four editions of 1554 (Alcalá de Henares, by Salcedo; Burgos, by Juan de Junta; Antwerp, by Martín Nuncio; and Medina del Campo, by Mateo and Francisco del Canto), we can add one in 1555 (Antwerp, by Guillermo Simón), one in 1573 (Madrid, by Pierres Cosin), one in 1587 (Milan, by Antoño de Antoni), two in 1597 (Antwerp, by the Oficina Plantiniana, and Bergamo, by Antoño de Antoni) and one in 1599 (Madrid, by Luis Sánchez). The Milan edition of 1587, having presented the novel as "almost forgotten and neglected by time," sold very poorly.[2] The novel's inclusion in the *Index of Prohibited Books* in 1559 may have significantly reduced its possibilities for editorial success, but the fact remains that between 1554 and its prohibition it did not do well by any stretch of the imagination.

This is not to say that the *Lazarillo* did not exert the considerable influence reserved for those few texts that give birth to a new genre. It certainly had notable readers and admirers, among whom the names of Miguel de Cervantes and Mateo Alemán stand out. Some of these admirers would write continuations to the *Lazarillo*, such as the enigmatic and anonymous one printed in Antwerp by Nuncio in 1555, which goes by the title *Segunda parte de la vida de Lazarillo de Tormes* (*Second Part of the Life of Lazarillo de Tormes*). This text offers transformations that remind one of Apuleius' *Golden Ass*; furthermore, it is obviously written in "code," as it were, a code that has to this day refused to yield its secrets to academic scrutiny. Another notable continuation (1620) is that of Juan de Luna, a Protestant Spaniard teaching in Paris. This work sports the same title as the 1555 continuation, and its author uses the genre's evident potential for social criticism to denounce the Inquisition and the Church. Juan de Cortés wrote his *Lazarillo de Manzanares* in Madrid this same year (1620), and several other texts, which bear little resemblance to the original *Lazarillo*, were published after this (*Lazarillo de Badalona*; *Vida y muerte del joven Lazarillo*; *Lazarillo de Duero* and others). Yet the *Lazarillo*'s ultimate contribution will be found not in its continuations, most of which are inadequate silhouettes of the original, but in its emulators, in novels like Mateo Alemán's *Guzmán de Alfarache* and Francisco de Quevedo's *Buscón*, and in the myriad tales and characters that populate the pages of books to our day, in Spain and well beyond its borders.

There remains the question of the *Lazarillo*'s author, one that has mystified generations of researchers and become a part of the novel's mythology. The first known attribution is made by the cleric José de Sigüenza in 1605. In a history of the Order of Saint Jerome, Sigüenza declares that the man who performed his priestly duties in the Order's Alba the Tormes (Salamanca) monastery and was "general" of the Order from 1552 to 1555, Juan de Ortega, wrote the *Lazarillo* as a student at the University of Salamanca. Sigüenza ostensibly supports his theory on the discovery, in Ortega's cell, of the *Lazarillo* manuscript written in his own hand. Ortega, he further explains, was very unconventional, loved literature, and was gifted with a quick wit and an intelligent sense of humor.[3] The weaknesses in Sigüenza's conjecture are apparent, for it was not unusual for priests, especially as young students, to copy books and keep those copies in their cells for future entertainment or reference. Moreover, the suggestion that the manuscript was in Ortega's own hand lends itself to further scrutiny.

The hypothesis that has shown the most resilience is that of Belgian bibliographer Valerio Andrés, who, in his 1607 compilation *Catalogus clarorum Hispaniae scriptorum* and without much foundation, contends that the diplomat and humanist don Diego Hurtado de Mendoza wrote the *Lazarillo*. This assertion is echoed by another Belgian, the Jesuit André Schott. In his 1608 work *Hispaniae Bibliotheca*, Schott argues that Hurtado de Mendoza wrote the *Lazarillo* during the time he spent as a law student in the University of Salamanca. When the novel was published, Hurtado de Mendoza had just finished his stint as governor of Spanish possessions in Italy (Siena) and ambassador to Rome and Venice. Such a solemn individual, it is argued, would not have wanted his name on this cheeky, feisty little text.

The Hurtado de Mendoza theory was deflated by French Hispanist Morel-Fatio in 1886,[4] but was taken up again by Ángel González Palencia and Eugenio Mele in 1946,[5] once more without conclusive substantiation. A new theory was the inspiration of Fonger de Haan,[6] who attributed the *Lazarillo* to Lope de Rueda based on the fact that in 1538 there was a town crier (Lázaro's last job) by that name in Toledo. He claims that this town crier was actually the young man who eventually became the playwright Lope de Rueda, and that the town crier episode in *Lazarillo* is told from personal experience. Also noted by de Haan was the fact that Lope de Rueda's short theatrical pieces (pasos and sainetes) in some ways resemble the *Lazarillo*'s short chapters. What de Haan doesn't explain is why Lope de Rueda did not put his name on the little novel.

Another theory came to light in 1914, when Julio Cejador believed he had proven conclusively that Toledan writer Sebastián de Orozco (also spelled Horozco) was the author of the *Lazarillo*. Cejador bases his hypothesis on the fact that some passages in Orozco's *Colección de varias noticias toledanas* have obvious parallels in the *Lazarillo*. He also finds similarities in Orozco's use of satire (in the poems of his *Cancionero*) and the *Lazarillo de Tormes*; the appearance of the character Lazarillo and his blind master in one of Orozco's short theatrical pieces in the same *Cancionero* reinforce Cejador's thesis. But the fact remains that the type of satire employed by Orozco and in the *Lazarillo* was common in sixteenth century Spain; moreover, the common passages can be attributed to the use of folk tales that were all too familiar to writers of the period. Cejador's contention that Orozco, being related to high authorities in the Church, did not find it expedient to acknowledge his creation, is a worn-out rationale applicable to half the writers in Spain.[7]

Alfred Morel-Fatio, for his part, was sure that the *Lazarillo* was written by an admirer of Dutch humanist Erasmus of Rotterdam. Hence he thought that the search for its author should focus on people like the Valdés brothers, especially Alfonso de Valdés, author of the *Diálogo de Mercurio y Carón.*[8] Marcel Bataillon rejects the Erasmian connection, arguing, with unassailable logic, that the *Lazarillo*'s roots are to be found in the medieval tradition of the *fabliaux* and the early Italian Renaissance. Nothing in the little novel is to be found outside the medieval tradition; from the anticlerical attitude to the string of mischievous misadventures, it is all traceable to the Middle Ages.[9]

Another noteworthy theory was advanced by Américo Castro, who saw in the *Lazarillo* the hand of a *converso*, a descendant of a Jew forced to convert to the Catholic faith. Castro hears in the pauper boy's voice the embittered and resentful cry of a people denied their faith, their traditions and their freedom.[10] If, as J. E. Gillet claims, the novel's lost first edition was printed in Antwerp in 1553, it is then very possible that the author was a Spaniard living in Flanders, perhaps in the very city of Antwerp. This would give credence to Castro's thesis, since commerce in that region was dominated by Spanish *conversos*. Yet as put forward, this hypothesis is based on Castro's unique interpretation of certain passages in the novel, and as such is extraordinarily assailable.[11]

The theory of a first Antwerp edition is supported by certain textual coincidences between the *Lazarillo* and the Flemish classic *Till Ulenspiegel.* Until fairly recently, scholars believed that the first edition of *Till Ulenspiegel* was a text printed in Germany in 1515, *Ein Kurzweilig Lesen von Dil Ulenspiegel.* In 1990, however, a part of an earlier edition (1510) was discovered, and since then many scholars have begun to identify Hermann Bote of Brunswick as the probable first compiler-author of the *Till Ulenspiegel* tales. The main character, Till Eulenspiegel or Ulenspiegel, was born at Kneitlingen in Brunswick at the end of the thirteenth or at the beginning of the fourteenth century. Folk tradition tells us he died near Lubeck in 1350. The jests and practical jokes ascribed to this son of a peasant were collected in 1483, according to information provided in an early printing. He was a poor yet witty country boy who loved to play pranks and tricks on the tradesmen and other townsfolk, most of all on the innkeepers, priests, noblemen, and even princes. His pranks are often brutal and obscene, but most of his jests are practical and his satire turns on class distinctions. Some students of the subject have described the *Till Ulenspiegel* as the retaliation of the peasant on the townsfolk who in the fourteenth and fifteenth centuries had begun to regard the country folk as dumb and inferior. Some of the *Ulenspiegel* misadventures have a parallel in the *Lazarillo*, and it may not be a coincidence, as Bataillon points out, that Jean Saugrain, Lyonese publisher of the French translation of *Till Ulenspiegel* in 1559, published the first French translation of the *Lazarillo* in 1560.[12]

Another proposed source for some of the Lazarillo exploits is the German *Liber Vagatorum* (*The Book of Vagabonds and Beggars*), first published shortly after 1509 in Pforzheim. Another early edition is one printed in Augsburg by Eghart Öglin (ca. 1512–1514.) By far the best known edition includes a preface by Martin Luther and was published in Wittenberg in 1528. The first English edition included Luther's preface and was published by Hotten in 1860. Besides the classification of beggars into twenty-eight different types, the *Liber Vagatorum* gives detailed information as to the tricks, jests and swindles used by beggars to separate the unsuspecting donor from his money and his wares, as well as a vocabulary (*rotwelsch*) of 107 slang words that beggars and vagabonds use to communicate with each other. Again, the *Lazarillo* offers some tantalizing parallels with the *Liber Vagatorum*, but the spirit of the Spanish novel is completely alien to the practical matters that concern the writer(s) of the *Liber*.

Whatever the source and whoever the author, it is clear that the original *Lazarillo* was altered in at least one edition — that of Alcalá in 1554, which includes some relatively long passages that are clearly not the work of the original author. Their incongruous style and content make them spectacularly out of place. For the benefit of the inquisitive, these passages are included in the present edition, but rendered in *italic type* for immediate recognition.

The foregoing comments on possible authors and sources are meant as a synopsis of the critical terrain negotiated by the Lazarillo in the hope that the interested reader will want to explore it. Perhaps this material is not essential for an understanding of the text, just as no selection of analytical opinions can do justice to this exceptional work. Regardless of its author or his original "purpose," the *Lazarillo* is a distinctive contribution ot the history of ideas in Spain, as well as a story the modern reader can enjoy.

Introduction: The Picaresque Novel *La vida de Lazarillo de Tormes*

Mid sixteenth-century Spain was awash in pastoral novels, romances of chivalry and sentimental novels. These productions set the action in faraway, exotic places during periods of time that were either not made clear or were very far removed from the realities of contemporary Spain. The one-dimensional heroes of these fictions bare no resemblance to normal human beings. They spent their time composing love songs to their beloved and unreachable damsels, surrounded by the most idyllic of forests and undisturbed by the lack of any basic necessity; they had marvelous adventures in remote places with nearly unpronounceable names, saving kingdoms from evildoers and marrying the grateful kings' daughters; they lived to love. These texts portrayed an idealized humanity into which the reader could insert himself and dream.

The author of the picaresque aims to throw some cold water on this self-indulgent exercise. His stylized version of daily life focuses on its most iniquitous aspects. In doing so, he places the picaresque text in competition with the pastoral and chivalrous texts by constructing a reverse mythology. But this mythology is more compelling than its competition because it gives the illusion of a strict adherence to reality.

The *Lazarillo's* anonymous author accomplishes this illusion through a number of strategies. His protagonist is a poor boy who has to fend for himself and find a way to survive; the time period in which the action is set is made obvious by a variety of hints; the geography through which the protagonist travels is central Spain (Salamanca, Escalona, Toledo), with well-known landmarks, such as the ancient stone bulls that grace the Salamanca countryside incorporated into the story. There is also an evident effort to portray a familiar environment that the reader will recognize: the bridge at Salamanca, the wines of Almorox, the neighborhoods of Toledo, the clothing, the money and the mores of different regions. All have a role in bringing the story to the reader's vicinity, underlying the text's more basic function of uncovering the false reality to which the sixteenth-century reader is accustomed. This approach to literary material gives the impression that the writer is familiar with the working side of a pulpit. In his little novel, indeed, he depicts the distressing yet constructive side of reality that is so frequent in clerical discourse, and he draws this portrayal from the stock of popular stories on which a cleric would rely for his homilies.

This "reality" should not be assumed to stand for 1554, the year of the first extant editions. Some of the historical events described in the book dispatch us to a former period, at least a quarter of a century earlier if one is to judge by the hints: the imprisonment of Francis I of France in Madrid after the Spanish victory at Pavía on February 24, 1525; the Courts of Toledo, held that same year; and the indication that Lázaro is eight years old when his father dies during the Gelves expedition (1510). The establishment of a time frame is important for the correct appreciation of the text's ideological tenets. The Spain of Lázaro (born in 1502) is a society that has refused to accept the new ideas (capitalism, mercantilism) that are flowing from northern Europe, a society that vilifies all who would better their lot by doing business (Jewish *conversos*) or by working with their hands (Moors from the eastern seaboard). Having derided these two groups, invalidating their principles and values, the Spain of the times must stand on hypothetical precepts that hinge upon the *hidalgo*, pure of blood, chaste and untainted by the "shameful" activities in which Jews, Moors and burgers engage to earn a living.

The confrontation between the two different interpretations of Spanish society—the traditional, Christian, closed model versus the capitalist, liberal, mercantile paradigm—comes to a head with the rebellion of the Castilian communities (the famed *comuneros*) against King Charles I in 1520. This rebellion has been touted as a Castilian uprising against the imperial project of Charles, who anticipated building his empire on the shoulders of Castile. It has also been asserted that the rebellion was directed against the foreign elements in Charles's court. The issue is more complex than that, and one important factor in this dynamic insurgence is the socio-economic one. It is no coincidence that the group fighting Charles was a conglomerate of artisans, merchants, small town bureaucrats, lesser nobles and the like, the burgeoning seed of what would have become the Castilian bourgeois class. They were fighting the iniquitous taxation system being put in place by Charles to finance his imperial designs—a system they knew would thwart any chance they had to achieve their economic objectives. If there had been any uncertainty about the king's intentions, the Cortes of Valladolid (2 February 1518), Santiago (31 March 1519) and La Coruña (19 May 1519) put an end to it. He needed money, lots of it, and he needed it now. These Cortes gave Charles 220 million maravedís to go to Germany and be crowned emperor as Charles V. As he departed Spain he left behind a climate of discontent that would explode as a generalized rebellion, beginning in Toledo and soon finding its way to Ávila, Burgos, Cuenca, Guadalajara, Salamanca, Segovia, Valladolid, Zamora and a host of smaller towns and villages, including some in Andalusia and Extremadura.

The fundamentally egalitarian nature of the rebellion has been amply proven, as the junta that the *comuneros* set up on 24 September 1520 in Tordesillas (Valladolid) called for equitable taxation of *everyone* in the kingdom, an idea that scandalized the nobles.[1] A level playing field where just about anyone could achieve economic and social prominence, without regard to lineage, must have seemed outrageous to many at the time. It was only to be expected that a coalition of the outraged would make use of their resources to help Charles I (now Emperor Charles V) destroy the rebellion. The decisive blow to the *comunero* uprising was struck on 23 April 1521 at the Battle of Villalar, where imperial troops led by the Count of Haro annihilated the rebels, capturing and decapitating the leaders Juan Bravo, Juan de Padilla and Francisco Maldonado.

At the end of that day in 1521, the Spain of the traders, merchants, bankers, artisans, burgers and laborers lay smashed amid the blood and mud of Villalar, while the Spain of the *hidalgo*, scornful of all of its enemies' values and ideals, paraded triumphantly with its archaic ideals and obsolete interpretations of dignity and honor. In this Spain the individual's lineage determines his worth; when this lineage is typified as a negation of the values embodied by the defeated at Villalar, we are left in a sorry state of affairs indeed, one where a person of worth, the paradigm for the national character, does not trade, does not work, does not sell, does not engage in lending, does not do the things needed to place the nation in step with those who eventually will become its rivals for world dominance.

The choice of characters and the backdrop for the *Lazarillo de Tormes* focus the readers' gaze upon the heart of the particular national dilemma as understood by forward-looking Spaniards after the events of the 1520s. Perhaps fueled by the economic stagnation these events caused, what would arguably become the world's leading military power had more than its share of social difficulties. Legions of poor and orphaned children, much like Lázaro, walked the streets looking for masters to serve or for a bit of bread to eat — and constantly got into trouble in the process. The punishments practiced upon little Lázaro, excessive and cruel to modern sensibilities, were not only common, but also encoded in contemporary law (Blecua: 1972, p. 17) — a fact that suggests the pervasiveness of the child problem. An adult Lázaro winds up as town crier in Toledo, a job that in real life was often filled by some of the legion of unsavory characters that roamed the region. Because there were not enough prisons to accommodate convicted law-breakers, men convicted of crimes frequently ended up in the galleys or as field auxiliaries in the army, like Lázaro's father. Blind men had governmental dispensations not given to other individuals, and were allowed to roam the country saying special prayers for a fee, much like

Lazarillo's first master. They had no other recourse. And, of course, the *hidalgo*, too proud to work but too poor to feed himself, is a master representation of the basic ailment of the nation. All the other characters that inhabit the novel's pages seem to come straight from the streets and byways of post–1520s Spain, including the priests with their well-documented lapses and dissipations.

That said, it would be a mistake to see in this picaresque novel an early attempt at realism. The author has not been walking the streets with pad and pencil in hand observing the people and their high jinks. It has been well established (Bataillon: 1968, pp. 27–46) that most stories and characters in the *Lazarillo* have their origins in folk tales; that is to say, the author uses contemporary reality as a frame on which to build what is, essentially, a text made of other texts. From the outset, then, we enter a world of literature, one made of received traditions, an anthology of anguish that is brought to life by the painfully plausible, contemporary context and the first-person narrative authority of the protagonist. Real picaresque individuals walking the roads of Spain do not totally explain Lázaro's genesis: The boy is a fabricated creature who transcends the physical realities of the writer's milieu, a Golem moving in step with the necessities of a new fictional aesthetic.

This all poses the question: What is the purpose and nature of this novelty? Many answers have been proposed, from an early interpretation of the novel as social criticism, to the opinion that the pícaro is a medium through which the reader can view society, to the interpretation of the picaresque as the textual photography of the "new man," the pícaro, come to life in sixteenth-century Spain, and everything in between. There are no clear answers. It seems evident that as a new genre, the picaresque, with *Lazarillo* at its forefront, employs the dominant fictional aesthetic of pastoral, chivalric and sentimental narratives as a reference point, and even while rejecting that aesthetic, still interacts with it in a way that sets picaresque discourse in competition with it. Picaresque fiction, for all its novelty, still attempts the conquest of the general geography occupied by the dominant forms, the colonization of a familiar terrain through characters from folk tales who had never before tread on that landscape. The general view of

Lázaro as an *antihero*, the novel as a sort of romance of chivalry turned upside down, suggests that the *Lazarillo* retains just enough of its competitor's features to be recognized as the irrepressible relative of the dominant discourse it aspires to replace.

In many ways, then, *Lazarillo de Tormes'* intelligibility hinges on the reader's awareness of competing claims on its general aesthetic topography. In this scenario, the novel's innovativeness has an apparent aesthetic genesis to which other considerations (social, moral, etc.) come second. But why does the innovation take *this* precise form and not another?

A close look at the protagonist might bring the issue further into focus. Lázaro is not an immoral individual; he is a pragmatic, intelligent survivor whose survival strategies insistently undermine the notion of morality offered by the competing discourse, destroying its claim to authenticity by the sheer semblance of truth that his plight projects. These strategies, in fact, constitute an aesthetic mechanism whereby the innovative critical discourse initiated by Lázaro lays down the new rules for this aesthetic contest: Viewed in the light of Lázaro's anguish, the competing discourse's moral code will seem like a bogus artifact lacking in human sensibility. At a time when literature was still ostensibly viewed as a vehicle for moral edification, the results of this strategy should have been devastating. Lázaro lies and steals to survive and, obviously, because everybody else does. The fact that he has to adapt painfully to these social behaviors is a sign of his natural virtue: He learns and conforms to his environment. Thus, unlike a knight errant or a pastoral lover, Lázaro does not create or change the moral environment in which he acts. Instead, the prevailing moral environment changes him; it creates him as a pícaro, molding his actions and giving them their particular complexion.

So it is that to the writer of an innovative fictional discourse, the competing, previous discourse becomes an institution whose coercive, constrictive forces must be negated in order to keep it from prolonging its dominance. It comes as no surprise, then, that the *Lazarillo* will invert the values and moral codes it has encountered in its competitor as the most viable method to achieve aesthetic supremacy. (For a groundbreaking and incisive study of competition among aesthetic discourses, see Gustavo Pérez Firmat's *Idle Fictions*, Durham, N.C.: Duke Univ. Press, 1982, espec. pages 3–38.) Consequently, what is a rebel-protagonist in the competing—and invalidated—discourse becomes an utter conformist in this novel, living out his life in the best manner available to him, as the cuckolded husband of a priest's concubine.

It is important to note that, in keeping with its objective of replacing the competing discourse and occupying its space, the *Lazarillo* adheres to what Father Sigüenza (1909, p. 45) conceptualizes as "propiedad y decoro"; that is to say, it does not considerably alter the rhetorical paradigm, an opinion largely shared by Bataillon (*Novedad y fecundidad del Lazarillo de tormes*. Salamanca: Anaya, 1968, pp. 63–65). The pícaro's discourse is structured upon a foundation of anecdotes, proverbs, popular beliefs, folk tales and the like, but properly assembled by the protagonist, an able rhetorician. The author thus erects for us a cosmos of deformity, of falsity and masquerade in which most characters participate and where truth and falsehood come together and interact in a most fecund manner within the "propiedad y decoro" model.

Nevertheless, it would be futile to deny the novel's social implications. Faced with his chosen context—contemporary Spain—the author had to assume a perspective; the fact that the result of his choice is the *Lazarillo de Tormes* indicates a certain predisposition to build his discourse in a socially relevant manner for which the existing literary and moral archetypes were unsuitable. It may be true that the context chosen by the author begins by serving a strictly bookish purpose, that it is a fundamental component in his aesthetic endeavor to prevail against the paradigm, but the fact that this context is pushed beyond its primarily functional purpose is evidenced by the author's resolute effort to generate a competing moral code to stand in opposition to that offered in the rival model. The image of Lázaro silently and anonymously feeding his master the "escudero"—while this same escudero strives to keep up appearances of wealth and power—speaks volumes in this regard. Lázaro, as an individual dissociated from the unsound conceptions of honor and ethical behavior that have become prevalent in his society, sheds rational light upon the absurd existence of those around him. The pícaro as a true-to-life individual and the Spanish concept of honor as social scourge carry with them the true meaning of the *Lazarillo*: the individual's confrontation with the insincerity and pretense of a decadent and degenerate society. To a Spaniard of the period, his final defeat comes across as one man's own personal Villalar.

The pícaro, subjugated and absorbed by a debauched social environment, tells his tale to a mysterious "Vuesa Merced" who never appears in the story. This puzzling interlocutor loses some of his mystery when we begin to study the way in which Lázaro addresses him. From the manner of speech, outline and structure of the pícaro's address to him, we can surmise that he is a consumer of chivalry romances, and that Lázaro wants to speak to him in his own language to make the story of his life intelligible to this unconcealed alternate for the reader. But he turns the basic premises of that language around to make the account of his life authentic and his anguish genuine. Conquered and overcome by society, the pícaro will be defeated only at the superficial, textual level; in the subtext, his great victory is that, in the end, he has told his story.

At work here too is a victory at the human level. Lázaro, in a way, represents an acceptance of the human condition. In a society of absolute values, absorbed in a psychosomatic topography of absolute good versus absolute evil devoid of gray areas, there is in the novel a reminder that this is a very heavy cross to bear. Lázaro is neither an ogre nor an angel, but a human being. There are some in sixteenth-century Spain who have certainly achieved sanctity, but they are atypical and extraordinary individuals, what is left for the rest of the human conglomerate is an everyday existence in which we strive to better our lot. It is rash to pretend to be a perfect representation of the social paradigm, as this venture usually corrupts people and propels them into a state of insincere pretentiousness, thrusting their daily existence into an underground world of unmentionable conduct. As the *hidalgo* "escudero" illustrates, it is just about impossible for us to will ourselves different from what we naturally are; Spain's collective unconscious makes people believe in the virtue of standards that none can live up to.

The lesson Lázaro teaches is that wisdom, righteousness and happiness depend on our behaving toward ourselves not with contempt and disapproval, but with a certain measure of fairness and compassion. Only if we accept the destiny fashioned by our limitations without bitterness can we recognize the privilege and dignity of being human. To do so, Lázaro reminds us, is the utmost accomplishment of human wisdom.

The Life of Lazarillo de Tormes

Prologue

I hold that admirable matters, such as have never before been seen nor heard, should by all measure be brought to the attention of the many, thus preventing them from being buried in the crypt of oblivion.[1] For it could be that some who read about them may well find something to their liking in them, while others that might not delve deeply into them could derive some pleasure from their endeavor. To this purpose Pliny maintains that there is no book so dreadful that it doesn't contain some benefit.[2] Considering that preferences vary, that what one man won't eat is another man's delicacy,[3] it shouldn't surprise us to see that what some disdain, others do not. And so it is that no thing should be broken and cast away — unless it be detestable — but communicated to all, especially if it isn't hurtful but rather able to yield profit. Were it otherwise, few would take pen in hand to write for only one person, for it is an arduous endeavor for which recompense is expected, not monetary, but with the celebrity stemming from having one's works seen and read, and, if there be cause, praised. To this end Tully writes: "Honor spawns the arts."[4]

Who would presume that the soldier who first scales the enemy wall is weary of life? Certainly, he is not; it is only the desire for praise that drives him to put his life in danger. And so it is in the arts and in literature. The theologian might preach very well, and he might be looking conscientiously after the souls of his flock, but just ask him if he finds it objectionable when they praise him: "Oh how wonderfully has Your Worship done it!" "Master so-and-so jousted very dastardly, yet he gave his undercoat to some fool just because he praised the way in which he handled his lances: what would he have given him if it had been true?"

This is how it is: I, confessing to be no holier than my neighbors, am satisfied that such as find any delight in this, my uncouth style, may see that a man lives who has endured so many perils, hazards and adversities.

I hence beseech Your Worship to receive this modest token from the hand of one who would make you richer if his power were the equal of his will. And therefore, being that Your Worship writes me commanding me to record and relate the case very extensively, I thought it prudent to begin not in the middle, but at the beginning, so that all may have full knowledge of my person, and so that all may consider how little praise is due to those who inherited great estates, for Fortune was generous to them; they may also consider how much commendation is deserved by those who, challenged by an adverse fate, with strength and ingenuity managed to row to a safe harbor.

Chapter One
Lázaro Relates His Life and Reports on His Parentage.

Know, Your Worship, before anything else, that they call me Lázaro de Tormes, son of Tomé Gonzales and Antona Pérez, natives of Tejares, a village of Salamanca. My birth was in the Tormes River, which is why I took the surname, and it happened thus: my father, may God forgive him, was in charge of supplying a water mill[5] at riverside, where he had been a miller for over fifteen years; being at the mill one night, my pregnant mother was surprised by her pains and gave birth to me then and there. I am thereby rightly entitled to say that I was born in the river.

I was a boy of eight when my father was accused of improperly bleeding his customers' grain sacks. For this he was imprisoned, and he confessed, and denied not, but suffered for justice.[6] May God have him in His Glory, for the Gospels call them blessed.[7] At this time an army was sent against the Moors, among whose combatants was my father, who at this juncture had been cast out by reason of the tragedy already mentioned. His task was to be mule-handler to a knight on that expedition; and this master, like a faithful servant, he followed to the grave.

My widowed mother, upon seeing herself without husband and destitute, decided to draw near the virtuous, she being one of them, and came to live in the city. Renting a little house, she began cooking for some students and doing the wash for certain grooms that worked in the Knight Commander de la Magdalena's stables.[8] This is how she began to frequent the stables, and how she and a black man, one of those that tended the beasts, came to know each other. At times he would come to our house and not leave until the next morning; other days he'd come to our door under the pretense of buying eggs from us, and he'd come into the house. I, at first, was not in favor of his access to our dwelling and was scared, seeing his color and repulsive countenance; but as soon as I saw that with his coming our meals improved, I began to love him, for he always brought bread, pieces of meat, and in winter gave us firewood with which to warm ourselves.

It was thus that, with the ongoing hospitality and association, my mother came to give me a very pretty little black boy with whom I played and whom I helped to warm in cold weather. I remember my black stepfather playing with the child, who, upon seeing that my mother and I were white and his father was not, would shriek: "Oh, mother, an ugly beast!" to which he'd reply: "you son of a whore."

Young as I was, my little brother's reaction made me consider: "How many people in the world shun others because they don't see themselves reflected in them!"[9]

As fate would have it, my mother and Zaide's (that was his name) correspondence was brought to the attention of the stable master, who initiated an investigation into the matter. The inquiry resulted in the discovery that my stepfather was stealing a full half of the barley that was intended for the beasts, as well as bran, wood, leather, currycombs and horse blankets. As if this were not enough, he would also unshoe the horses; the profits from all of these takings would be delivered to my mother for my little brother's maintenance.[10] Seeing how clerics steal from the poor and friars steal from the convent to give to their female admirers, it shouldn't outrage us that a poor slave should steal for love.

Everything I say was proved against him, and even more, for under the threat of punishment I told everything I knew, including the business of some horseshoes that my mother had sent me to sell to a blacksmith.

My poor stepfather was whipped and had boiling bacon grease poured over the open wounds. My mother was found guilty and received the customary one hundred lashes; she was also prohibited from entering the Knight Commander's house and from allowing the wounded Zaide into hers.

Resolving to make the best out of a bad situation, my sad mother made the effort and complied. And in order to avoid further dangers and not give the gossips further cause for their chatter, she went to serve people who presently live at the Solana Inn[11]; there, shouldering a thousand burdens, she managed to bring up my little brother until he could walk, and me until I became a young man, running errands for the guests, bringing them wine, candles, and anything else they needed.

At this time a blind man happened to pass by the inn; judging me fit to guide him, he asked my mother for me, and she gave me to him, telling him that I was the son of an honest man who died during the Gelves campaign[12] in the defense of the faith. Adding that she hoped by the grace of God I would not turn out any worse a man than my father, she begged he treat me well and watch after me, as I was an orphan. He responded that he would do as she requested and more, for he would take me not as his servant, but as his son. And this is how I began to serve and guide my new, old master.

We spent a few days in Salamanca, but seeing as my master felt that business was not as good as he'd like, he decided to leave. Before departing, I went to visit my mother. As we both cried, she blessed me and said: "Son, I know that I shall never see you again. Strive to be good and may God guide you; I've brought you up and given you a good master. Fend for yourself now."

Then I went to my master, who was waiting for me.

We left Salamanca and arrived at the bridge; there is a stone animal shaped more or less like a bull there, and the blind man asked me to approach it. Once I had complied, he told me: "Lázaro, put your ear next to this bull and you will hear a great noise within it."

I simply approached, believing this to be true, and as soon as he thought my head was next to the stone, he stiffened his hand and gave such a blow that the ensuing headache lasted over three days. He then told me: "You fool. This should teach you that a blind man's servant must always stay one step ahead of the devil himself."

The incident proved good sport to him, and he laughed heartily.

It seemed to me that at that moment I awakened from the simplicity in which, like a child, I was dormant. And I said to myself: "This man is right. I must get my wits about me and keep my eyes open, for I am alone in the world, and I must fend for myself."

We took to the road, and in a few days he taught me the particular language in which blind men of his trade communicate with each other. When he saw my proficiency in this subject, he was very pleased and said: "I can give you neither gold nor silver,[13] but I will supply you with devices that will help you survive." And so it was that, after God, it was this man who gave me life, and being blind, enlightened me and taught me the art of living.[14]

I take the time to recount these trivialities to Your Worship in order to show how much virtue resides in those who, though having been low-born, manage to rise, and how much vice attends those of high birth who degenerate from their quality.

But returning to my good blind man, Your Worship should know that since God created the world there has never been a more cunning or astute fellow. In his trade he was peerless: he knew and recited over a hundred prayers by heart, using a low, calm, grave voice that resonated in any church where he prayed. With a visage of humility and piety, he would pray without the staged grimaces incident to others of his profession. Besides this, he had a thousand other means to extract money from his clients. He pretended to have special prayers to induce many and diverse outcomes: for barren women,[15] for those about to give birth and for unhappily married wives so that their husbands would love them. He moreover foretold the gender of their future children to women who were with child. In medicine, he'd maintain that Galen didn't know half of what he knew in the matter of curing toothaches, fits and feminine illness. Finally, when someone complained to him of some pain, he'd immediately prescribe: "Do this, do that, boil such and such an herb, take this root." By these methods he drew a multitude of followers, especially women, who believed everything he told them. It was from women that he derived the greatest profit, and by the use of these artifices he alone attained better revenue in a month than a hundred blind men in a year.[16]

But I'd also like Your Worship to know that, in spite of all the profits generated by his endeavors, I never saw a greedier nor a more miserly man, so much so that he was killing me with hunger, not allowing me even a half of the necessary sustenance for me to keep body and soul together. I tell the truth: if it weren't for my wits and craft, I wouldn't be around to tell the story, for many times I should have died of hunger. But notwithstanding all of his knowledge and vigilance, I fooled him to such an extent that always, or most of the time, I came away with the most and best of the take. To accomplish this I duped him hellishly; some of these hoodwinkings I shall relate, although I did not come away unscathed from them all.

He'd bring bread and everything else in a canvas sack whose opening would be closed with an iron ring, lock and key. When adding or extracting anything from this sack, he'd do it with such vigilance and assessment that there isn't a man born who could wrest a crumb from its contents. I would take the pittance he gave me, which, all accounted for, didn't add up to two mouthfuls. After he closed the lock and became unwary, thinking that I was engaged in some other endeavor, I'd undo some loose stitches at the side of the avaricious sack, partake of its contents, and sew the evanescent opening; from it I acquired not just good chunks of bread, but sweetmeats and sausage. Thus I found a convenient way to return, not the ball,[17] but the infernal misery with which the pernicious blind man grieved me.

For the money that I could swindle and fleece out of him I had a scheme that worked like a charm: the moment a customer reached to pay him for a special prayer I, intercepting the coin, feigned giving it a kiss. I then instantly swapped it for another coin, worth half as much, which I had stashed in my mouth. Being blind, he never perceived that the currency that eventually reached his outstretched hand was devalued by half. The wicked blind man would complain, for upon touching the coin he would recognize its insignificant worth. At that point he'd say: "What the hell is the matter, that after you've joined me they only pay me with half-pences, when formerly I never got less than a full pence or a double? You must be the source of this misfortune!"

He also cut his prayers short, reducing them by half their length, for he had commanded me to pull on his cape as soon as the customer had left. Once I had done so, he'd stop praying and would begin attracting new clients by shouting "Prayers here, who needs such and such a prayer?" as they say.

He used to keep a small jar of wine next to him when we ate. Well I'd quickly grab this jar and quietly take a couple of sips before putting it back. This didn't last long, for he quickly found his draught shortened, and in order to safeguard it, he never again let it out of his hand, never letting go of the handle. Yet no magnet in the world attracted with such lure as I drew on the wine with a long reed that I had prepared for the occasion. This reed I'd introduce through the mouth of the jar and, sucking on the wine, would leave my master in the dark as to the whereabouts of the liquid. The traitor being so cunning—perhaps after hearing me suck—he changed his strategy and began placing the jar between his legs while covering its mouth with his hand. Thus, he'd drink to his heart's delight. I was already fond of wine; in fact I was dying for it, and seeing as the reed ploy was no longer viable, I decided to make a small hole in the bottom of the jar which I would delicately cover up with a dab of wax. At dinner time I'd insert myself between the sad blind man's legs, feigning cold and a desire to warm myself next to the poor fire that we could muster. In the heat of this fire the wax would start to melt, as it was only a small dab, and a little fountain would begin to distill the precious liquid into my mouth. This I accomplished with such finesse that not a drop escaped my desire. When the poor sod attempted to drink, he found that there was nothing left; horrified, he cursed himself and conveyed jar and wine to the devil, not knowing what to make of it. "You can't say, uncle, that I drink it — I'd say — for you never take your hand from it."

He put the jar through so many turns and tactile investigations that eventually he found the fountain and discovered the deception. But he acted as if he hadn't uncloaked the mystery. The next day, looking forward to the fine distillations and not foreseeing the injury that was in store for me nor the malicious blind man's designs, I sat as usual. Receiving the sweet liquor, my face towards heaven, eyes half closed to better delight in the exquisite fluid, I didn't discern that the desperate blind man was preparing his vengeance. Using all his strength, raising that sweet and bitter jar, he let it drop on my mouth, helping it on its way to its target, as I said, with all the strength of his arms. Thus it was that poor Lázaro, unaware of the lurking danger, careless and blithe as usual, felt what seemed to be heaven and all that it contains drop on his head.

Such was the little whack that I fainted and blacked out, bits and pieces of the jar lodging in my face and cutting it in many places. It furthermore smashed my teeth, without which I remain to this day. From that time forward I hated the bad blind man, and although he loved me and gave me things and took care of me, he proved excessive in the application of this cruel punishment. Washing my injuries with wine, he said smiling: "What do you say, Lázaro? That which injured you now cures and restores you to health."[18]

And added other delightful witticisms that I found quite distasteful.

When I had almost recovered from the clobbering, and considering that a couple more like that and the cruel blind man would do away with me, I resolved to be rid of him, but at a time and place of my own choosing. And although I may have wished to appease my heart and forgive the jarring blow, I found it impossible because of the ill treatment with which the wicked blind man subsequently handled me. He rained blows on me without rhyme or reason, knocking on my head and pulling my hair at a whim. If anyone asked him why the ill treatment, he'd answer with the story of the wine jar, saying: "Do you think that this servant of mine is some innocent? Well tell me if the devil himself could come up with such an exploit."

Those who heard him made the Sign of the Cross and said: "Look at that! Who'd think that such a young boy could be capable of such wickedness!" And they'd find much mirth in the account of my deeds, adding: "Punish him, punish him, for God will reward you!" He, after such recommendations, never ceased to do so.

Because of this, I always and purposely led him through the worst trails in order to cause him harm. If there were stones, there we'd go, if mud, through the deepest part of it.[19] Although I wasn't on dry ground myself, I would gladly forfeit an eye to take two from he who had none himself.[20] For this he was always hitting me in the head with the handle end of his cane, so that I was never without my share of lumps and bald spots from his ill usage of me. I swore that I took those paths not with malice, but because I was searching for the best route, but he didn't trust or believe me, such was the slyness and great shrewdness of the traitor.

And so that Your Worship understand the great resourcefulness of this astute blind man, I'll tell you one of the many incidents that I endured with him. This way you will get a true idea of his great shrewdness. When we left Salamanca, his reason was to come to this land of Toledo, where he said people were wealthier though not very generous.[21] He firmly believed the saying "The rich miser gives more than the charitable beggar." So we made our way here through the best places: where he found good reception and profit, we stayed, where he did not, on the third day we picked up and left.[22]

It so happened that we arrived at a place they call Almorox[23] during the vintage, and a harvester gave him a bunch by way of alms. Since the grapes were bruised in the basket and by that time they were also very ripe, they fell from the bunch in his hand. Putting the grapes in his sack would have been a mistake, so he resolved to have a banquet, not only because the grapes could not travel, but to show me a little kindness on a day spent kneeing me and regaling me with miscellaneous blows. When we sat on a fence, he said: "Now I'll be generous with you. Let us partake of this bunch of grapes, and I want you to have as many as me. We'll share them in this manner: you take one, and I'll take another, but you must promise not to take more than one at a time. I'll do the same until we finish them; this way there will be no tricks."

Having agreed on the terms, we began, but on the second turn the traitor bent the rules and began taking two at a time, thinking that I was doing the same. Seeing how he disregarded the agreement, I wasn't content merely to keep up with him, so I took not only by twos, but by threes as the situation allowed. Having finished the bunch, he held the stalk in his hand, and shaking his head stated: "Lázaro, you have cheated me. I'll swear to God that you have taken three at a time." "I didn't — said I —, but why do you suspect such a thing?" The insidious blind man answered: "Do you want to know how I found that you were eating three at a time? Because I was eating two and you remained silent."

To this I did not respond.[24]

Walking another day under some buttresses in Escalona,[25] where we were at the time, we happened upon the house of a shoemaker, outside of which there hung all sorts of ropes and other artifacts made of esparto. Some of these touched my master on the head as we strolled by; he, raising his hand and touching them, said to me: "Step lively, boy, let's withdraw from this place of dangerous foods, that choke you even if you don't eat them."

I was not paying much attention to him, but I looked up to see what he was going on about. Seeing only ropes and belts, none of which were edible, I said to him: "Uncle,[26] why do you say that?" To which he responded: "Quiet, nephew. From what I've seen of your ways, you'll find out soon enough, and you'll discover that what I say is true."

And thus we passed by the portal and arrived at an inn. Next to its door there were several horns protruding from a wall for mule drivers to tie up their beasts. As he felt around the horns to determine if that was the same inn where each day he prayed a certain prayer of the Emparedada for the lady innkeeper, he grabbed a horn and with a great sigh declared: "Oh, you evil thing, more terrible than your menacing countenance proclaims! How many aspire to place you on their neighbor's head, and how few are those who would welcome you on their own, even trembling at the news of your approach!"

As I was listening to what he was saying, I asked him: "Uncle, what is this that you're saying?" "Quiet, nephew; some day this I hold in my hand will give you a dire method of earning your vittles."[27] *"I won't eat from that plate—said I—nor will fill my saucer."*

"I speak the truth, and you will see it come to pass, if you live."

And thus we proceeded to the door of the inn, one I wish to God we'd never crossed, seeing what happened to me inside.

He was constantly saying prayers for women innkeepers, storekeepers, bakers, whores and other such bad women, for I never saw him say a prayer for a man.[28]

I laughed at all this, and though just a boy, I couldn't help but discern the discreet considerations of the blind man. But in order to be brief, I'll forego informing you of many a funny and remarkable event that came to pass while I was in the company of this, my first master. I'll relate the last one, and with that, I'll finish. We were at an inn in Escalona, a village that belongs to its duke,[29] and he gave me a piece of sausage to roast. When the sausage swelled and began to ooze, my master started savoring the drippings with a piece of bread. He then gave me a coin and told me to get some wine at the tavern. But the devil put the opportunity in front of my eyes, and since, as they say, opportunity makes the thief, I chanced to spy a longish, measly little turnip abandoned by the fire, unworthy, I suppose, for the stew.

Seeing as he and I were alone at the moment, as I was getting hungry due to the aromatic wafts surging from the pleasant morsel, and knowing that these wafts would be my only enjoyment of it, I decided to act. Not considering the consequences and subordinating my fear to my desire, as the blind man took his money from his purse I purloined the sausage and put the turnip in its place on the skewer. After handing me the money for wine, he began to turn the skewer, trying to cook that which, because of its demerits, had escaped the pot.

I went for the wine, with the help of which I didn't take much time to do away with the sausage. When I returned I found the blind sinner squeezing the turnip between two slices of bread, not knowing the true contents of his buffet as he had not felt it with his hands. Once he took a bite of the collation, the cold turnip coldly astonished him. He became altered and said: "What is this, Lazarillo?"

"Woe is me — I said —, now you want to accuse me of something? Am I not just returned from fetching wine? Someone must have come by and played a joke on you."

"No, no — said he —, I haven't let go of the skewer. It's not possible."

I again swore and affirmed that I had nothing to do with the replacement and substitution, but it was for naught, for the astute blind man wasn't having any of it. Getting up from his seat, he grabbed me by the head and approached to smell me. Like an anxious hound, he must have sniffed the remnants of the morsel in my breath, but in order to be sure, he clutched my face and opened my mouth wide, putting his long, pointed nose deep into it. His great obsession must have elongated his nose, for with it he managed to reach my epiglottis.

The great fear with which I was seized; the little time to assimilate the black sausage; the long nose choking me; all these factors combined and caused the fact and the morsel to manifest themselves and prompted the assets to return to their rightful proprietor. Thus it was that before the bad blind man took his nose out of my mouth, the alteration in my stomach made restitution of the stolen goods unto it,[30] in such a way that his nose and the ill-digested sausage exited my mouth at one and the same time.

Oh, Dear God! What I would have given to be buried under ground at that moment, for I was as good as dead. The perverse blind man's anger reached such a point that if people hadn't come to see what the racket was all about, he certainly would have ended my life then and there. They tore me from his hands, which were full of my hair — the little that remained from our past skirmishes —; my face was scratched and my neck and throat were clawed. And well did my throat deserve this treatment, for only on account of its excesses was I suffering such treatment.[31]

The evil blind man would tell everyone about my tragedy, and related the stories time and again: the jar debacle, the incident with the grapes, and now this latest calamity. The hilarity was such that people passing by the door would come in to join in the festivity; he recounted the story of my notorious exploits with such wit and levity, that, bruised and crying as I was, I thought I'd do him wrong if I didn't laugh as heartily as the rest.

While all this was going on, it suddenly came to me that I had been cowardly and craven. I cursed myself: having been given a fair opportunity, I should have bitten his nose off. I'd had the chance, the road was halfway traveled already; if I'd just squeezed my teeth together, it would have come off. Being that it belonged to the treacherous blind man, I'm sure my stomach would have done a better job of retaining it than it did for the sausage. There being no body of evidence, I could have denied all accusations. I wish to God I had done it, for it would have made no difference in the way I was treated.

The lady innkeeper and those present had us make up, and my face and throat were washed with the wine I had procured earlier. Upon this cure and remedy the evil blind man dissertated and exercised his wit: "In truth I must say this: that young rascal costs me more in wine for washings, in one year, than I drink in two. You are certainly more obliged to the vine, Lázaro, than to your own father, for he engendered you once, whereas wine has given you life a thousand times over."[32]

He then spoke about the many times he clobbered and ripped my face, and how I had been cured with wine. "I'll tell you — he continued — if there's a man in this world that will be blessed by wine, that man is you."

Though I was cursing, those who were washing me laughed riotously. But the blind man's prophecy would prove correct, for from that time to now I've had occasion to remember him, as without a doubt he possessed a prophetic spirit. I'm sorry for the tribulations I caused him, although I was only paying him back. What he told me that day came true just like he said, as Your Worship will hear shortly.

Because of the ill usage I received and the dirty tricks the blind man played on me, I decided to leave him. I had thought about it for a while and set my mind to it; this last caper of his only strengthened my resolve. It happened thus: the following day we went into town to beg, it having rained quite a bit the night before. It was still raining as he prayed, keeping dry under some arcades there. We observed that nightfall approached and the rain wasn't letting up, so the blind man told me: "Lázaro, this rain is not likely to stop anytime soon, and the later it gets the harder it comes down. Let's seek shelter at the inn before it's too late."

In order to get there, we had to cross a stream that had grown considerably with all the rain. I told him: "Uncle, the stream is very wide, but if you wish, I see a spot where we can cross it without getting wet. It is very narrow at that spot, so that with one leap we can reach the other side with dry feet."

He thought this was good advice and said: "You are discreet, that is why I'm so fond of you. Take me to that place where the stream narrows, for this is winter and water can be dangerous, especially when your feet are wet."

Seeing my dream come true, I took him from under the arcade and led him to a pillar or stone column that was in the square, one of the supports for the covered passage's overhanging arches. I told him: "Uncle, this is the narrowest place in the stream."

It was raining hard and the wretch was getting wet. With the urgency we felt to get out of the downpour that was drenching us, and what's most important, because of the fact that God blinded his judgment at that precise moment (to grant me my vengeance),[33] he trusted me and said: "Point me in the right direction, and then you go over first."

I set him precisely in front of the pillar, jumped and placed myself behind it, and looking at him as one looks upon a mad, charging bull, I said to him: "Now jump as far as you can so that you may reach this side of the water."

I had barely finished telling him this when like a goat the blind man charged with all his strength, having taken a step back to gather more speed. His head came with such a vengeance against the pillar that it sounded like a hollow pumpkin had hit it. He then fell over backwards, half dead and with a great indentation on his skull. "What, you smelled the sausage and not the pillar? Smell! Smell!" said I.

I left him in the care of the many people who had come to help him, took the road out of the village at a brisk pace, and before nightfall I reached Torrijos.[34] I never knew what became of him, nor did I ever make an effort to find out.

Chapter Two

How Lázaro Came to Serve a Priest, and What Came to Pass While in His Service.

The next day, not feeling quite safe in that town, I went to a place they call Maqueda,[35] where, for my sins, I met a certain priest who was begging for alms. He asked me if I knew how to serve at Mass, to which I answered truthfully that yes, I could. Although he mistreated me, the sinner of the blind man taught me a thousand things, this particular one among them. Thus it was that the priest took me into his service.

In this manner I escaped the frying pan and fell into the fire,[36] for compared to this individual the blind man was as generous as Alexander the Great. This priest was the quintessence of avarice itself. I will only say that all the greed in the world was enclosed within him (I don't know if it was because of his natural disposition or if he seized it after donning his priestly garb.)

He owned an old chest that he kept under lock and key, hanging this key from a piece of lace that he made fast on his jacket. Taking pieces of milk-bread from the offerings at the church, he'd toss them into the coffer and close it. There was not a thing to eat in the whole house; in other houses a being will rarely fail to spot a piece of bacon hanging from the chimney, some cheese set on a cutting-board or in a cupboard, or a basket with left-over pieces of bread: stuff from whose sight I might take some comfort, even if I were excluded from its consumption.

There was only a rope of onions under lock and key in a garret. I was allowed one of these for my provision every four days, and when I asked for the key to take my measure, if anyone else was around, he'd put his hand in his pocket and, taking on an air of magnificence, he'd hand me the key, saying: "Take it and bring it back immediately, and do not overindulge."

One might think that all the confections of Valencia were stored in the curate's garret, though, as I said before, there was nothing there but the onions hanging from a nail. So well did he know the exact number of onions on the rope, that if I, sinner that I am, decided to take more than my share, I would surely pay a terrible price for my transgression. Finally, I was dying of hunger.

Although on me he exercised little charity, he proved quite generous with his own person. Five coins' worth of meat was his daily portion for lunch and dinner. It is true enough that he allowed me to slurp up some of the broth, but as for the meat, I didn't even get a scent. A bit of bread with that allowance, and God help me should I consume half of what I needed to subsist.

On Saturdays it is the custom in these parts to eat sheep's heads, so he sent me off to obtain one that cost three maravedíes.[37] He would cook the head and eat the eyes, tongue, neck, brain and all the flesh around the jaws, reducing it to the bare bone; this he would give to me on a plate, saying: "Take, feast on this banquet, eat, satisfy your desires, be victorious, for the world is yours. Child, you live better than the Pope!"

"May God give you such a life as this," I whispered.

After three weeks of living with him, I came to such an emaciated state that I could hardly stand on my feet from sheer hunger. I saw my way clear to the grave, where I would certainly have ended up were it not for God and my wits. The problem was that there wasn't an object on which to exercise my faculties, and if there had been one, I could not take advantage of blindness, as I did with my previous master, may God forgive him (if, indeed, he survived his encounter with the pillar), who, though shrewd, was missing this very precious sense and couldn't detect me. Of this new master I can truly say that there is no one with such an acute sense of sight.

When we received the offering, not a coin fell into the plate but that he recorded it: one eye he placed on the parishioners and the other on my hands. His eyes danced in his head as if they were made of quicksilver. He tallied every penny that was put in, and once the offering was over, he'd take the plate from my hands and place it upon the altar.

I was unable to get hold of a single coin in all the time I lived with him, or more accurately, died with him. He never sent me to the tavern for even a drop of wine; whatever he brought back from the offering he locked in his trunk, rationing it so that it lasted him the whole week. And in order to hide his colossal parsimony, he'd tell me: "Listen, child, we priests must exercise exemplary sobriety in our eating and drinking. That is why I do not overindulge like others do."

But the miser lied like the devil, for when we prayed at ceremonial dinners and funerals, seeing how others paid for the food, he'd eat like a wolf and drink like a fish.

Now that I've mentioned funerals, as God is my witness I was never the enemy of humankind except for then, as it was only during funerals that we ate well and I satisfied my severe want. Therefore, it was my earnest wish and prayer to God that each day He'd call to his eternal rest at least one of our parishioners. When we administered the Sacraments to the sick, especially the Extreme Unction, the priest bid everyone in attendance to pray. I was of my own accord sufficiently inclined to do so, but I prayed not that they be disposed of according to the Lord's Holy Will, but that they be swiftly and without further hindrance delivered from this world. And when any of the ailing escaped the fate I craved for him and managed to recover, a thousand times (God forgive me) I wished perdition and death on him, as well as several other niceties I reserved for such occasions. During the time I was there, which must have been about six months, only twenty people died, and these I believe I killed myself, or better yet, they died at my request. For seeing my unremitting and rabid death, the Lord I think killed them to give me life. Yet for my enduring penury I obtained little comfort, for if on burying days I found life, on days when no one died my misery exceedingly increased, for the memory of the good days made my hunger that much more unbearable. Thus I came to little contentment other than in the anticipation of death, my death as well as that of others, but it never came, although it was always in me.

I often entertained the thought of leaving that miserly master, but I was deterred from it for two reasons: first, because my legs couldn't carry me far as a result of my hunger; second, I considered that my first master made me go hungry, but my second had me with one foot in the grave; taking account of this progression, I concluded that a third would surely make an end of me.

Contemplating my predicament, I didn't dare make a move, for I was sure that each movement would be to a lower note on the scale. And if I descended one more step, not another sound would ever again be heard from Lázaro.

Being trapped in this quandary (may God release all good Christians from it), not knowing what to do and seeing how I was going from bad to worse, it came to pass that one day, when my miserable, vile and despicable master was out of town, a tinker arrived at my door. To me he seemed like an angel in tinker's garb sent down by the Hand of God. He asked me if I had any pots or pans to repair. "If you could put right my wretched life, you'd have much work, but you'd accomplish a great objective if you mended me," I whispered, and he didn't hear me.

Having no time to waste on witticisms, as if enlightened by the Holy Spirit I told him: "Uncle, I've lost the key to this chest and I'm afraid my master will whip me. Please look to see if among those that you carry there is one that will fit the lock, and I'll pay you for your trouble."

The angelic tinker began to try key after key from a great cluster he had on a chain. I supported his efforts with my feeble prayers. All of a sudden I saw the face of God, as they say, formed by the loaves inside the chest.[38] Seeing the chest open, I told him: "I don't have money with which to pay you, but you can take your payment from there."

So he took a loaf from the chest, the one he thought best, and handing me the key he went on his way very pleased, leaving me even more so.

I presently touched nothing, being afraid that the tinker's loaf might be missed. Besides, being now the master of a treasure such as this, it seemed to me that my relentless hunger didn't dare show its face, fearing its quick demise. My miserable master returned, but God willed that he not look in the chest to spot the loaf that the angel had carried off.

Another day, no sooner had my master left the house, I opened my breadly paradise and sank my hands and teeth into a loaf, making it invisible in less time than it takes to say the Nicene Creed twice. Closing the chest, I began to sweep the house merrily, thinking that my sad life was about to improve with this newly found remedy. Thus I spent that day and the next in happy thoughts. But it wasn't meant for me to enjoy that state of affairs for long, for on the third day I was hit with tertian fever.[39]

As it happened, the man who was starving me began searching in the chest, tallying the loaves time and again, shifting them from side to side. I played dumb and secretly pleaded, implored and begged, saying: "Saint John, blind him."

After calculating for a great while, tallying the days with his fingers, he said: "If I didn't keep such a thorough assessment of the contents of this chest, I'd say that someone has taken loaves from it. From now on, just to shut the door on all my misgivings, I'll keep a stricter account of them: there are nine and a piece of another. "May God send you nine calamities!" I whispered.

When I heard his words I felt as if an arrow had pierced my heart. My stomach, contemplating the prospect of returning to its previous diet, began to rumble violently. When my master again went out, I, in order to soothe my spirit, opened the chest and, upon seeing the bread, began to worship it, not daring to receive it.[40] I counted the loaves, hoping against hope that the miser had erred in his reckoning, but his computation was truer than I would have liked it to be. The most I could do was to kiss the bread a thousand times and, as delicately as humanly possible, I peeled a tiny fraction off the partially eaten loaf.[41]

But because my hunger intensified, mostly because I had become accustomed to eating bread those previous two or three days, I was dying a grim death. So much so that I did nothing else but open and close the chest to witness inside it the Face of God, as children say. But this same God, who comes to the aid of the afflicted, upon seeing my dire circumstances suggested a thought that would procure me some assistance. Considering the great exigency of my affairs, I said to myself: "this chest is old and large and has small holes in places. It can well be believed that mice, entering it, could cause damage to this bread. Taking whole loaves is not convenient, as the deficit would surely be noticed by he who makes me live in deficit. This can be done."

I began to crumb the bread over some inexpensive tablecloths he had there, taking one loaf and sparing others, so that from every three or four I took scraps from one. Then, as one who gobbles up grated candy, I ate it and was somewhat gratified. He came to eat and opened the chest, saw the mutilation, and undoubtedly believed it to be mice: I had expertly counterfeited their method to my benefit. He inspected the chest from one side to the other and discovered the holes, suspecting these were the entry-points for the vermin. He called me, saying: "Lázaro! Look, look at the mischief that has been visited upon our bread last night!"

I feigned astonishment, asking him what it could be.

"What else — said he — but mice? They get into everything."

We began to eat, and God willed that I meet with success here as well. During that meal I partook of more than my usual paltry share, for using his knife, he scraped off some bits from the parts where he thought the mice had been, saying: "Eat that, for mice are clean creatures."

So that day, after enjoying a bonus ration that I earned with the toil of my own hands (or rather my own fingernails), we finished our meal, although it seemed to me that I never started.

And then another surprise. I saw him busily pulling nails off the walls and looking for bits of board; with these he closed up all of the holes in the old chest.

"Oh my God!" I said then. Misery, misfortune and calamity are the lot of mortals; pleasure lasts but a fleeting instant in our arduous lives. Here I was thinking that this poor and sad cure would remedy my misery, and I was happy, delighted at my good fortune. But my ill luck deemed it necessary to supply my master with the proper means to destroy my happiness. Employing more diligence than I ever thought nature had given him (although misers are well endowed with it), he closed the holes in the chest, closing with them the doors to my joy and opening them to my labors.

Thus did I lament as the industrious carpenter finished nailing and boarding, saying: "Come now, Mr. Mouse, you traitor. I rather think that you'd better change the venue for your sport, for in this house you'll have no consolation."

As soon as he left the house I ran to inspect his work. I found that he left no hole through which even a mosquito could enter. I opened the chest with my now useless key, not harboring any hope of profiting from it. Therein I spied the two or three loaves we had begun to eat and on which my master thought the mice had chewed. From these I was able to reap some poor shavings, touching them very lightly with the skill of a master fencer.[42] As necessity is the mother of invention,[43] I, being shackled to it night and day, was constantly pondering ways to keep body and soul together. I believe that hunger lit a path to ease my grief, for as they say, it sharpens the wit as much as gluttony blunts it. I was living proof of that.

So being awake one night, deep in consultations with myself and trying to find the best method of renewing my assault on the chest, I noticed, from the customary loud snoring and heavy breathing, that my master was fast asleep. I got up very quietly, and having previously planned what I would do and having laid out an old, rusty knife for the purpose, I went to the sad chest. Determining the spot where it was most defenseless, I began to work on it with the knife, and the chest, being old and wasted away, soft, rotten and heartless, surrendered to my aggression, consenting to the opening of a great breach upon its side. Having accomplished this, I opened the chest very slowly and partook of the bread that was already broken, as I had done in the past. Obtaining some consolation from those crumbs, I closed the chest and returned to my straw mat; on it I took my repose and managed to get some sleep. Prior to that night I had been sleeping little and badly, owing to, I suppose, the poor diet that I was forced to follow. And that surely must have been the reason for my lack of sleep, for that night the King of France's troubles could not have kept me awake.[44]

The next day my master took a look at the damage done — both to the chest and the bread — and began to curse the mice, saying: "How can this be explained? We've never had mice in this house until now!"

What he was saying was true, without a doubt. If there was a house in this kingdom that enjoyed an exemption from the depredations of rodents it was this one, and with good reason: mice seldom frequent places where there's nothing to eat. So he again searched on the walls and around the house looking for nails and boards with which to repair the hole. As night fell I'd get to work with my own tools, undoing by night what he had accomplished by day. We counteracted each other's deeds so quickly, that now I understand the meaning of the saying "When one door closes, another opens." Finally, we seemed to be imitating the work of Penelope, for what he wove by day, I undid by night. After a few days and nights we had mistreated the poor chest to such a point, that more than a chest it resembled an antique piece of armor, seeing the profusion of nails and tacks with which it was burdened.

At last he began to consider the futility of his endeavor, saying to himself: "This chest is so worn, its wood so old and weak, that there is not a mouse in the world against which it could mount a credible defense. Indeed it's in such a state that, should we insist in using its services, it'll certainly leave us exposed to the depredations of these foul vermin. But what's worse, in spite of its decrepitude, it's the only one I have; should I decide to replace it, the new one will surely set me back anywhere from three to four crowns.[45] I'll employ another strategy, as up to now nothing has worked, and set a trap inside the chest for my cursed enemies."

He then went out and got someone to lend him a mousetrap, and with the cheese rinds that he got from his neighbors, he set the trap inside the chest.

This turned out to be an unexpected windfall for me. Not being what one would call a fastidious or demanding diner, I feasted on the cheese rinds that I took from the mousetrap and didn't even spare the bits of bread on which I had heretofore come to depend.[46]

When he saw that the bread had been got to, that the cheese was gone and the perpetrator mouse had escaped, he began to curse, asking every neighbor how anything could eat the cheese, spring the trap and get away in one piece. The neighbors agreed that the offender could not possibly be a mouse, for a mouse would have been trapped. One neighbor told him: "I remember that your house used to be frequented by a snake. Undoubtedly, this is the unwelcome guest. It stands to reason, for only an animal that is that long can take the bait and still gain release from the trap, as it is too large to be held in it."

Everyone agreed that it must be a snake, a revelation that perturbed my master to no end. He stopped sleeping soundly as was his habit, and any woodworm that made a sound at night he took to be the snake that was getting at the chest. He'd spring to his feet immediately and grab a club that he kept standing at his bedside. Thus armed, he would strike the chest in order to frighten the snake, laying into it with such fury and vigor that he'd wake the neighbors and allowed me little sleep in the bargain. After that he'd come to the straws where I slept and began to turn them over with me inside them, thinking that the animal had sought refuge in my straws or in my coat. It was said that at night these creatures seek warmth in children's cribs, going so far as to bite them or otherwise endanger them.[47]

Most of the time I feigned to be asleep, so the next morning he would ask me: "Last night, young man, did you not feel anything? I was in hot pursuit of the snake, and I think it got into your mat, for snakes are cold and commonly seek warmth wherever they are."

"I hope to God that it doesn't bite me — I'd say — because I'm terribly afraid of it."

In this manner he ran around at night, all agitated and restless, making such a racket that the snake (boy-snake, I should say) didn't dare to go out for its evening dinner or even approach the chest. But during the day, when he was in church or making his rounds, I'd renew my assault on it. Seeing the continuing mischief and the futility of his attempts at ending it, he began to wander at night like a goblin.

I started to fear that with his constant meanderings he'd eventually spot the key that I was hiding under the straws. This is why I came to believe that the best way to safeguard the key was to place it inside my mouth at night. This was facilitated by the fact that, because of my apprenticeship with the blind man, my mouth had acquired the storage capacity of a purse: in it I could hold twelve to fifteen maravedís, all in small change, and be able to eat simultaneously. Otherwise, I would not have been master of a penny that the cursed blind man didn't find, accustomed as he was to searching every seam and patch of my garments. So, as I was saying, each night I put the key in my mouth and slept without a care, not expecting that my bewitched master would stumble onto it. But when misfortune is in the cards, nothing you do can prevent its bite; if you're born to be a hammer, you can expect the nails to rain from Heaven.

Fate (or my sins) saw to it that one night, as I slept, the key shifted inside my mouth — which must have been open — so that my breath blew directly into it. As it was made from pipe, it whistled very loudly and, as a consequence, propitiated my forthcoming disaster. My astonished master heard the noise and took it to be the snake that surely must be about. I truly must have sounded like one. He got up very quietly with his club in his hand and approached me stealthily, not wanting to be noticed by the snake. As he got closer, he assumed that it had slithered into the straw where I was sleeping, looking for warmth. Raising his club high enough that the ensuing blow would exterminate the troublesome creature, he discharged such a formidable and well-placed wallop on my skull that I was left unconscious and very dreadfully battered. As he later informed me, when he saw that he'd hit me (I must have cried out when I felt the furious blow), he came to me, and shouting my name he attempted to revive me. As he touched me with his hands he detected that I was bleeding profusely and became aware of the full extent of the damage. Hurriedly he went for a light, returning with it to find me moaning with the key still hanging from my mouth, for I never forsook it. It must have been in that position when it began to whistle.

The snake exterminator was surprised, wondering what the meaning and purpose of that key might be. He took it from my mouth and looked carefully at it, noticing that it resembled his own key very closely. He then tried it on the lock in the chest and discovered the mystery. The ruthless hunter must have said to himself: "I've found the mouse and the snake that had plagued me and were consuming my estate."

Of what happened during the next three days I shall not give an account, for I spent them in the belly of the whale.[48] What I've just told I heard from my master after I came to, it being the discourse with which he entertained anyone who called on us.

After three days I regained consciousness and saw myself lying on my straws, my head plastered with rags, oils and ointments. Frightened, I said: "What is this?"

To which the cruel priest responded: "Truly, the mice and snakes that were overthrowing me have finally been vanquished."

I looked at myself, saw my condition and began to suspect the nature of the problem.

At this point some neighbors came in with an old woman that cured folks with prayers and ointments. She began to take the rags off my head and treat the wound. When they realized that I had revived, they rejoiced and said: "He's come to, God willing he won't be the worse for wear."

They again took up the recital of my adventures and derived much sport and amusement from it. I, sinner that I am, only managed to cry. With all this they decided to feed me, since I was famished, giving me barely enough to survive. Thus it transpired that, slowly but surely, after fifteen days I managed to get up from my mat and, once out of danger (but not out of hunger) I was able to think of myself as a halfway healthy person again. Soon after that, one morning I was awakened by my master. Taking me by the hand, he brought me to the door and, once I was in the street, he told me: "Lázaro, from this day on you're on your own, for I'll have nothing more to do with you. I have no occasion for such a diligent servant. You could only have come to be as you are from having served a blind man."[49]

And making the Sign of the Cross as if I were possessed, he went back in the house and shut the door.

Chapter Three
How Lázaro Took Up with a Squire, and What Happened to Him in His Company.

Thus it happened that I was forced to generate strength from weakness and, step by step and with the help of good folk, I managed to arrive at this renowned metropolis of Toledo. Here, by the Grace of God, in fifteen days my wound healed. While I was ailing people always gave me some alms, but after I recovered, they'd say: "You are a lazy scoundrel. Go on, look for a master whom you might serve."[50]

"And where am I going to find him — I thought — unless God makes him from scratch, just like He created the world."

Roaming thus from door to door and meeting with little success — charity seemed to have moved out of town and gone to Heaven — God saw it fit to have me meet up with a squire that was walking down the street. He was reasonably well dressed, coiffured and had the gait and bearing of a true gentleman. We looked at each other, and he said to me: "You there, boy, are you looking for a master?"

I responded "Yes, sir."

"Well then, follow me — he replied — for God has been merciful to you this day, having you run into me. You must have said a very effective prayer today."

I followed him, thanking God for what I'd just heard and also for sending me a suitable master, for that is what he seemed as far as I could tell from his clothes and his deportment.

I met my third master at daybreak; from that first moment I set to scurrying behind him as he led me through the greater part of the city. Our expedition took us through several squares where people were selling bread and other victuals. I thought (and even expected) that he was meaning to load me up with these conveniences, as it was a proper hour for it, but he hurried by these places without stopping. "He's probably searching for better quality foodstuffs — I fancied — and will purchase them elsewhere when he finds them."

In this manner we jogged around the city until eleven. He then entered the cathedral with me in tow; there he assisted very devoutly at Mass and other holy offices until all ended and everyone left. Leaving the church, we started down the street at a good clip. I was the happiest person in the world, seeing that we hadn't even bothered to look for food. I well considered that this, my new master, must be a man who provides for his household in great quantities at a time. Such being the case, our meal must be prepared and awaiting our arrival, just as I desired, or better yet, just as I needed it to be.

By this time the clock struck one hour past noon, marking our arrival at a house in front of which my master stopped, and so did I. Throwing one end of his cloak over his left shoulder, he took a key from his sleeve, opened the door, and we entered the house. The entrance was dark and gloomy to the point of inspiring a feeling of dread. Inside the house were a small patio and reasonably sized rooms.

When we went in the house he took off his cloak, asking me if my hands were clean before allowing me to help him shake it and fold it. He blew the dust off a stone bench there, placed the cloak on top of it and sat himself next to it. He then proceeded to ask me extensively about my background: where I was from, how I came to Toledo and the like. I gave him more answers than I would have wanted, as it seemed to me that it was quite unseasonable to enter into such discourse at a time when the cloth should be laid on the table and the victuals set upon it. In spite of it I satisfied his curiosity as best I could with lies, dwelling on my good qualities and passing over my shortcomings, as this was not the right place to give an account of them. This being concluded, he mused upon my answers for a while; I saw this as a bad omen, since it was almost two o'clock and he showed no more desire to eat than a dead man. After this I began to consider how the door was locked and there wasn't a sound to be heard in the whole house: neither upstairs nor down was there any noise to serve as proof of life. All I could see were walls: no chairs, no stools, no benches, no tables, not even a chest like the priest's. In short, the house seemed bewitched. While I thought about this he asked me: "You, boy, have you eaten?" "No, sir," I said. "It wasn't even eight o'clock when I met Your Mercy."

"Well, although it was still morning I had already breakfasted, and when I eat in the morning you must know that I never touch food until nighttime. Get along as best you can; we'll have supper later."

Your Worship must believe that when I heard this I nearly fainted, not so much from hunger as from the knowledge that fate would always be cruel to me.[51] All my former despair came afresh to my mind, and I began to cry over my latest adversity. Right then and there all the premonitions I experienced when leaving the priest entered my mind. I remember thinking then that, although the priest was mean and miserable, I'd surely end up with someone worse. Finally I cried over my arduous life and my impending demise. And with all that, I concealed my anguish as best I could and told him 'sir, I'm young and I don't trouble myself much over food, God be praised. I'm proud to say that among my peers I'm the lightest eater, and because of that I've always been praised by every master I've had."

"That's truly a virtue — he said — and I shall have a better opinion of you for it. It is for swine to stuff themselves; good men are moderate in their eating habits."

"I understand you well," I said to myself. "Damn the therapy and virtue that all my masters find in my starvation."

I withdrew to a corner of the yard and from my shirt took a few pieces of bread that had been left over from my morning's begging. Spotting this, he said to me: "Come hither, boy. What are you eating?"

I approached him and showed him the bread. He took a piece, the best and biggest of the three I had, and exclaimed, "Upon my faith, this does seem to be good bread."

"Indeed, Sir — I said — it is good!"

"I'll swear to that," he said. "Where did you get it? Did its baker have clean hands?"[52]

"That I couldn't say — I answered — but that doesn't change its taste as far as I'm concerned."

"Pray God it is so," said my poor master, and putting it in his mouth he began to bite into it as ferociously as I was tearing into my piece.

"Delicious bread, this is, by God," he said.

As I immediately understood his situation, I thought it convenient to make haste with my loaf, for I saw him well disposed to help me finish it. Thus, we both finished at the same time. My master then shook off the few little crumbs that had fallen on his chest and went off into a small room, whence he exited with a worn out old jug. After taking a draught from it he offered it to me, and I, feigning moderation, told him "sir, I don't drink wine."

"It's water — he responded — you may well drink." I then took the jug and drank, though not much, for it wasn't thirst that was troubling me.

Thus we spent the rest of the day until nighttime, he asking me questions, I answering as best I could. He then took me to the little room where he kept the jug from which he had drunk and said "Boy, stand there and observe how we prepare this bed so that you'll be able to prepare it yourself from now on."

I stood on one side, he on the other and we prepared the black bed. There really wasn't much to do because it was only a wicker frame; it supported a mattress that, having been washed far too many times, didn't much look like a mattress but rather like a thin blanket. Having stretched it out he attempted to soften it, but it was impossible. You can hardly make soft that which is innately hard. That hellish mattress appeared to have nothing inside; when placed upon the frame every wicker strut showed through it like the ribs of a starving pig. Over that hungry mattress was placed a cover of the same ilk whose color I was unable to make out.

Once the bed was prepared and the night was upon us, he told me "Lázaro, it's very late and the market is a long way off; besides, there are many thieves in this city that ply their trade at night. Let's get along as well as we can tonight, for tomorrow God will provide. Having formerly been alone, I haven't stocked any foodstuffs but have eaten out. From now on we'll do things differently."

"Sir — I said — Your Mercy must not worry. I well know how to spend a night and even more, if need be, without eating."

"You will live longer and in better health for it — he responded — for, as we discussed today, there is nothing better for longevity than a modest diet."

"If that's the case — I said to myself— I'll never die; circumstances have always forced that variety of diet upon me and I expect, in my misfortune, to keep it all my life."

And he lay down on the bed, using his pants and jacket as a pillow. He told me to lie down at his feet, which I did. But damn it if I got a wink of sleep: the wicker struts and my protruding bones engaged in a ferocious quarrel all night long. With all my hardships, anguish and hunger I believe that my body wasn't carrying a pound of flesh; on top of that, I hadn't eaten almost anything that day and was rabid with hunger, a sensation that doesn't go well with sleep. Lying there I cursed myself a thousand times (God forgive me) and my miserable fate, and what's worse, not daring to move lest I wake my master, I asked God for death many times.

In the morning we got up and he began to clean his pants, jacket, coat and cape. I stood around loitering. He got dressed at his leisure, very slowly. I brought water for him to wash his hands; he combed his hair, put his sword in its sheath, and as he began placing his swordbelt around his waist he said to me "Boy, if you only knew what a blade this is! There is no fortune in the world for which I'd trade it. Its steel has been crafted with such precision that none of those that Antonio[53] forged can compare to it."

And he unsheathed it and felt it with his fingers, saying: "take a good look at it. I bet I can slice a ball of wool with it."

And I said to myself, "and I with my teeth, though they're not made of steel, could slice a four-pound loaf of bread."

He sheathed it again and finished strapping it on. He then hung a string of large beads on the sword-belt and began to walk with a stately gait, his body straight but swaying gracefully along with his head. Flinging the edge of his cape now over his shoulder, now under his arm, and placing his right hand on his side, he slipped out the door. He said as he went: "Lázaro, take care of the house while I go to Mass, make the bed and fill the jug with water from the river, which is right below us. And lock the door to insure that nothing is stolen. You can put the key on the stoop so that I may enter should I return before you."

Then he went up the road with such a genteel air and countenance that anyone who didn't know him might have mistaken him for a close relative of the Count of Arcos,[54] or at least for his valet. "You are blessed, Lord — I said as I watched him — for You never send a disease without a cure."[55] Anyone encountering my master on the street will fancy — observing his contentment — that he dined lavishly last night and slept on a fine bed. Although it is yet early in the morning, people undoubtedly will assume that he has enjoyed a hearty breakfast already. Great and mysterious are Your ways, oh Lord, and much ignored by folks![56] Who could help but be fooled by his fine disposition and fair cape and coat? Who could possibly believe that such a gentleman got by yesterday on a humble piece of bread that his servant Lázaro had been carrying all day and night in the coffer of his bosom, where not much cleanliness could have rubbed off on it? And that today, when he washed his hands and face, he dried them on his shirttail for lack of towels? No one, of course, could suspect such a thing. Oh, Lord, how many others like him have You scattered around the world, who suffer for that black whore they call honor what they'd never suffer for You!

Thus I stood by the door, looking out and considering all these things and many others, until my master slipped out of sight up the long, narrow street. I then went back into the house and in the time it takes to say the Nicene Creed I walked throughout it, upstairs and down, neither stopping anywhere nor anywhere finding a reason to do so. So I made the hard black bed, took the jug and made it to the river, where I chanced to spot my master in a garden engaged in a sweet discourse of seduction with two veiled ladies, the likes of which abound in that place. Such ladies make it their custom to saunter down to the riverside on summer mornings to take the air and breakfast without actually bringing any food with them. In fact they go to the cool riverbank trusting that there will always be gentlemen from the neighborhood that will treat them to an early morning repast.

As I was saying, there he was between them like the troubadour Macías,[57] showering them with more sweet words and compliments than even Ovid ever wrote.[58] Seeing him burning in the heat of passion, they felt no shame in asking him for breakfast, making it clear that he should expect the standard reward in return. Recalling that his purse was icy though his groin was on fire, he began to have the chills and the color drained from his face. His speech became blurred and he began to give them daft excuses; they, who were obviously well practiced in these matters, quickly ascertained his limitations and abandoned him there for what he was worth.

I had busied myself in dispatching some cabbage stalks that I had for my breakfast. When I saw my master's downfall I concluded that, as a new servant, the best course of action would be to return home diligently without being seen by him. Once there I thought I should sweep, as it was much needed, but I didn't find anything with which to do it. So I began to consider what I should do, and I resolved to wait for him until noon in the hopes he'd bring something to eat. But my hopes were in vain.

Once I saw that it was two o'clock, that he hadn't shown up and hunger had me in its clutches, I closed the door, put the key where he had ordered and went out begging. With a low, sickly voice and hands on my chest; with God before my eyes and His Name on my tongue, I began to beg for bread at the doors of the largest houses that I saw. I had sucked in all the secrets of this profession like mother's milk from that great master the blind man, and I proved to be such an accomplished disciple that, even though in this town there wasn't any charity to be found even in the best of times, I made use of my faculties so effectively that before the clock struck four I had as many pounds of bread in my belly and more than two others in my sleeves and under my shirt. On the way back home I went by the meat market where I beseeched one of the women there; she gave me a piece of a cow's hoof and some boiled tripe.

When I got home my good master had already arrived and folded his cape, which he'd placed on the stone bench. He was strolling in the yard, and when I entered he dashed toward me with a design, I thought, to scold me for my tardiness. But God had other designs. He asked me where I had been, and I told him: "Sir, I was here until two, and when I saw that Your Mercy was not coming, I roamed through the city to recommend myself to the charity of well-disposed folk; they have given me this you see here."

I showed him the bread and the tripe that I had stowed in my shirttail, and he clearly rejoiced at the sight. He said: "Well, I was waiting for you in order to eat, but when I saw you weren't coming, I ate. But you've acted as a good man in this matter, for it is better to beg in God's name than to steal. As God is my witness that's my honest opinion, only be very careful, for the sake of my honor, not to let out that you live with me. It should be easy to keep it a secret, for in this town I'm not well known. Would to God I had never come here."

"Don't worry about that, sir"—I told him. "Nobody cares enough to ask me such questions, so I'd never have an occasion to answer them."

"Well, then, eat, poor boy, for God willing we'll soon be rid of this wretchedness. I'll tell you, after I came to this house nothing has gone right for me; its floor must be cursed. In some houses the bad luck rubs off on the people who live in them. This, without a doubt, must be one of them, but I promise you that by the end of the month we won't be living here, even if they give it me as a gift."

I sat next to the bench and kept quiet about my previous meal so that he wouldn't take me for a glutton. I began to dine, chewing my tripe and bread and watching my master all the while out of the corner of my eye. He wasn't taking his eyes from my shirttail, which I was using as a plate. May God pity me as much as I pitied him at that moment, for I was painfully aware of what he was feeling, as daily experience had made me sensible to his predicament. I wasn't sure whether I should invite him to join me, but since he had told me that he'd already eaten, I feared that he would not accept. In the end I was wishing he'd help himself to my earnings and breakfast like he had done the day before; unlike yesterday, there was better fare this day, and I wasn't as hungry.

God made my wish come true, as well as my master's. As I ate and he walked around, he came close and said "I'll tell you, Lázaro, I've never seen a man eat with as much enthusiasm as you, so much so that even a one who has already feasted will have a mind to partake of the meal."

"The great feast you've had — thought I — makes mine seem so terribly attractive."

Still, I felt I should help him, since he was offering me a way to do so, and I said: "Sir, good tools make the craftsman; this bread is delicious, and the cow's foot so nicely cooked and well seasoned that it seduces with its fine flavor."

"It's a cow's foot?"

"Indeed, sir."

"I tell you that's the tastiest morsel in the world. I even prefer it to pheasant."

"Well taste it, sir, and you'll see just how good it is."[59]

I put the cow's foot in his hand and three or four loaves of the whitest bread. He sat by my side and began to exercise his great appetite on the victuals, gnawing on each little bone more diligently than any hound of his would have done.

"Prepared with an oil, garlic and cheese sauce — he said — is this singular treat."

"Your hunger is the best seasoning," I said under my breath.

"By God, its taste makes me enjoy it as if I had not had a bite to eat all day."

"That's true as sure as I'm sitting here next to you," I thought.

He asked me for the jug of water and I gave it to him, still full. That was a sure sign that my master had not eaten all day; if he had, he would have drunk some water. So we drank and happily went to bed like the night before.

To make a long story short, we spent the next eight or ten days this way: the poor man would leave in the morning with his air of contentment and measured step to dawdle about the streets, leaving me with the care of providing for him.

I often reflected upon my disastrous fate; fleeing the hands of two miserable masters and ending up in the hands of a third who not only doesn't feed me, but whom I have to support.[60] In spite of it all I wished him well, seeing how it was not in his power to improve our lot. I felt sorrow for him, rather than enmity, and many times I went hungry just so he'd have something to eat.

I behaved in this manner for a simple reason: one morning he got up from bed in his shirttails and went upstairs, needing to relieve himself; to satisfy my curiosity, I unfolded his jacket and pants, which he had left at the head of the bed. I found a small velvet purse that was folded up a hundred times, without a coin or sign that it had ever contained one for long. "This man — I said to myself— is poor, and no man can give what he doesn't have. On the other hand the miserly blind man and the scrounging, mean priest had assets: the one gained them by kissing hands, the other with a quick tongue. These two I had reason to abominate, for they starved me needlessly, but the squire is only deserving of pity."

As God is my witness, even nowadays when I run into one such as he, walking with the same gait, dressing in his style and affecting that air of pompous pageantry, I pity him just thinking that he might be going through the same misery that I saw this one endure. With all his poverty, for the reasons I've mentioned I'd rather serve him than my two previous masters. Only one thing displeased me about him: I wish he hadn't been so presumptuous and had controlled his vanity a bit, seeing as his needs were also out of control. But as far as I can see, this is an incurable distemper in people of his sort: even if there isn't a red cent in their purse, their bonnet must be on straight. May God forgive them, for they'll go to their graves without ever being cured of this disease.

Well, being in this situation, living the life I've described, my adverse fortune, never weary of persecuting me, saw to it that this hard, shameful lifestyle didn't continue. The year's wheat harvest had been bad,[61] so the town authorities decided to get rid of all outsiders who begged in the city. The town crier announced it: all persons foreign to Toledo caught begging would be punished with a taste of the whip. The law was enforced, and four days after the pronouncement went into effect I saw a procession of unfortunates being led down Cuatro Calles being duly flogged.[62] The sight frightened me to such an extent that I no longer dared to go out begging.

Anyone who had cared to look into our affairs would have witnessed a vision of famine, gloom and silence; a house whose inhabitants were mired in misery, not even tasting a crumb or saying a word for two or three days. I was kept alive by some women who spun cotton to make bonnets; since they lived right next door, I had formerly made their acquaintance. From their meager means they were able to provide some small assistance that somewhat decelerated the progression of my demise.

I didn't feel as much pity for myself as I felt for my aching master, who in eight days didn't have a damned bite to eat. At least in the house I didn't see him eat a thing. I don't know how or where he went or what he ate. And who in the world could have detected his dire circumstances, seeing him come down the street at noon holding his body straight, longer than a pureblooded greyhound? And on account of that black whore they call honor, he'd take a piece of straw, the type of which we have no need for in this house, and go out the door picking at the empty space between his teeth. He'd then abuse that awful dwelling by saying: "Things are certainly not looking up. It is this damned house that brings us all this misfortune. As you see, it is gloomy, sad and dark. While we stay here we will suffer. I'm wishing this month were over so that we might be quit of it."

Such was our miserable, starving condition when one day, I don't know by what stroke of good luck or fortune, my poor master became the master of a real.[63] He came home with it as proud as if he had just become the owner of all the treasures of Venice; smiling very happily, he handed it to me and said: "take it, Lázaro, for Heaven is beginning to open its hand. Go to the market and buy bread, wine and meat. Let's splurge and spite the Devil, and to complete our joy, you should understand that I have rented another house. We'll only stay in this cursed habitation until the month is out. Damn this house and the fellow who put the first tile on its roof, and damn the day I first set foot in it![64] As God is my witness, in all the time that I've lived here I have not had a drop of wine nor have I tasted any meat; in fact, there's been no end to my tribulations. Just look at its dark and gloomy aspect! Go, fly, for today we eat like nobility."

I took my coin and my jug and hurried up the street, heading merrily towards the square. But what's the use of believing that my luck could turn, when it's my fate that no happiness can come without much pain and suffering? And thus I was walking up the street, thinking of the best ways to spend the cash and giving God a thousand thanks for bestowing it upon my master, when, for my disaster, I met up with a corpse that was being carried down the street on a litter by many priests and other folk. Pinning myself to the wall to let them pass, I saw the corpse go by attended by a woman dressed in black. She was in turn accompanied by a large group of women.[65] The widow was crying out in her grief, saying: "my husband and master, where are they taking you? To the sad, unhappy abode; to the dark and frightful habitation where neither meal nor drink is to be had."

When I heard that, I thought that heaven and earth were coming together, and I exclaimed: "Oh, woe is me, they're taking this corpse to my house!"

Engrossed in this apprehension and forgetting my errand, I made my way through the crowd and started down the street, running as fast as I could towards the house. When I arrived, I entered and closed the door quickly, calling out to my master. Embracing him, I begged his assistance to defend the entrance to the house. Startled, thinking that it might be something else, he told me: "Boy, what are you going on about? What is this hollering? Why do you close the door with such fury?"

"Oh, sir — I replied — come here quickly, for they're bringing us a cadaver!"

"What do you mean?" he replied.

"I met it up the street, and his wife was saying: 'my husband and master, where are they taking you? To the sad, unhappy abode; to the dark and frightful habitation where neither meal nor drink is to be had.' They're delivering it here to us, sir!"

And certainly, when my master heard this, even though he had no reason to be merry, he laughed so heartily that is was a great while before he could speak. While he laughed I barred the door and put my shoulder against it to aid in its defense. The procession went by with its corpse, but I was still afraid that they'd try to bring it into the house. As soon as my master had his fill of laughter — laughter is the only thing that filled him at that point — he said: "It is true enough, Lázaro, that as the widow described it, you were right to think what you did. But as you can see, God has otherwise disposed of it. Open the door, open it and go get us something to eat."

"Let them be out of the street first, sir," said I.

Finally he came to the door and restored my confidence. I sorely needed it, as I was so afraid and distressed. Through the door, I started up the street again.

Although we ate well that day, I enjoyed not a damned bit of it: in those three days the color didn't return to my cheeks, although my master had many a merry moment when considering my recent predicament.

Thus I remained a few days with this, my poor third master, and all the while I was itching to know why he came and why he stayed in these lands. From the first day I met him I knew him to be foreign to these parts and a stranger to everyone around him. At last my wish came true and I found out what I wanted to know, for one day after we had eaten reasonably well and he was in good humor, he decided to give me the following account of his affairs:

He told me that he was from Old Castile and that he left his country only because he didn't want to take off his hat to a gentleman of quality from his vicinity. "Sir," I said, "If he was who you say and by birth and estate was your superior, you did well to salute him first, since, as you say, he never failed to make you a civil return."

"That is true enough, he always returned my civilities by removing his hat after I had done mine, but it would not be too much to ask for him to take the initiative and remove his hat first for once."

"It seems to me — I told him — that I wouldn't have been bothered by such a thing, especially when dealing with people who are my superiors and have more than I."

"You're just a boy — he responded — and a stranger to the sentiment of honor in which the riches of those that now profess it do principally consist. I'll have you know that, though I'm a simple squire, if I met a count on the street and he didn't take his hat completely off his head for me, the next time I saw him come down the street I'd duck right into a house pretending I had business there, or I'd cross over to another street, if there was one, that I might not be obliged to salute him. For an hidalgo yields to no one but God and the king. It's not right, if he be a man of honor, to disregard his worth and self-respect. I remember that one day I dishonored a craftsman, and almost pummeled him, for every time he came across me he'd say: "may God keep Your Mercy." "You miserable scoundrel," I told him, "why don't you mind your manners? How dare you address me by saying May God keep you as if I were just anybody?" From that day on he began to take his hat off and speak properly."

"Isn't that a good way for a man to greet another — I said — by exclaiming 'God keep you?'"

"For goodness' sake!" he said. "That is good enough for ordinary folk, but for higher ups like me the least you must say is 'I kiss Your Mercy's hands,' or at the very least 'Sir, I kiss your hand' if he who addresses one is a gentleman. You may see by that whether it was proper for me to submit to my countryman's treatment, why I wouldn't put up with it, and why I'll never accept that anyone that is not the king himself greet me by saying 'may God keep you.'"

"Sinner me," I said to myself, "that is the reason He has such little concern for your sustenance, since you won't tolerate anyone imploring it of Him on your behalf."

"In the main," he said, " I am not so poor that I don't have in my country, sixteen leagues from where I was born, on Costanilla Street in Valladolid,[66] a building site for houses which, if standing and well-finished, would be valued at more than two hundred thousand maravedís, as they could be made large and splendid. And I have a dovecote that, were it not in ruins, would produce more that two hundred pigeons yearly. And there are other things about which I hold my piece, for I forsook them all for the sake of my honor. And I came to this city in the hopes of meeting with a good position, but have been deceived in my expectations. Canons and men of the church I've met quite a few, but these people are so stingy that it is impossible to change their habits. Gentlemen of lesser nobility also requested me; but serving them is a cause of stress, for you have to change from man into a jack-of-all-trades, and if you don't comply with all their fancies, they show you the door. You can expect the payments to be few and far between, and most of the time the only remuneration you're apt to get is a meal. And when they want to clear their conscience by somehow paying you for your toil, your compensation comes from their clothes closet in the form of a sweat-logged jacket or a ragged cape or coat. And even when a man obtains a position with a noble, his troubles don't diminish. For goodness' sake, am I not able enough to serve them and make them happy? By God, if one of them were to give me the chance, I believe I'd quickly recommend myself to his favor and do a thousand things for him. I could lie to him as well as any man; I'd flatter him impressively and laugh at his jokes and yarns even if they weren't exactly funny. I'd never tell him anything that would upset him, even if he'd profit from the advice. I would be very diligent in caring for his good name, both in word and in deed, and I certainly wouldn't kill myself to do things right if he wasn't going to see them. I'd scold the servants whenever he was close enough to hear me so he'd think I was very concerned about his interests. And if he were reprimanding one of his servants, I'd intervene with some pointed remarks about the culprit that would make the nobleman irate; I'd do this while appearing to take the servant's side. I would praise the things he already found praiseworthy, and I'd ridicule and disparage household members and outsiders alike. I'd snoop around and try to discover juicy tidbits about other people's business so I could tell him about them. In short, I would not omit any of those practices that are so well appreciated by nobles and grandees nowadays. These people won't endure the presence of virtuous men in their homes. In fact, they hate them, belittle them and call them foolish. They say you can't deal with them and that a nobleman can't ever turn his back on them. Clever people today deal with the nobles in the way I've described. But fate hasn't decreed that I meet any one of them."

And so my master bemoaned his adverse fortune while telling me about his admirable person.

The pleasing subject of his discourse was interrupted when a man and an old woman came through the door. The man asked him for the house-rent, while the old woman requested money for the rental of the bed. After adding up the amount owed, which was for a period of two months, the total turned out to be more than the squire's yearly revenue. I believe that it was twelve or thirteen reales. The squire was very complaisant, desiring them to come back in the evening so as to give him time to go to the market and change a two-castellano piece.[67] He never returned.

His creditors came back at the appointed time, but too late. I told them that he hadn't returned. The night having arrived but not my master, I became frightened at the prospect of staying in the house by myself. I therefore went next door to the lady neighbors, told them what had happened, and was lodged for the night.

The next morning the creditors returned and enquired after the squire, not finding him next door. The women replied: "see, here is his servant and the key to the door."

They asked me about him and I told them I didn't know where he was, as he never returned to the house after he'd left to change the piece. I also told them I thought he'd left both them and me high and dry.

When they heard all of this, they went for a sheriff and a notary. They returned with them a bit later, took the key, summoned me, summoned witnesses, opened the door and entered, determined to seize my master's possessions pending reimbursement. They searched the place and found it bare, as I've said. They then told me: "What has become of your master's possessions: His chests, tapestries and furnishings?"

"I don't know about that," I replied.

"Undoubtedly," they said, "last night they must have packed up and carried it off somewhere. Master sheriff, seize this boy, for he knows where it is."

At this the sheriff came over and grabbed me by the collar, saying: "Boy, you are going to jail if you don't reveal where your master's goods are."

Having never seen myself in such a predicament (for, though I'd been held by the collar an infinite number of times, it was gently that I might show the road to he who could not see it), I was scared and, weeping, promised to tell them what they asked of me.

"That's good," they said. "Then tell us what you know and don't be afraid."

The notary sat down on a stone bench in order to take down the inventory, asking me what his possessions were.

"Gentlemen," I said, "what my master owns, according to what he told me, is a very fine plot for manor houses and a ruined dovecote."

"Very well," they said; "however little that may be worth, it should be enough to discharge the debt. And in what part of the city does he have this?" they asked me.

"In his own country," I replied.

"By God, this business is going well," they said. "And where is his country?"

"He told me he was from Old Castile," I said.

The sheriff and the notary laughed enthusiastically, saying: "Your tale is good enough to pay off your debt, even if it were greater than it actually is."

The lady neighbors, who were present, said: "Gentlemen, this is just an innocent child that's been with this squire only a few days and doesn't know any more of him than do your worships. The little sinner came here to our house and we fed him as well we could, for the sake of charity; at night he went back to sleep with his master.

My innocence demonstrated, they let me go, granting me my freedom. Then the sheriff and the notary asked the man and the woman for their fees, a request that caused a great quarrel and commotion. The creditors claimed they weren't required to pay, since the property they came to seize wasn't to be had. The others said they'd given up other, more lucrative business to participate in this undertaking.

Finally, after much shouting, a deputy took away the old woman's aged bedcovers; his burden was light enough. All five left screaming. I don't know how it wound up: It seems that the sinful bedcovers paid for everything. And just as well, since at a time when the bedcovers should have been relaxing and resting from earlier service, they were running around being let out to rent.

Thus it was, as I have related, that my poor third master forsook me. That's how I became thoroughly acquainted with my ruinous fortune, for in arranging itself systematically against me, it upset all my dealings to such an extent that, while it is usually the servant who leaves the master, in my case it was the reverse: it was my master who left and ran away from me.

Chapter Four

Which Tells How Lázaro Came to Serve a Friar of the Order of Mercy,[68] and What Came to Pass While in His Service.

I had to search for the fourth master, and this turned out to be a friar of the Mercedarian Order who was recommended to me by the lady neighbors. These ladies were given to calling him their kinsman.[69] He was a great enemy of devotions and of eating in the monastery, and cared for nothing but idle strolling, lay business and visiting at such a rate that I think he wore out more shoes than the rest of the monastery put together. This one gave me the first shoes I've worn out in my life, and they lasted me only eight days, for I was unable to put up with his scurrying any longer than that. For this and for other little things I will not report, I left him.

Chapter Five

How Lázaro Came to Attend a Purveyor of Indulgences[70] and What Came to Pass While in His Service.

The fifth master to which my fortune led me was a purveyor of indulgences. He was the greatest, most confident and unashamed dealer in absolutions that I ever saw, hope to see, or in my estimation anybody in the world ever came across. For although he was already lord and master of a myriad of cunning schemes, he constantly searched for ever-new ways and means and ever-more subtle fabrications to ply his trade.

Upon entering the villages where he was to promote the bulls, his first visit was to the vicar and his curates, whom he always endeavored to bring over to his interests by way of some little gifts devoid of much value or substance. These consisted of lettuce from Murcia, if it was in season, a couple of limes or oranges, an apricot, a couple of peaches, and green pears for each and every one of his targets. Thus he sought to induce them to favor his design by promoting his business among their parishioners and calling on them to take up the bull.

After they thanked him for the presents, he took care to inform himself of their abilities. If they told him they understood Latin he didn't speak a word of it, lest he slip up, but rather made use of a genteel and well trimmed vernacular and of his very nimble tongue. But if he learned that these clerics were reverends (those who were ordained not so much for their learning as for their wealth and the references of powerful acquaintances), he would become a Saint Thomas among them and speak two hours in Latin. At least that's what it seemed to be, although it wasn't.

When they didn't take up his bulls voluntarily, he sought out ways in which he might bring his business to bear anyway. For this he'd often harass the townsfolk, while at other times he used cunning artifices to get his way. And because it would be an endless story to tell you of all the hoaxes I saw him draw on, I will speak of a very sly and witty one with which I shall well prove his ability.[71]

In a place of the Sagra de Toledo[72] he had preached for two or three days, going through the customary motions, and no one had taken a bull nor, in my estimation, were they in any disposition to do so. Giving himself to the devil and thinking of ways to overcome this adverse situation, he resolved to convene the townsfolk the next day in order to dispense the bull.

That night, after supper, he and the sheriff began to gamble to see who would pay for the meal. They started to quarrel over the game and exchanged fiery words. He called the sheriff a thief, and the sheriff called him a con artist. At that point my master the purveyor grabbed a large spear that was kept by the portal where they were playing. The sheriff countered by reaching for a sword that he carried in his belt.

In response to the shouting and the noise we all began to make, the guests and neighbors came running, got between them and tried to break it up. Each man was irate and seemed eager to decide the quarrel by killing his opponent, struggling to get away from those who were holding them back. With the racket they made many people had come rushing in and the house was full; seeing that they couldn't get at their antagonist with their weapons, they continued hurling all manner of opprobrious remarks at each other. Among these the sheriff said my master was a con man and that all the indulgences he was selling were forged.

Finally the townsfolk, seeing that there was no way to reconcile them, decided to remove the sheriff from the inn and take him somewhere else. My master remained, still fuming. But after the guests and neighbors pleaded with him to calm down and go to bed, he left, and then so did we all.

Come morning my master went to the church and asked them to ring for mass and sermon so he'd have a chance to sell indulgences. And the townsfolk gathered, mumbling about the indulgences, saying that they were forgeries and that the sheriff himself had divulged it during the squabble. So, if they weren't well disposed to take any pardons before, they were downright reluctant now.

The purveyor my master mounted the pulpit. Starting his sermon, he began to exhort the people not to snub so great a blessing and indulgence as offered by the holy bull that he brought with him.

As he was reaching the climax of his sermon, the sheriff entered the church and, after praying a bit, got up and with a loud and composed voice began to say gravely: "Good people, I would have a word with you, after which I leave it to you to judge the merits of this man's discourse. I came here with this con man that's preaching to you. I confess that I was seduced by his cunning: he said that if I favored him in his business, he'd split the profits with me. But now, considering the injury I would do my own conscience and your estate, and repenting of ever having enlisted in this venture, I come now openly to declare that the indulgences he's selling are forgeries. Don't believe him and don't buy them. I'll concern myself no more with them in any way, be it directly or indirectly. From this moment on I'm giving up my staff, emblem of the office I hold, and casting it on the ground. If he should ever come to be punished for his deception, you as witnesses may testify that I am not in league with him nor do I help him in any way; instead of such treachery, I give you timely notice of his wickedness and villainy." With these words he ended his discourse.

Hoping to avoid a scandal, some honest men who were in attendance wanted to get up and throw the sheriff out of the church, but my master forbad them under pain of excommunication, ordering them to allow the lawman to say anything he wanted. He also kept silent until the sheriff finished saying everything I've reported.

When he finished my master asked him if he wanted to say anything else, and informed him that, if he so desired, he could proceed with his harangue.

To this the sheriff responded: "There is much more to reveal about you and about your trickery, but for now I have said enough."

The indulgence seller then kneeled at the pulpit and, joining the open palms of his hands and looking up to heaven, said: "Lord God to Whom nothing is hidden, Who knows all things and to Whom nothing is impossible, You know the truth and appreciate how unjustly I am being accused. As far as I'm concerned, I forgive him, even as I desire You to forgive me. Forgive them who know not what they do or say[73], but as for the injury he does You, I ask and beg of You, for the sake of justice, to show a sign so that the truth may be confirmed. For if anyone here desired to take the holy bull and is impeded by that man's false words, it would be a great harm. I therefore implore You, Lord, that by means of a miracle You persuade these good people of my sincerity. And I beg You to do it thusly: if what that man says about my malice and wickedness is true, let this pulpit collapse with me on it and plunge fifty feet into the ground, where neither it nor I shall ever be found. But if what I say is true, and my accuser, persuaded by the devil to deprive those who are here present from such a great blessing, is shown to speak evil of me, let him in turn be punished and let his malice be known to all."[74]

As soon as my devout master had finished his prayer the corrupt sheriff fell to the floor, hitting it so hard that the blow made the whole church resonate. He then began to roar and froth at the mouth, twisting it and making weird faces, kicking, punching and rolling around on the floor.

The commotion was so fierce and the folks shouted so loudly that no one could hear anyone else. Some were shocked and terrified.

Some said: "May God help him and give him comfort." Others said: "He had it coming, for he was giving false witness."

Finally, some of those present (and not without much foreboding, as far as I could tell) approached him and grabbed a hold of his arms, as he was punching violently at anyone who got close to him. Others pulled at his legs, holding on to them for dear life, for no fiendish mule in the world could deliver a punt as solidly as this man. In this manner they held him down for a while. There were more than fifteen men on him and he still managed to hit them, clobbering the noses of the less cautious among them.

All the while my master was before the pulpit upon his knees, hands and eyes raised to heaven, so much taken up by his devotion that all the noise and confusion in the church could not divert him from those divine contemplations.

Those good men approached him and, through much shouting,

managed to arouse him. After this they begged him to help that poor, dying man, telling him to forget his past actions and his calumnies, for he surely had obtained his just retribution. Furthermore they entreated him, for God's sake, to do what he could to free him from the perils and agony that he was experiencing, since all were sufficiently convinced of the sheriff's guilt and of my master's goodness and honesty, qualities that had been so visibly approved by the hand of Heaven.

At that my master the pardoner, as if awakened from a pleasant slumber, looked at them, at the felon and at the assembled crowd, and solemnly said: "Good people, you need not pray for a man against whom God has so clearly manifested His irritation. But since God has commanded us not to return evil for evil and to forgive those who trespass against us, let us apply to Him with confidence in the hopes that He will be pleased to pardon one who has offended Him by placing obstacles before His holy Faith. Let us all pray."

And so, descending from the pulpit, he urged them to pray very devoutly to Our Lord for the sinner's recovery, that He would be pleased to cast the devil out of him if, as punishment for his sins, He had allowed that unclean spirit to enter into him.

They all fell upon their knees in front of the altar and, in the company of the priests, began to sing the Litanies in a soft voice. My master brought the Cross and holy water, and after he had chanted over the sheriff, he thrust his hands upward to heaven and rolled his eyes so that only their whites were showing. He then began a prayer that was as long as it was pious, making all the folks cry (just like in Passion sermons, when both preacher and audience are pious). He implored Our Lord, asking Him to will not the death of the sinner but rather his health and life, so that a man like him, led by the devil and guided by sin and death, may come to repent and confess his transgressions.[75]

Having done this, he called for the bull and placed it on the sinner's head. Gradually, the sheriff began to come to his senses and feel better. As soon as he recovered his wits, he threw himself at my master the pardoner's feet and implored his forgiveness. He confessed that the words that had come out of his mouth were instigated by the devil himself, seeking to take revenge on the good pardoner and, more importantly, trying to deprive all these folks of the great benefits that the distribution of the bulls would bring them.

My master forgave him and they renewed their friendship. This occasioned such a rush to take the bulls, that there was hardly a soul in the place that didn't purchase one of these pardons: husbands and wives, sons and daughters, boys and girls.

The news of what had happened spread around the region, so that as we arrived in the neighboring villages there was no need of any sermon or preaching in the church: People came straight to the inn to get the bulls as if they were free pears. So in the ten or twelve places that we visited in the area, my master sold what must have been a thousand indulgences in each place without even giving a sermon.

When he performed the miracle, I must confess that I was amazed and believed it to be authentic much like everybody else. But when I saw the way my master and the sheriff laughed and joked about the business later on, I came to understand that it had all been cooked up by my shrewd and ingenious master.[76]

In yet another place, whose name I'll not mention lest I injure its reputation, something else happened that is well worth noting. After giving two or three sermons, my master observed that no one was purchasing the pardons. Weighing the situation, and seeing how they would not take them even upon the offer of a year's credit, he judged his efforts to have been in vain. He had the bells toll so that he could say goodbye to the folks, which he did from the pulpit. As he came down from the pulpit, he called the scribe and me — I was weighed down with saddlebags — and had us come up to the first step. He took the pardons that the sheriff had in his hands and the ones I was carrying in the saddlebags and laid them down next to his feet. Turning towards the parishioners with a happy face, he began to take the bulls and throw them at the assembly ten and twenty at a time, saying: "take, my brethren, take the blessings that God has sent to you, take them home and don't fret, for the rescue of Christian captives from Moslem lands is truly a pious endeavor.[77] *Your charity, along with five Lord's Prayers and five Hail Marys will help them be free of their captivity and so keep them from renouncing our Holy Faith and burning in the fires of hell. And you can help the parents, siblings and friends that you have in Purgatory, as you will see in this holy bull.*

As soon as the people saw the pardons being thrown like that, free of charge and from the hand of God, they began to pick them up with both hands: for the babies in their cribs, for their dead and for every child and minor servant they had, counting with their fingers to ensure they had everyone covered. In the ensuing commotion the throng finished ripping a poor old shirt that I was wearing, but I can assure Your Worship that in little more than an hour there wasn't one bull left in the saddlebags and that it was necessary to go back to the inn for more.

After everyone had taken his fill of the pardons, my master called from the pulpit on his scribe and on the Council member, requesting they get up and record the names of all who were to benefit from the holy indulgence and pardons of the sacred bull. The folks declared very willingly the number of pardons they had taken, counting in an orderly fashion those obtained for their children, their servants, and the dearly departed.

Having thus taken stock, he asked the town officials to order the scribe to surrender authority over this inventory of names to him; from here he deduced that more than two thousand pardons were now in the hands of the townsfolk.

After he said his goodbyes with much talk of peace and love, we quit the place. But before we left my master was approached by the town priest and officials, asking if the bulls were good for infants that were still in their mothers' bellies. To this he responded that, according to the books he'd read, unborn children were not covered by the bull, but that they'd have to consult the matter with men more learned than he. These were his views on the subject.

Then we left, delighted at the way this business had turned out. My master remarked to the sheriff and the scribe: "How do you like that? These villains think that just by saying that they're old Christians[78] *they'll be saved, and that this will happen without their throwing any part of their savings into the deal. Well, I swear by the life of Bachelor Pascasio Gómez that more than ten captives will be freed with money from their pockets!"*

Then we went to another place in that region of Toledo, towards what is called La Mancha, where we found people that obstinately refused to take the bulls. Even after all of us completed the customary deals, less than thirty pardons were bought in the two town festivals that we attended.

Seeing my master the great losses and considerable expenses that he was having to assume, he came up with yet another devious design to unload his bulls. And it was this: That day he said High Mass, and after the sermon he returned from the pulpit to the altar and took a cross of about six inches in length. He then took a brazier that was on the altar (which they had put there to warm their hands, for it was very cold) and hid it behind a missal without anyone noticing it. He then put the cross on the hot coals very stealthily, and as soon as he finished saying Mass and offered the blessing, he picked up the cross with a handkerchief he had prepared in his right hand for the occasion. With his left he picked up the bull and descended to the bottom step of the altar, where he pretended to kiss the cross. He then gave a signal for all to draw closer and venerate the cross. The officials came first with the village elders, one by one as is the custom.

The first to arrive, an old official, burned his lips and quickly stepped aside, although the cross had been offered to him very gently. My master saw this and exclaimed: "Behold, Mr. Official, a miracle!" The same thing happened with another seven or eight of them, and to all he said: Behold, gentlemen, a miracle!"

When he saw that there were enough smoldering lips to testify to his miracle, he stopped offering up the cross to be kissed. He climbed to the base of the altar and from there he began to declare awe-inspiring things. He claimed that God had caused the miracle owing to the small charity shown by those townsfolk. He also said that the cross should be taken to the main church of that diocese, for the lack of charity being shown by that town was causing the cross to burn.

This all caused such a rush to take the bull that the two scribes, the clerics and the sacristans had their hands full just trying to record the transactions. I firmly believe that more than three thousand bulls were taken, as I've told Your Mercy.

Afterwards, as we were about to leave, he went with great reverence to retrieve the holy cross, as is proper, saying that he was going to have it dipped in gold, as was proper. But the Town Council and the local clerics begged him to leave that holy cross, in memory of the miracle that had taken place there. He absolutely refused, but eventually, after being begged by so many, he agreed to leave it. In return they gave him another old cross they had, an antique made of solid silver that must have weighed two or three pounds, as they said.[79]

Thus we left the place, happy with the exchange and with the way the business had turned out. And no one saw what happened but me. At the time I had gone up to the altar to see if there was any wine left in the communion vessels: I wanted to polish it off as was my custom. When he saw me there, he put his finger to his lips, signaling me to keep quiet. And I did so because it was my obligation, and although after I saw the miracle I wanted to open my mouth and tell everyone about it, I did not for fear of my astute master. And I never spoke about it to anyone after that; he made me swear not to reveal the truth about the miracle, and I've ever since kept my word.

And although a boy, it greatly amused me and I said to myself: "These con artists must hoodwink so many innocent people with these scams!"

Finally, I spent close to four months with this, my fifth master. During this time I also experienced ample privation, although by and large he fed me well at the expense of the priests and other clerics where he went to preach.

Chapter Six

How Lázaro Served a Chaplain, and What Came to Pass with Him.

After this, I settled with a master tambourine painter to grind his colors for him; I endured a thousand calamities with him as well.[80]

Being already a grown lad by this time, one day I chanced to enter the cathedral, where its chaplain saw me and took me into his service. He gave a good ass, four casks and a whip into my care with which I commenced to deliver water about the city. This was the first step in my ascent to the good life, for my voice was ideal for calling out the customers. Every day I gave my master thirty maravedís from my take;

anything above that I could keep, as well as everything I made on Saturdays.

I managed this affair so well, that at the end of four years I was able to save enough to dress myself decently in second-hand clothes. I purchased an old cotton pile doublet, a threadbare tunic with braided sleeves and open collar, a cape that had once been velvet, and a sword of the old type, of the first that were made in Cuéllar.[81] When I finally saw myself in the habit of a gentleman, I told my master to take back his donkey, for I didn't wish to engage in that profession any longer.

Chapter Seven
How Lázaro Established Himself with a Sheriff, and What Happened with Him.

After I left the chaplain I established myself as bailiff with a sheriff. But I didn't stay with him for long, as the job seemed too perilous to me. For example, one night a band of felons that had taken refuge in a church,[82] sallying out with a robust quantity of stones and stout rods in their hands, came at us with a naughty disposition. They did most confoundedly belabor my patron, who was fool enough to hang about and wait for them, but as for me, I fled at such a speed that they were unable to catch me. With this I abandoned that employment.

I applied all my thoughts to finding some source of revenue that would allow me to live peacefully and to save some money for my old age. And God saw it fit to light my way and put me on the road to success. With the good will and favor of some friends and gentlemen, all the trials and tribulations to which I'd been subjected up to then finally paid off, seeing how I obtained a government job. A job like that is the only way to thrive.

And this is what I do to this day, in the service of God and Your Worship. The details of the job are these: I am charged with publicly announcing the wines that are sold in this city. I also call out at auctions and broadcast my voice around town enquiring after lost objects.

And I escort people who are suffering punishment by justice and call out their crimes. In short, I'm a town crier, to put it bluntly.[83]

While in the pursuance of the duties of my office, one day as we were hanging a rag maker in Toledo using a good esparto rope, I recalled the good advice given me in Escalona by my blind master, and I felt sorry for having repaid him in the way I did. He taught me much. After God, he gave me the resources to reach the position in which I find myself today.

This business has gone so well for me, and I am so adept at it, that almost every deal that requires the services of a crier ends up in my charge. So much so that in this city, if anyone has wine or anything else to sell, if Lázaro de Tormes is not involved it will certainly not show a profit.

By this time I was announcing the wines of the Archpriest of San Salvador, my master and Your Worship's servant and friend.[84] Seeing my industrious nature, my honest way of life, and having good reports on my person, he was well pleased to bestow his lady housekeeper upon me. Considering how only good and favorable circumstance could come from a person like the Archpriest, I consented to take her hand in marriage. And so I married her, and to this day I haven't had occasion to regret it.

Because, besides being a decent sort and a good housewife, I obtain much favor and assistance from the Archpriest on her account. Every year he gives her close to a full load of wheat, on Easter a considerable amount of meat, bread on holidays, and I get his discarded old pants.[85] He had us rent a little house next to his and we commonly ate at his house almost every Sunday and holiday.

But as ill tongues are never still, they are apt to disturb the repose of folk like us, tattling I don't know what about my wife going to make the Archpriest's bed and prepare his food. May God help them speak the truth.[86]

It is true that I've had occasion to doubt her honesty, and many a time I've had bitter dinners waiting for her until the break of dawn[87] and even longer. At those times I am reminded of what my blind master told me in Escalona while holding the horn in his hand.[88] Although, to tell the truth, I always suppose the Devil brings forth this recollection to make me unhappy in my marriage, yet it profits him not.

Because, besides the fact that she's not the kind of woman who takes these scandalmongers seriously, my master made me a promise, and I believe that he is a man of his word. One day he talked to me for a long time in front of her, and he said to me: "Lázaro of Tormes, he who pays attention to gossips will never prosper. I tell you this because it wouldn't surprise me if gossips made a butt of your wife, seeing how she goes in and out of my house. But she enters for your honor and for hers, and this I pledge to you. So don't fret about what people say. Just think about the advantages ... I mean, about your profits."

"Sir," I said, "some time ago I determined to dwell among the virtuous. It is true that some of my friends have told me something to that effect, saying that before we were married she bore more than three children, speaking with reverence to Your Grace, as she is here before us."

At this my wife began to make such terrible execrations that I thought the house was going to sink with us in it. Then she began to cry most bitterly, cursing the man who had married her to me. It got to the point where I thought I should have died before ever speaking those words. But I pleaded with her from one side and my master from the other, agreeing to so much that we prevailed on her to cease her lamentations. I had to swear that never again in my life would I mention anything of that nature and that I was comfortable and happy with her entering and leaving his house, be it night or day, since I was confident of her virtue. And thus the three of us reached conformity. To this day no one has heard one word from us about the case; when I sense someone wants to say something about her, I cut him off and say: "Look, if you are my friend, tell me nothing that will annoy me, for he who offends me is not my friend. Above all, I can't endure to hear any reflections upon my wife, whom I love better than the entire world, even better than myself. God has blessed me a thousand times in giving her to me; indeed, she is more than I deserve. I will swear upon the consecrated Host that she is as virtuous a woman as lives in all of Toledo.[89] Whoever says otherwise will have to fight me to the death." After that declaration they refrain from saying anything and I am able to live in peace at home.

This was the same year that our victorious emperor entered into this illustrious city of Toledo,[90] where his court was kept with great feasts, as Your Worship must have heard. It was then that I was in my prosperity and at the very pinnacle of all good fortune.

Of what may happen to me henceforth, I shall inform Your Worship.[91]

La Vida de Lazarillo de Tormes

Prólogo

Yo por bien tengo que cosas tan señaladas, y por ventura nunca oídas ni vistas, vengan a noticia de muchos y no se entierren en la sepultura del olvido, pues podría ser que alguno que las lea halle algo que le agrade, y a los que no ahondaren tanto los deleite; y a este propósito dice Plinio que no hay libro, por malo que sea, que no tenga alguna cosa buena; mayormente que los gustos no son todos unos, mas lo que uno no come, otro se pierde por ello. Y así vemos cosas tenidas en poco de algunos, que de otros no lo son. Y esto, para ninguna cosa se debería romper ni echar a mal, si muy detestable no fuese, sino que a todos se comunicase, mayormente siendo sin perjuicio y pudiendo sacar della algún fructo; porque si así no fuese, muy pocos escribirían para uno solo, pues no se hace sin trabajo, y quieren, ya que lo pasan, ser recompensados, no con dineros, mas con que vean y lean sus obras, y si hay de qué, se las alaben; y a este propósito dice Tulio: "La honra cría las artes."

¿Quién piensa que el soldado que es primero del escala, tiene más aborrecido el vivir? No, por cierto; mas el deseo de alabanza le hace ponerse en peligro; y así, en las artes y letras es lo mesmo. Predica muy bien el presentado, y es hombre que desea mucho el provecho de las ánimas; mas pregunten a su merced si le pesa cuando le dicen: "¡Oh, qué maravillosamente lo ha hecho vuestra reverencia!" Justó muy ruinmente el señor don Fulano, y dio el sayete de armas al truhán, porque le loaba de haber llevado muy buenas lanzas. ¿Qué hiciera si fuera verdad?

Y todo va desta manera: que confesando yo no ser más santo que mis vecinos, desta nonada, que en este grosero estilo escribo, no me pesará que hayan parte y se huelguen con ello todos los que en ella algún gusto hallaren, y vean que vive un hombre con tantas fortunas, peligros y adversidades.

Suplico a Vuestra Merced reciba el pobre servicio de mano de quien lo hiciera más rico si su poder y deseo se conformaran. Y pues Vuestra Merced escribe se le escriba y relate el caso por muy extenso, parecióme no tomalle por el medio, sino por el principio, porque se tenga entera noticia de mi persona, y también porque consideren los que heredaron nobles estados cuán poco se les debe, pues Fortuna fue con ellos parcial, y cuanto más hicieron los que, siéndoles contraria, con fuerza y maña remando salieron a buen puerto.

Tratado Primero

Cuenta Lázaro su vida, y cúyo hijo fue.

Pues sepa Vuestra Merced ante todas cosas que a mí llaman Lázaro de Tormes, hijo de Tomé Gonzáles y de Antonia Pérez, naturales de Tejares, aldea de Salamanca. Mi nacimiento fue dentro del río Tormes, por la cual causa tomé el sobrenombre, y fue desta manera. Mi padre, que Dios perdone, tenía cargo de proveer una molienda de una aceña, que está ribera de aquel río, en la cual fue molinero más de quince años; y estando mi madre una noche en la aceña, preñada de mí, tomóle el parto y parióme allí; de manera que con verdad me puedo decir nacido en el río.

Pues siendo yo niño de ocho años, achacaron a mi padre ciertas sangrías mal hechas en los costales de los que allí a moler venían, por lo que fue preso, y confesó, y no negó, y padeció persecución por justicia. Espero en Dios que está en la Gloria, pues el Evangelio los llama bienaventurados. En este tiempo se hizo cierta armada contra moros, entre los cuales fue mi padre, que a la sazón estaba desterrado por el desastre ya dicho, con cargo de acemilero de un caballero que allá fue; y con su señor, como leal criado, feneció su vida.

Mi viuda madre, como sin marido y sin abrigo se viese, determinó arrimarse a los buenos por ser uno dellos, y vínose a vivir a la ciudad, y alquiló una casilla, y metióse a guisar de comer a ciertos estudiantes, y lavaba la ropa a ciertos mozos de caballos del Comendador de la Magdalena, de manera que fue frecuentando las caballerizas. Ella y un hombre moreno, de aquellos que las bestias curaban, vinieron en conoscimiento. Este algunas veces se venía a nuestra casa, y se iba a la mañana; otras veces de día llegaba a la puerta, en achaque de comprar huevos, y entrábase en casa. Yo, al principio de su entrada, pesábame con él y habíale miedo, viendo el color y mal gesto que tenía; mas de que vi que con su venida mejoraba el comer, fuile queriendo bien, porque siempre traía pan, pedazos de carne, y en el invierno leños, a que nos calentábamos.

De manera que, continuando con la posada y conversación, mi madre vino a darme un negrito muy bonito, el cual yo brincaba y ayudaba a calentar. Y acuérdome que, estando el negro de mi padre trebajando con el mozuelo, como el niño vía a mi madre y a mí blancos, y a él no, huía dél con miedo para mi madre, y señalando con el dedo decía:

—¡Madre, coco!

Respondió él riendo:

—¡Hideputa!

Yo, aunque bien mochacho, noté aquella palabra de mi hermanico, y dije entre mí: "¡Cuantos debe de haber en el mundo que huyen de otros porque no se veen a sí mesmos!"

Quiso nuestra fortuna que la conversación del Zaide, que así se llamaba, llegó a oídos del mayordomo, y hecha pesquisa, hallóse que la mitad por medio de la cebada, que para las bestias le daban, hurtaba, y salvados, leña, almohazas, mandiles, y las mantas y sábanas de los caballos hacía perdidas, y cuando otra cosa no tenía, las bestias desherraba, y con todo esto acudía a mi madre para criar a mi hermanico.

No nos maravillemos de un clérigo ni fraile, porque el uno hurta de los pobres y el otro de casa para sus devotas y para ayuda de otro tanto, cuando a un pobre esclavo el amor le animaba a esto.

Y probósele cuanto digo y aun más, porque a mí con amenazas me preguntaban, y como niño respondía, y descubría cuanto sabía con miedo, hasta ciertas herraduras que por mandado de mi madre a un herrero vendí.

Al triste de mi padrastro azotaron y pringaron, y a mi madre pusieron pena por justicia, sobre el acostumbrado centenario, que en casa del sobredicho Comendador no entrase, ni al lastimado Zaide en la suya acogiese.

Por no echar la soga tras el caldero, la triste se esforzó y cumplió la sentencia; y por evitar peligro y quitarse de malas lenguas, se fue a servir a los que al presente vivían en el mesón de la Solana; y allí, padesciendo mil importunidades, se acabó de criar mi hermanico hasta que supo andar, y a mí hasta ser buen mozuelo, que iba a los huéspedes por vino y candelas y por lo demás que me mandaban.

En este tiempo vino a posar al mesón un ciego, el cual, paresciéndole que yo sería para adestralle, me pidió a mi madre, y ella me encomendó a él, diciéndole cómo era hijo de un buen hombre, el cual por ensalzar la fe había muerto en la de los Gelves, y que ella confiaba en Dios no saldría peor hombre que mi padre, y que le rogaba me tratase bien y mirase por mi, pues era huérfano. Él le respondió que así lo haría, y que me recibía no por mozo, sino por hijo. Y así le comencé a servir y adestrar a mi nuevo y viejo amo.

Como estuvimos en Salamanca algunos días, paresciéndole a mi amo que no era la ganancia a su contento, determinó irse de allí; y cuando nos hubimos de partir, yo fui a ver a mi madre, y ambos llorando, me dio su bendición y dijo:

—Hijo, ya sé que no te veré más. Procura ser bueno, y Dios te guíe. Criado te he y con buen amo te he puesto. Válete por ti.

Y así me fui para mi amo, que esperándome estaba. Salimos de Salamanca, y llegando a la puente, está a la entrada della un animal de piedra, que casi tiene forma de toro, y el ciego mandóme que llegase cerca del animal, y allí puesto, me dijo:

—Lázaro, llega el oído a este toro, y oirás gran ruido dentro dél.

Yo simplemente llegué, creyendo ser ansí; y como sintió que tenía la cabeza par de la piedra, afirmó recio la mano y dióme una gran calabazada en el diablo del toro, que más de tres días me duró el dolor de la cornada, y díjome:

—Necio, aprende, que el mozo del ciego un punto ha de saber más que el diablo.

Y rió mucho la burla.

Parescióme que en aquel instante desperté de la simpleza en que, como niño, dormido estaba. Dije entre mí: "Verdad dice éste, que me cumple avivar el ojo y avisar, pues solo soy, y pensar cómo me sepa valer."

Comenzamos nuestro camino, y en muy pocos días me mostró jerigonza. Y, como me viese de buen ingenio, holgábase mucho y decía:

—Yo oro ni plata no te lo puedo dar; mas avisos para vivir muchos te mostraré.

Y fue ansí que, después de Dios, éste me dio la vida, y, siendo ciego, me alumbró y adestró en la carrera de vivir.

Huelgo de contar a Vuestra Merced estas niñerías para mostrar cuánta virtud sea saber los hombres subir siendo bajos, y dejarse bajar siendo altos cuánto vicio.

Pues, tornando al bueno de mi ciego y contando sus cosas, Vuestra Merced sepa que desde que Dios crió el mundo ninguno formó más astuto ni sagaz. En su oficio era un águila: ciento y tantas oraciones sabía de coro; un tono bajo, reposado y muy sonable, que hacía resonar la iglesia donde rezaba; un rostro humilde y devoto, que, con muy buen continente ponía cuando rezaba, sin hacer gestos ni visajes con boca ni ojos como otros suelen hacer. Allende de esto, tenía otras mil formas y maneras para sacar el dinero. Decía saber oraciones para muchos y diversos efectos: para mujeres que no parían; para las que estaban de parto; para las que eran malcasadas, que sus maridos las quisiesen bien. Echaba pronósticos a las preñadas si traían hijo o hija. Pues en caso de medicina, decía que Galeno no supo la mitad que él para muelas, desmayos, males de madre. Finalmente, nadie le decía padecer alguna pasión, que luego no le decía:

—Haced esto, haréis esto otro, cosed tal yerba, tomad tal raíz.

Con esto andábase todo el mundo tras él, especialmente mujeres, que cuanto les decía creían. De éstas sacaba él grandes provechos con las artes que digo, y ganaba más en un mes que cien ciegos en un año.

Mas también quiero que sepa Vuestra Merced que, con todo lo que adquiría y tenía, jamás tan avariento ni mezquino hombre no vi; tanto, que me mataba a mí de hambre, y así no me demediaba de lo necesario. Digo verdad: si con mi sutileza y buenas mañas no me supiera remediar, muchas veces me finara de hambre; mas con todo su saber y aviso, le contaminaba de tal suerte que siempre, o las más veces, me cabía lo más y mejor. Para esto le hacía burlas endiabladas, de las cuales contaré algunas, aunque no todas a mi salvo.

Él traía el pan y todas las otras cosas en un fardel de lienzo, que por la boca se cerraba con una argolla de hierro y su candado y su llave; y al meter de todas las cosas y sacallas, era con tanta vigilancia y tanto por contadero, que no bastara hombre en todo el mundo hacerle menos una migaja. Mas yo tomaba aquella laceria que él me daba, la cual en menos de dos bocados era despachada. Después que cerraba el candado y se descuidaba, pensando que yo estaba entendiendo en otras cosas, por un poco de costura, que muchas veces del un lado del fardel descosía y tornaba a coser, sangraba el avariento fardel, sacando no por tasa pan, más buenos pedazos, torreznos y longaniza. Y ansí, buscaba conveniente tiempo para rehacer, no la chaza, sino la endiablada falta que el mal ciego me faltaba.

Todo lo que podía sisar y hurtar traía en medias blancas, y cuando le mandaban rezar y le daban blancas, como él carecía de vista, no había el que se la daba amagado con ella, cuando yo la tenía lanzada en la boca y la media aparejada, que por presto que él echaba la mano, ya iba de mi cambio aniquilada en la mitad del justo precio. Quejábaseme el mal ciego, porque al tiento luego conocía y sentía que no era blanca entera, y decía:

—¿Qué diablo es esto, que después que conmigo estás, no me dan sino medias blancas, y de antes una blanca y un maravedí hartas veces me pagaban? En ti debe estar esta desdicha.

También él abreviaba el rezar y la mitad de la oración no acababa, porque me tenía mandado que, en yéndose el que la mandaba rezar, le tirase por cabo del capuz. Yo así lo hacía. Luego él tornaba a dar voces diciendo:

—¿Mandan rezar tal y tal oración?—como suelen decir.

Usaba poner cabe sí un jarrillo de vino cuando comíamos, y yo muy de presto le asía y daba un par de besos callados y tornábale a su lugar. Mas turóme poco, que en los tragos conocía la falta, y, por reservar su vino a salvo, nunca después desamparaba el jarro, antes lo tenía por el asa asido. Mas no había piedra imán que así trajese a sí como yo con una paja larga de centeno, que para aquel menester tenía hecha, la cual metiéndola en la boca del jarro, chupando el vino lo dejaba a buenas noches. Mas como fuese el traidor tan astuto, pienso que me sintió, y dende en adelante mudó propósito y asentaba su jarro entre las piernas y atapábale con la mano, y ansí bebía seguro.

Yo, como estaba hecho al vino, moría por él, y viendo que aquel remedio de la paja no me aprovechaba ni valía, acordé en el suelo del jarro hacerle una fuentecilla y agujero sutil, y delicadamente, con una muy delgada tortilla de cera, taparlo. Al tiempo de comer, fingiendo haber frío, entrábame entre las piernas del triste ciego a calentarme en la pobrecilla lumbre que teníamos, y al calor de ella luego derretida la cera, por ser muy poca, comenzaba la fuentecilla a destilarme en la boca, la cual yo de tal manera ponía, que maldita la gota se perdía. Cuando el pobreto iba a beber, no hallaba nada. Espantábase, maldecíase, daba al diablo el jarro y el vino, no sabiendo qué podía ser.

—No diréis, tío, que os lo bebo yo—decía—, pues no le quitáis de la mano.

Tantas vueltas y tientos dio al jarro, que halló la fuente y cayó en la burla; mas así lo disimuló como si no lo hubiera sentido.

Y luego otro día, teniendo yo rezumando mi jarro como solía, no pensando el daño que me estaba aparejado ni que el mal ciego me sentía, sentéme como solía; estando recibiendo aquellos dulces tragos, mi cara puesta hacia el cielo, un poco cerrados los ojos por mejor gustar el sabroso licor, sintió el desesperado ciego que agora tenía tiempo de tomar de mí venganza, y con toda su fuerza, alzando con dos manos aquel dulce y amargo jarro, le dejó caer sobre mi boca, ayudándose, como digo, con todo su poder, de manera que el pobre Lázaro, que de nada desto se guardaba, antes, como otras veces, estaba descuidado y gozoso, verdaderamente me pareció que el cielo, con todo lo que en él hay, me había caído encima.

Fue tal el golpecillo, que me desatinó y sacó de sentido, y el jarrazo tan grande, que los pedazos de él se me metieron por la cara, rompiéndomela por muchas partes, y me quebró los dientes, sin los cuales hasta hoy día me quedé.

Desde aquella hora quise mal al mal ciego, y aunque me quería y regalaba y me curaba, bien vi que se había holgado del cruel castigo. Lavóme con vino las roturas que con los pedazos del jarro me había hecho, y sonriéndose decía:

—¿Qué te parece Lázaro? Lo que te enfermó te sana y da salud.

Y otros donaires que a mi gusto no lo eran.

Ya que estuve medio bueno de mi negra trepa y cardenales, considerando que a pocos golpes tales el cruel ciego ahorraría de mí, quise yo ahorrar dél; mas no lo hice tan presto, por hacello más a mi salvo y provecho. Y aunque yo quisiera asentar mi corazón y perdonalle el jarrazo, no daba lugar el maltratamiento que el mal ciego dende allí adelante me hacía, que sin causa ni razón me hería, dándome coscorrones y repelándome.

Y si alguno le decía por qué me trataba tan mal, luego contaba el cuento del jarro, diciendo:

—¿Pensaréis que este mi mozo es algún inocente? Pues oíd si el demonio ensayara otra tal hazaña.

Santiguándose los que lo oían, decían:

—¡Mirá quién pensara de un mochacho tan pequeño tal ruindad!

Y reían mucho el artificio y decíanle:

—¡Castigaldo, castigaldo, que de Dios lo habréis!

Y él, con aquello, nunca otra cosa hacía. Y en esto yo siempre le llevaba por los peores caminos, y adrede, por hacerle mal y daño; si había piedras, por ellas; si lodo, por lo más alto; que, aunque yo no iba por lo más enjuto, holgábame a mí de quebrar un ojo por quebrar dos al que ninguno tenía. Con esto, siempre con el cabo alto del tiento me atentaba el colodrillo, el cual siempre traía lleno de tolondrones y pelado de sus manos. Y, aunque yo juraba no hacerlo con malicia, sino por no hallar mejor camino, no me aprovechaba ni me creía, mas tal era el sentido y el grandísimo entendimiento del traidor.

Y porque vea Vuestra Merced a cuánto se extendía el ingenio de este astuto ciego, contaré un caso de muchos que con él me acaecieron, en el cual me parece dio bien a entender su gran astucia. Cuando salimos de Salamanca, su motivo fue venir a tierra de Toledo, porque decía ser la gente más rica, aunque no muy limosnera. Arrimábase a este refrán: "Más da el duro que el desnudo". Y venimos a este camino por los mejores lugares. Donde hallaba buena acogida y ganancia, deteníamonos; donde no, a tercero día hacíamos San Juan.

Acaesció que, llegando a un lugar que llaman Almorox al tiempo que cogían las uvas, un vendimiador le dio un racimo dellas en limosna. Y como suelen ir los cestos maltratados, y también porque la uva en aquel tiempo está muy madura, desgranábasele el racimo en la mano. Para echarlo en el fardel, tornábase mosto, y lo que a él se llegaba. Acordó de hacer un banquete, ansí por no poder llevar como por contentarme, que aquel día me había dado muchos rodillazos y golpes. Sentámonos en un valladar y dijo:

—Agora quiero yo usar contigo de una liberalidad, y es que ambos comamos este racimo de uvas y que hayas dél tanta parte como yo. Partillo hemos de esta manera: tú picarás una vez y yo otra, con tal que me prometas no tomar cada vez más de una uva. Yo haré lo mismo hasta que lo acabemos, y de esta suerte no habrá engaño.

Hecho así el concierto, comenzamos; mas luego al segundo lance, el traidor mudó propósito, y comenzó a tomar de dos en dos, considerando que yo debría hacer lo mismo. Como vi que él quebraba la postura, no me contenté ir a la par con él, mas aún pasaba adelante: dos a dos y tres a tres y como podía las comía. Acabado el racimo, estuvo un poco con el escobajo en la mano, y meneando la cabeza dijo:

—Lázaro, engañado me has. Juraré yo a Dios que has tú comido las uvas tres a tres.

—No comí— dije yo—; mas ¿por qué sospecháis eso?

Respondió el sagacísimo ciego:

—¿Sabes en qué veo que las comiste tres a tres? En que comía yo dos a dos y callabas.

A lo cual yo no respondí. Yendo que íbamos así por debajo de unos soportales, en Escalona, adonde a la sazón estábamos, en casa de un zapatero había muchas sogas y otras cosas que de esparto se hacen, y parte dellas dieron a mi amo en la cabeza. El cual, alzando la mano, tocó en ellas, y viendo lo que era díjome:

—Anda presto, mochacho; salgamos de entre tan mal manjar, que ahoga sin comerlo.

Yo, que bien descuidado iba de aquello, miré lo que era, y como no vi sino sogas y cinchas, que no era cosa de comer, díjele:

—Tío, ¿por qué decís eso?

Respondióme:

— Calla, sobrino; según las mañas que llevas, lo sabrás y verás cómo digo verdad.

Y ansí pasamos adelante por el mismo portal y llegamos a un mesón, a la puerta del cual había muchos cuernos en la pared, donde ataban los recueros sus bestias, y como iba tentando si era allí el mesón adonde él rezaba cada día por la mesonera la oración de la emparedada, asió de un cuerno, y con un gran sospiro dijo:

—¡Oh, mala cosa, peor que tienes la hechura! ¡De cuántos eres deseado poner tu nombre sobre cabeza ajena y de cuán pocos tenerte ni aun oír tu nombre por ninguna vía!

Como le oí lo que decía, dije:

—Tío, ¿qué es eso que decís?

— Calla, sobrino, que algún día te dará éste que en la mano tengo alguna mala comida y cena.

— No le comeré yo — dije — y no me la dará.

— Yo te digo verdad; si no, verlo has, si vives.

Y así pasamos adelante hasta la puerta del mesón, adonde pluguiere a Dios nunca allá llegáramos, según lo que me sucedió en él.

Era todo lo más que rezaba por mesoneras y por bodegoneras y turroneras y rameras y ansí por semejantes mujercillas, que por hombre casi nunca le vi decir oración.

Reíme entre mí y, aunque mochacho, noté mucho la discreta consideración del ciego.

Mas por no ser prolijo, dejo de contar muchas cosas, así graciosas como de notar, que con este mi primer amo me acaescieron, y quiero decir el despidiente y, con él, acabar.

Estábamos en Escalona, villa del duque della, en un mesón, y dióme un pedazo de longaniza que le asase. Ya que la longaniza había pringado y comídose las pringadas, sacó un maravedí de la bolsa y mandó que fuese por él de vino a la taberna. Púsome el demonio el aparejo delante los ojos, el cual, como suelen decir, hace al ladrón, y fue que había cabe el fuego un nabo pequeño, larguillo y ruinoso, y tal que, por no ser para la olla, debió ser echado allí. Y como al presente nadie estuviese, sino él y yo solos, como me vi con apetito goloso, habiéndoseme puesto dentro el sabroso olor de la longaniza, del cual solamente sabía que había de gozar, no mirando qué me podría suceder, pospuesto todo el temor por cumplir con el deseo, en tanto que el ciego sacaba de la bolsa el dinero, saqué la longaniza y muy presto metí el sobredicho nabo en el asador, el cual, mi amo, dándome el dinero para el vino, tomó y comenzó a dar vueltas al fuego, queriendo asar al que, de ser cocido, por sus deméritos había escapado. Yo fui por el vino, con el cual no tardé en despachar la longaniza, y cuando vine, hallé al pecador del ciego que tenía entre dos rebanadas apretado el nabo, al cual aún no había conoscido por no haberlo tentado con la mano. Como tomase las rebanadas y mordiese en ellas pensando también llevar parte de la longaniza, hallóse en frío con el frío nabo. Alteróse y dijo:

—¿Qué es esto, Lazarillo?

—¡Lacerado de mí!— dije yo—. ¿Si queréis a mí echar algo? ¿Yo no vengo de traer el vino? Alguno estaba ahí y por burlar haría esto.

— No, no — dijo él —, que yo no he dejado el asador de la mano; no es posible.

Yo torné a jurar y perjurar que estaba libre de aquel trueco y cambio; mas poco me aprovechó, pues a las astucias del maldito ciego nada se le escondía. Levantóse y asióme por la cabeza y llegóse a olerme. Y como debió sentir el huelgo, a uso de buen podenco, por mejor satisfacerse de la verdad y con la gran agonía que llevaba, asiéndome con las manos, abríame la boca más de su derecho y desatentadamente metía la nariz, la cual él tenía luenga y afilada, y a aquella sazón, con el enojo, se había aumentado un palmo; con el pico de la cual me llegó a la gulilla.

Y con esto, y con el gran miedo que tenía, y con la brevedad del tiempo, la negra longaniza aún no había hecho asiento en el estómago; y lo más principal: con el destiento de la cumplidísima nariz medio cuasi ahogándome, todas estas cosas se juntaron y fueron causa que el hecho y golosina se manifestase y lo suyo fuese vuelto a su dueño. De manera que, antes que el mal ciego sacase de mi boca su trompa, tal alteración sintió mi estómago, que le dio con el hurto en ella, de suerte que su nariz y la negra mal maxcada longaniza a un tiempo salieron de mi boca.

¡Oh gran Dios, quién estuviera aquella hora sepultado, que muerto ya lo estaba! Fue tal el coraje del perverso ciego, que, si al ruido no acudieran, pienso no me dejara con la vida. Sacáronme de entre sus manos, dejándoselas llenas de aquellos pocos cabellos que tenía, arañada la cara y rascuñado el pescuezo y la garganta. Y esto bien lo merecía, pues por su maldad me venían tantas persecuciones.

Contaba el mal ciego a todos cuantos allí se allegaban mis desastres, y dábales cuenta una y otra vez, así de la del jarro como de la del racimo, y agora de lo presente. Era la risa de todos tan grande, que toda la gente que por la calle pasaba entraba a ver la fiesta; mas con tanta gracia y donaire contaba el ciego mis hazañas, que, aunque yo estaba tan maltratado y llorando, me parecía que hacía sinjusticia en no se las reír.

Y en cuanto esto pasaba, a la memoria me vino una cobardía y flojedad que hice, por que me maldecía, y fue no dejalle sin narices, pues tan buen tiempo tuve para ello, que la mitad del camino estaba andado; que con sólo apretar los dientes se me quedaran en casa, y con ser de aquel malvado, por ventura lo retuviera mejor mi estómago que retuvo la longaniza, y no pareciendo ellas, pudiera negar la demanda. ¡Pluguiera a Dios que lo hubiera hecho, que eso fuera así que así!

Hiciéronnos amigos la mesonera y los que allí estaban, y con el vino que para beber le había traído laváronme la cara y la garganta. Sobre lo cual discantaba el mal ciego donaires, diciendo:

—Por verdad, más vino me gasta este mozo en lavatorios al cabo del año, que yo bebo en dos. A lo menos, Lázaro, eres en más cargo al vino que a tu padre, porque él una vez te engendró, mas el vino mil te ha dado la vida.

Y luego contaba cuántas veces me había descalabrado y arpado la cara, y con vino luego sanaba.

—Yo te digo—dijo—que si hombre en el mundo ha de ser bienaventurado con vino, que serás tú.

Y reían mucho los que me lavaban con esto, aunque yo renegaba. Mas el pronóstico del ciego no salió mentiroso, y después acá muchas veces me acuerdo de aquel hombre, que sin duda debía tener espíritu de profecía, y me pesa de los sinsabores que le hice, aunque bien se lo pagué, considerando lo que aquel día me dijo salirme tan verdadero como adelante Vuestra Merced oirá.

Visto esto y las malas burlas que el ciego burlaba de mí, determiné de todo en todo dejalle, y como lo traía pensado y lo tenía en voluntad, con este postrer juego que me hizo afirmélo más. Y fue así que luego otro día salimos por la villa a pedir limosna, y había llovido mucho la noche antes; y porque el día también llovía, y andaba rezando debajo de unos portales que en aquel pueblo había, donde no nos mojamos, mas como la noche se venía y el llover no cesaba, díjome el ciego:

—Lázaro, esta agua es muy porfiada, y cuanto la noche más cierra, más recia. Acojámonos a la posada con tiempo.

Para ir allá habíamos de pasar un arroyo, que con la mucha agua iba grande. Yo le dije:

—Tío, el arroyo va muy ancho; mas si queréis, yo veo por donde travesemos más aína sin mojarnos, porque se estrecha allí mucho, y saltando pasaremos a pie enjuto.

Parecióle buen consejo y dijo:

—Discreto eres, por esto te quiero bien; llévame a ese lugar donde el arroyo se ensangosta, que agora es invierno y sabe mal el agua, y más llevar los pies mojados.

Yo que vi el aparejo a mi deseo, saquéle de bajo de los portales y llevéle derecho a un pilar o poste de piedra que en la plaza estaba, sobre el cual y sobre otros cargaban saledizos de aquellas casas, y dígole:

—Tío, éste es el paso más angosto que en el arroyo hay.

Como llovía recio y el triste se mojaba, y con la priesa que llevábamos de salir del agua, que encima de nos caía, y, lo más principal, porque Dios le cegó aquella hora el entendimiento (fue por darme dél venganza), creyóse de mí y dijo:

—Ponme bien derecho y salta tú el arroyo.

Yo le puse bien derecho enfrente del pilar, y doy un salto y póngome detrás del poste, como quien espera tope de toro, y díjele:

—¡Sús, saltad todo lo que podáis, porque deis de este cabo del agua!

Aun apenas lo había acabado de decir, cuando se abalanza el pobre ciego como cabrón y de toda su fuerza arremete, tomando un paso atrás de la corrida para hacer mayor salto, y da con la cabeza en el poste, que sonó tan recio como si diera con una gran calabaza, y cayó luego para atrás medio muerto y hendida la cabeza.

—¿Cómo, y olisteis la longaniza y no el poste? ¡Olé! ¡Olé!—le dije yo.

Y dejole en poder de mucha gente que lo había ido a socorrer, y tomo la puerta de la villa en los pies de un trote, y antes de que la noche viniese, di conmigo en Torrijos. No supe más lo que Dios dél hizo ni curé de saberlo.

Tratado Segundo

Cómo Lázaro se asentó con un clérigo, y de las cosas que con él pasó.

Otro día, no pareciéndome estar allí seguro, fuime a un lugar que llaman Maqueda, adonde me toparon mis pecados con un clérigo, que llegando a pedir limosna, me preguntó si sabía ayudar a misa. Yo dije que sí, como era verdad; que, aunque maltratado, mil cosas buenas me mostró el pecador del ciego, y una de ellas fue ésta. Finalmente, el clérigo me recibió por suyo.

Escapé del trueno y di en el relámpago, porque era el ciego para con éste un Alejandro Magno, con ser la misma avaricia, como he contado.

No digo más, sino que toda la laceria del mundo estaba encerrada en éste (no sé si de su cosecha era o lo había anexado con el hábito de clerecía).

Él tenía un arcaz viejo y cerrado con su llave, la cual traía atada con una agujeta del paletoque. Y en viniendo el bodigo de la iglesia, por su mano era luego allí lanzado y tornada a cerrar el arca. Y en toda la casa no había ninguna cosa de comer, como suele estar en otras algún tocino colgado al humero, algún queso puesto en alguna tabla o en el armario, algún canastillo con algunos pedazos de pan que de la mesa sobran; que me parece a mí que, aunque de ello no me aprovechara, con la vista de ello me consolara.

Solamente había una horca de cebollas, y tras la llave, en una cámara en lo alto de la casa. De éstas tenía yo de ración una para cada cuatro días, y, cuando le pedía la llave para ir por ella, si alguno estaba presente, echaba mano al falsopeto y con gran continencia la desataba y me la daba diciendo:

—Toma y vuélvela luego, y no hagáis sino golosinar.

Como si debajo della estuvieran todas las conservas de Valencia, con no haber en la dicha cámara, como dije, maldita la otra cosa que las cebollas colgadas de un clavo. Las cuales él tenía tan bien por cuenta, que si por malos de mis pecados me desmandara a más de mi tasa, me costara caro. Finalmente, yo me finaba de hambre.

Pues ya que conmigo tenía poca caridad, consigo usaba más. Cinco blancas de carne era su ordinario para comer y cenar. Verdad es que partía conmigo del caldo, que de la carne ¡tan blanco el ojo!, sino un poco de pan, y ¡pluguiera a Dios que me demediara!

Los sábados cómense en esta tierra cabezas de carnero, y enviábame por una, que costaba tres maravedís. Aquélla le cocía, y comía los ojos y la lengua, y el cogote y sesos, y la carne que en las quijadas tenía, y dábame todos los huesos roídos, y dábamelos en el plato, diciendo:

—Toma, come, triunfa, que para ti es el mundo: ¡Mejor vida tienes que el Papa!

"¡Tal te la dé Dios!", decía yo paso entre mí.

A cabo de tres semanas que estuve con él vine a tanta flaqueza, que no me podía tener en las piernas de pura hambre. Vime claramente ir a la sepultura, si Dios y mi saber no me remediaran. Para usar de mis mañas no tenía aparejo, por no tener en qué dalle salto, y aunque algo hubiera, no podía cegalle, como hacía al que Dios perdone (si de aquella calabazada feneció), que todavía, aunque astuto, con faltalle aquel preciado sentido, no me sentía; mas estotro, ninguno hay que tan aguda vista tuviese como él tenía.

Cuando al ofertorio estábamos, ninguna blanca en la concha caía que no era dél registrada: el un ojo tenía en la gente y el otro en mis manos. Bailábanle los ojos en el caxco como si fueran de azogue. Cuantas blancas ofrecían tenía por cuenta, y acabado el ofrecer, luego me quitaba la concha y la ponía sobre el altar.

No era yo señor de asirle una blanca todo el tiempo que con él viví, o, por mejor decir, morí. De la taberna nunca le traje una blanca de vino; mas aquel poco que de la ofrenda había metido en su arcaz compasaba de tal forma que le duraba toda la semana. Y por ocultar su gran mezquindad, decíame:

—Mira, mozo, los sacerdotes han de ser muy templados en su comer y beber, y por esto yo no me desmando como otros.

Mas el lacerado mentía falsamente, porque en cofradías y mortuorios que rezamos, a costa ajena comía como lobo y bebía más que un saludador.

Y porque dije de mortuorios, Dios me perdone, que jamás fui enemigo de la naturaleza humana sino entonces. Y esto era porque comíamos bien y me hartaban. Deseaba y aun rogaba a Dios que cada día matase el suyo. Y cuando dábamos sacramento a los enfermos, especialmente la extremaunción, como manda el clérigo rezar a los que están allí, yo cierto no era el postrero de la oración, y con todo mi corazón y buena voluntad rogaba al Señor, no que le echase a la parte que más servido fuese, como se suele decir, mas que le llevase de aqueste mundo. Y cuando alguno de éstos escapaba, ¡Dios me lo perdone!, que mil veces le daba al diablo; y el que se moría, otras tantas bendiciones llevaba de mí dichas. Porque en todo el tiempo que allí estuve, que serían casi seis meses, solas veinte personas fallescieron, y éstas bien creo que las maté yo, o, por mejor decir, murieron a mi recuesta; porque, viendo el Señor mi rabiosa y continua muerte, pienso que holgaba de matarlos por darme a mí vida. Mas de lo que al presente padecía, remedio no hallaba; que, si el día que enterrábamos yo vivía, los días que no había muerto, por quedar bien vezado de la hartura, tornando a mi cotidiana hambre, más lo sentía. De manera que en nada hallaba descanso, salvo en la muerte, que yo también para mí como para los otros deseaba algunas veces; mas no la veía, aunque estaba siempre en mí.

Pensé muchas veces irme de aquel mezquino amo, mas por dos cosas lo dejaba: la primera, por no me atrever a mis piernas, por temer de la flaqueza que de pura hambre me venía; y la otra, consideraba y decía: "Yo he tenido dos amos: el primero traíame muerto de hambre y, dejándole, topé con este otro que me tiene ya con ella en la sepultura; pues si de éste desisto y doy en otro más bajo, ¿qué será, sino fenecer?".

Con esto no me osaba menear, porque tenía por fe que todos los grados había de hallar más ruines. Y a abajar otro punto, no sonara Lázaro ni se oyera en el mundo.

Pues estando en tal aflicción, cual plega al Señor librar de ella a todo fiel cristiano, y sin saber darme consejo, viéndome ir de mal en peor, un día que el cuitado, ruin y lacerado de mi amo había ido fuera del lugar, llegóse acaso a mi puerta un calderero, el cual yo creo que fue ángel enviado a mí por la mano de Dios en aquel hábito. Preguntóme si tenía algo que adobar. "En mí teníades bien que hacer, y no haríades poco si me remediásedes", dije paso, que no me oyó.

Mas como no era tiempo de gastarlo en decir gracias, alumbrado por el Espíritu Santo, le dije:

—Tío, una llave de este arcaz he perdido, y temo mi señor me azote. Por vuestra vida, veáis si en ésas que traéis hay alguna que le haga, que yo os lo pagaré.

Comenzó a probar el angélico calderero una y otra de un gran sartal que de ellas traía, y yo ayudalle con mis flacas oraciones. Cuando no me cato, veo en figura de panes, como dicen, la cara de Dios dentro del arcaz, y abierto, díjele:

—Yo no tengo dineros que daros por la llave; mas tomad de ahí el pago.

Él tomó un bodigo de aquéllos, el que mejor le pareció, y dándome mi llave, se fue muy contento, dejándome más a mí.

Mas no toqué en nada por el presente, porque no fuese la falta sentida, y aun porque me vi de tanto bien señor, parecióme que la hambre no se me osaba allegar. Vino el mísero de mi amo, y quiso Dios no miró en la oblada que el ángel había llevado.

Y otro día, en saliendo de casa, abro mi paraíso panal y tomo entre las manos y dientes un bodigo y en dos credos le hice invisible, no olvidándoseme el arca abierta. Y comienzo a barrer la casa con mucha alegría, pareciéndome con aquel remedio remediar dende en adelante la triste vida. Y así estuve con ello aquel día y otro gozoso; mas no estaba en mi dicha que me durase mucho aquel descanso, porque luego, al tercero día, me vino la terciana derecha. Y fue que veo a deshora al que me mataba de hambre sobre nuestro arcaz, volviendo y revolviendo, contando y tornando a contar los panes. Yo disimulaba, y en mi secreta oración y devociones y plegarias decía: "¡San Juan y ciégale!"

Después que estuvo un gran rato echando la cuenta, por días y dedos contando, dijo:

—Si no tuviera a tan buen recaudo esta arca, yo dijera que me habían tomado de ella panes; pero de hoy más, sólo por cerrar la puerta a la sospecha, quiero tener buena cuenta con ellos: nueve quedan y un pedazo.

"¡Nuevas malas te dé Dios!", dije yo entre mí.

Parecióme con lo que dijo pasarme el corazón con saeta de montero y comenzóme el estómago a escarbar de hambre, viéndose puesto en la dieta pasada. Fue fuera de casa. Yo, por consolarme, abro el arca y, como vi el pan, comencélo de adorar, no osando rescebillo. Contélos, si a dicha el lacerado se errara, y hallé su cuenta más verdadera que yo quisiera. Lo más que yo pude hacer fue dar en ellos mil besos, y, lo más delicado que yo pude, del partido partí un poco al pelo que él estaba, y con aquél pasé aquel día, no tan alegre como el pasado.

Mas, como la hambre creciese, mayormente que tenía el estómago hecho a más pan aquellos dos o tres días ya dichos, moría mala muerte; tanto, que otra cosa no hacía, en viéndome solo, sino abrir y cerrar el arca y contemplar en aquella cara de Dios, que así dicen los niños. Mas el mismo Dios que socorre a los afligidos, viéndome en tal estrecho, trajo a mi memoria un pequeño remedio: que, considerando entre mí, dije: "Este arquetón es viejo y grande y roto por algunas partes, aunque pequeños agujeros. Puédese pensar que ratones, entrando en él, hacen daño a este pan. Sacarlo entero no es cosa conveniente, porque verá la falta el que en tanta me hace vivir. Esto bien se sufre".

Y comienzo a desmigajar el pan sobre unos no muy costosos manteles que allí estaban, y tomo uno y dejo otro, de manera que, en cada cual, de tres o cuatro desmigajé su poco. Después, como quien toma gragea, lo comí y algo me consolé. Mas él, como viniese a comer y abriese el arca, vio el mal pesar y sin duda creyó ser ratones los que el daño habían hecho, porque estaba muy al propio contrahecho de como ellos lo suelen hacer. Miró todo el arcaz de un cabo a otro y viole ciertos agujeros por do sospechaba habían entrado. Llamóme, diciendo:

—¡Lázaro, mira, mira, qué persecución ha venido aquesta noche por nuestro pan!

Yo híceme muy maravillado, preguntándole qué sería.

—¿Qué ha de ser?—dijo él—. Ratones, que no dejan cosa a vida.

Pusímonos a comer, y quiso Dios que aun en esto me fue bien: que me cupo más pan que la laceria que me solía dar, porque rayó con un cuchillo todo lo que pensó ser ratonado, diciendo:

—Cómete eso, que el ratón cosa limpia es.

Y así, aquel día, añadiendo la ración del trabajo de mis manos, o de mis uñas por mejor decir, acabamos de comer, aunque yo nunca empezaba.

Y luego me vino otro sobresalto, que fue verle andar solícito quitando clavos de las paredes y buscando tablillas, con las cuales clavó y cerró todos los agujeros de la vieja arca.

"¡Oh Señor mío—dije yo entonces—, a cuánta miseria y fortuna y desastres estamos puestos los nacidos, y cuán poco duran los placeres de esta nuestra trabajosa vida! Heme aquí, que pensaba con este pobre y triste remedio remediar y pasar mi laceria, y estaba ya cuanto que alegre y de buena ventura. Mas no quiso mi desdicha, despertando a este lacerado de mi amo y poniéndole más diligencia de la que él de suyo se tenía (pues los míseros por la mayor parte nunca de aquélla carecen), agora, cerrando los agujeros del arca, cerrase la puerta a mi consuelo y la abriese a mis trabajos".

Así lamentaba yo, en tanto que mi solícito carpintero, con muchos clavos y tablillas, dio fin a sus obras, diciendo:

—Agora, donos traidores ratones, conviéneos mudar propósito, que en esta casa mala medra tenéis.

De que salió de su casa, voy a ver la obra, y hallé que no dejó en la triste y vieja arca agujero ni aun por donde le pudiese entrar un mosquito. Abro con mi desaprovechada llave, sin esperanza de sacar provecho, y vi los dos o tres panes comenzados, los que mi amo creyó ser ratonados, y dellos todavía saqué alguna laceria, tocándolos muy ligeramente, a uso de esgrimidor diestro. Como la necesidad sea tan gran maestra, viéndome con tanta siempre, noche y día estaba pensando la manera que tendría en sustentar el vivir. Y pienso, para hallar estos negros remedios, que me era luz la hambre, pues dicen que el ingenio con ella se avisa, y al contrario con la hartura, y así era por cierto en mí.

Pues estando una noche desvelado en este pensamiento, pensando cómo me podría valer y aprovecharme del arcaz, sentí que mi amo dormía, porque lo mostraba con roncar y en unos resoplidos grandes que daba cuando estaba durmiendo. Levantéme muy quedito, y habiendo en el día pensado lo que había de hacer y dejado un cuchillo viejo que por allí andaba en parte do le hallase, voyme al triste arcaz, y, por do había mirado tener menos defensa, le acometí con el cuchillo, que a manera de barreno de él usé. Y como la antiquísima arca, por ser de tantos años, la hallase sin fuerza y corazón, antes muy blanda y carcomida, luego se me rindió y consintió en su costado, por mi remedio, un buen agujero. Esto hecho, abro muy paso la llagada arca y, al tiento, del pan que hallé partido hice según de yuso está escrito. Y con aquello algún tanto consolado, tornando a cerrar, me volví a mis pajas, en las cuales reposé y dormí un poco, lo cual yo hacía mal, y echábalo al no comer. Y así sería, porque cierto, en aquel tiempo no me debían de quitar el sueño los cuidados del rey de Francia.

Otro día fue por el señor mi amo visto el daño, así del pan como del agujero que yo había hecho, y comenzó a dar a los diablos los ratones y decir:

—¿Qué diremos a esto? ¡Nunca haber sentido ratones en esta casa, sino agora!

Y sin duda debía de decir verdad, porque si casa había de haber en el reino justamente de ellos privilegiada, aquélla de razón había de ser, porque no suelen morar donde no hay qué comer. Torna a buscar clavos por la casa y por las paredes, y tablillas a atapárselos. Venida la noche y su reposo, luego yo era puesto en pie con mi aparejo, y cuantos él tapaba de día, destapaba yo de noche.

En tal manera fue y tal prisa nos dimos, que sin duda por esto se debió decir: "donde una puerta se cierra, otra se abre." Finalmente, parecíamos tener a destajo la tela de Penélope, pues cuanto él tejía de día rompía yo de noche. Ca en pocos días y noches pusimos la pobre despensa de tal forma que, quien quisiera propiamente de ella hablar, más corazas viejas de otro tiempo, que no arcaz, la llamara, según la clavazón y tachuelas sobre sí tenía.

De que vio no le aprovechar nada su remedio, dijo:

—Este arcaz está tan maltratado y es de madera tan vieja y flaca, que no habrá ratón a quien se defienda. Y va ya tal, que si andamos más con él nos dejará sin guarda. Y aun lo peor, que aunque hace poca, todavía hará falta faltando, y me pondrá en costa de tres o cuatro reales. El mejor remedio que hallo, pues el de hasta aquí no aprovecha: armaré por de dentro a estos ratones malditos.

Luego buscó prestada una ratonera, y con cortezas de queso que a los vecinos pedía, contino el gato estaba armado dentro del arca. Lo cual era para mí singular auxilio, porque, puesto caso que yo no había menester muchas salsas para comer, todavía me holgaba con las cortezas del queso que de la ratonera sacaba, y sin esto no perdonaba el ratonar del bodigo.

Como hallase el pan ratonado y el queso comido y no cayese el ratón que lo comía, dábase al diablo, preguntaba a los vecinos qué podría ser comer el queso y sacarlo de la ratonera y no caer ni quedar dentro el ratón, y hallar caída la trampilla del gato.

Acordaron los vecinos no ser el ratón el que este daño hacía, porque no fuera menos de haber caído alguna vez. Díjole un vecino:

—En vuestra casa yo me acuerdo que solía andar una culebra, y ésta debe de ser sin duda. Y lleva razón, que como es larga, tiene lugar de tomar el cebo, y, aunque la coja la trampilla encima, como no entre toda dentro, tórnase a salir.

Cuadró a todos lo que aquél dijo y alteró mucho a mi amo, y dende en adelante no dormía tan a sueño suelto, que cualquier gusano de la madera que de noche sonase pensaba ser la culebra que le roía el arca. Luego era puesto en pie, y con un garrote que a la cabecera, desde que aquello le dijeron, ponía, daba en la pecadora del arca grandes garrotazos, pensando espantar la culebra. A los vecinos despertaba con el estruendo que hacía, y a mí no me dejaba dormir. Íbase a mis pajas y trastornábalas, y a mí con ellas, pensando que se iba para mí y se envolvía en mis pajas o en mi sayo; porque le decían que de noche acaecía a estos animales, buscando calor, irse a las cunas donde están criaturas, y aún mordellas y hacerles peligrar.

Yo las más veces hacía del dormido, y en la mañana, decíame él:

—¿Esta noche, mozo, no sentiste nada? Pues tras la culebra anduve, y aun pienso se ha de ir para ti a la cama, que son muy frías y buscan calor.

—¡Plega a Dios que no me muerda — decía yo —, que harto miedo le tengo!

Desta manera andaba tan elevado y levantado del sueño, que, mi fe, la culebra (o culebro por mejor decir) no osaba roer de noche ni levantarse al arca; mas de día, mientras estaba en la iglesia o por el lugar, hacía mis saltos. Los cuales daños viendo él, y el poco remedio que les podía poner, andaba de noche, como digo, hecho trasgo.

Yo hube miedo que con aquellas diligencias no me topase con la llave, que debajo de las pajas tenía, y parecióme lo más seguro metella de noche en la boca, porque ya, desde que viví con el ciego, la tenía tan hecha bolsa que me acaeció tener en ella doce o quince maravedís, todo en medias blancas, sin que me estorbase el comer, porque de otra manera no era señor de una blanca que el maldito ciego no cayese con ella, no dejando costura ni remiendo que no me buscaba muy a menudo.

Pues, así como digo, metía cada noche la llave en la boca y dormía sin recelo que el brujo de mi amo cayese con ella; mas cuando la desdicha ha de venir, por demás es diligencia. Quisieron mis hados, o por mejor decir mis pecados, que una noche que estaba durmiendo la llave se me puso en la boca, que abierta debía tener, de tal manera y postura que el aire y resoplo, que yo durmiendo echaba, salía por lo hueco de la llave, que de cañuto era, y silbaba, según mi desastre quiso, muy recio, de tal manera que el sobresaltado de mi amo lo oyó, y creyó sin duda ser el silbo de la culebra, y cierto lo debía parecer.

Levantóse muy paso con su garrote en la mano, y al tiento y sonido de la culebra se llegó a mí con mucha quietud, por no ser sentido de la culebra. Y como cerca se vio, pensó que allí en las pajas, do yo estaba echado, al calor mío se había venido. Levantando bien el palo, pensando tenerla debajo y darle tal garrotazo que la matase, con toda su fuerza me descargó en la cabeza un tan gran golpe que sin ningún sentido y muy mal descalabrado me dejó.

Como sintió que me había dado, según yo debía hacer gran sentimiento con el fiero golpe, contaba él que se había llegado a mí y, dándome grandes voces, llamándome, procuró recordarme. Mas, como me tocase con las manos, tentó la mucha sangre que se me iba y conoció el daño que me había hecho. Y con mucha prisa fue a buscar lumbre y, llegando con ella, hallóme quejando, todavía con mi llave en la boca, que nunca la desamparé, la mitad fuera, bien de aquella manera que debía estar al tiempo que silbaba con ella.

Espantado el matador de culebras qué podría ser aquella llave, miróla, sacándomela del todo de la boca, y vio lo que era, porque en las guardas nada de la suya diferenciaba. Fue luego a proballa, y con ella probó el maleficio. Debió de decir el cruel cazador: "El ratón y culebra que me daban guerra y me comían mi hacienda he hallado".

De lo que sucedió en aquellos tres días siguientes ninguna fe daré, porque los tuve en el vientre de la ballena, mas de cómo esto que he contado oí, después que en mí torné, decir a mi amo, el cual a cuantos allí venían lo contaba por extenso.

A cabo de tres días yo torné en mi sentido, y vime echado en mis pajas, la cabeza toda emplastada y llena de aceites y ungüentos, y espantado dije:

—¿Qué es esto?

Respondióme el cruel sacerdote:

—A fe que los ratones y culebras que me destruían ya los he cazado.

Y miré por mí, y vime tan maltratado que luego sospeché mi mal.

A esta hora entró una vieja que ensalmaba, y los vecinos. Y comiénzanme a quitar trapos de la cabeza y curar el garrotazo. Y como me hallaron vuelto en mi sentido, holgáronse mucho y dijeron:

—Pues ha tornado en su acuerdo, placerá a Dios no será nada.

Ahí tornaron de nuevo a contar mis cuitas y a reírlas, y yo, pecador, a llorarlas. Con todo esto, diéronme de comer, que estaba transido de hambre, y apenas me pudieron demediar. Y así, de poco en poco, a los quince días me levanté y estuve sin peligro (mas no sin hambre) y medio sano.

Luego otro día que fui levantado, el señor mi amo me tomó por la mano y sacóme la puerta fuera y, puesto en la calle, díjome:

—Lázaro, de hoy más eres tuyo y no mío. Busca amo y vete con Dios, que yo no quiero en mi compañía tan diligente servidor. No es posible sino que hayas sido mozo de ciego.

Y santiguándose de mí, como si yo estuviera endemoniado, tórnase a meter en casa y cierra su puerta.

Tratado Tercero

Cómo Lázaro se asentó con un escudero y de lo que le acaeció con él.

Desta manera me fue forzado sacar fuerzas de flaqueza, y poco a poco, con ayuda de las buenas gentes, di conmigo en esta insigne ciudad de Toledo, adonde, con la merced de Dios, dende a quince días se me cerró la herida. Y mientras estaba malo, siempre me daban alguna limosna; mas después que estuve sano, todos me decían:

—Tú, bellaco y gallofero eres. Busca, busca un buen amo a quien sirvas.

"¿Y adónde se hallará ése—decía yo entre mí—, si Dios agora de nuevo, como crió el mundo, no le criase?"

Andando así discurriendo de puerta en puerta, con harto poco remedio, porque ya la caridad se subió al cielo, topóme Dios con un escudero que iba por la calle, con razonable vestido, bien peinado, su paso y compás en orden. Miróme y yo a él, y díjome:

—Mochacho, ¿buscas amo?

Yo le dije:

—Sí, señor.

—Pues vente tras mí—me respondió—, que Dios te ha hecho merced en topar conmigo; alguna buena oración rezaste hoy.

Y seguíle, dando gracias a Dios por lo que le oí, y también que me parecía, según su hábito y continente, ser el que yo había menester.

Era de mañana cuando éste mi tercero amo topé, y llevóme tras sí gran parte de la ciudad. Pasábamos por las plazas do se vendía pan y otras provisiones. Yo pensaba, y aun deseaba, que allí me quería cargar de lo que se vendía, porque ésta era propia hora cuando se suele proveer de lo necesario, mas muy a tendido paso pasaba por estas cosas. "Por ventura no lo ve aquí a su contento—decía yo—, y querrá que lo compremos en otro cabo".

Desta manera anduvimos hasta que dio las once. Entonces se entró en la iglesia mayor, y yo tras él, y muy devotamente le vi oír misa y los otros oficios divinos, hasta que todo fue acabado y la gente ida. Entonces salimos de la iglesia. A buen paso tendido comenzamos a ir por una calle abajo. Yo iba el más alegre del mundo en ver que no nos habíamos ocupado en buscar de comer. Bien consideré que debía ser hombre, mi nuevo amo, que se proveía en junto, y que ya la comida estaría a punto y tal como yo la deseaba y aun la había menester.

En este tiempo dio el reloj la una después de mediodía, y llegamos a una casa ante la cual mi amo se paró, y yo con él, y derribando el cabo de la capa sobre el lado izquierdo, sacó una llave de la manga y abrió su puerta y entramos en casa. La cual tenía la entrada oscura y lóbrega de tal manera, que parece que ponía temor a los que en ella entraban, aunque dentro della estaba un patio pequeño y razonables cámaras.

Desque fuimos entrados, quita de sobre sí su capa, y preguntando si tenía las manos limpias, la sacudimos y doblamos, y muy limpiamente, soplando un poyo que allí estaba, la puso en él. Y hecho esto, sentóse cabo della, preguntándome muy por extenso de dónde era y cómo había venido a aquella ciudad. Y yo le di más larga cuenta que quisiera, porque me parecía más conveniente hora de mandar poner la mesa y escudillar la olla que de lo que me pedía. Con todo eso, yo le satisfice de mi persona lo mejor que mentir supe, diciendo mis bienes y callando lo demás, porque me parecía no ser para en cámara. Esto hecho, estuvo así un poco, y yo luego vi mala señal por ser ya casi las dos y no verle más aliento de comer que a un muerto. Después desto, consideraba aquel tener cerrada la puerta con llave, ni sentir arriba ni abajo pasos de viva persona por la casa. Todo lo que yo había visto eran paredes, sin ver en ella silleta, ni tajo, ni banco, ni mesa, ni aun tal arcaz como el de marras. Finalmente, ella parescía casa encantada. Estando así, díjome:

—Tú, mozo, ¿has comido?

—No, señor—dije yo—, que aún no eran dadas las ocho cuando con Vuestra Merced encontré.

—Pues, aunque de mañana, yo había almorzado, y cuando así como algo, hágote saber que hasta la noche me estoy así. Por eso, pásate como pudieres, que después cenaremos.

Vuestra Merced crea, cuando esto le oí, que estuve en poco de caer de mi estado, no tanto de hambre como por conocer de todo en todo la fortuna serme adversa. Allí se me representaron de nuevo mis fatigas y torné a llorar mis trabajos; allí se me vino a la memoria la consideración que hacía cuando me pensaba ir del clérigo, diciendo que, aunque aquel era desventurado y mísero, por ventura toparía con otro peor. Finalmente, allí lloré mi trabajosa vida pasada y mi cercana muerte venidera. Y con todo disimulando lo mejor que pude, le dije:

—Señor, mozo soy que no me fatigo mucho por comer, bendito Dios. Deso me podré yo alabar entre todos mis iguales por de mejor garganta, y así fui yo loado della hasta hoy día de los amos que yo he tenido.

—Virtud es ésa—dijo él—, y por eso te querré yo más, porque el hartar es de los puercos y el comer regladamente es de los hombres de bien.

"¡Bien te he entendido!— dije yo entre mí—. ¡Maldita tanta medicina y bondad como aquestos mis amos que yo hallo hallan en la hambre!"

Púseme a un cabo del portal y saqué unos pedazos de pan del seno, que me habían quedado de los de por Dios. Él, que vio esto, díjome:

— Ven acá, mozo. ¿Qué comes?

Yo lleguéme a él y mostréle el pan. Tomóme él un pedazo, de tres que eran, el mejor y más grande, y díjome:

— Por mi vida, que parece éste buen pan.

—¡Y cómo agora — dije yo —, señor, es bueno!

— Sí, a fe — dijo él —. ¿Adónde lo hubiste? ¿Si es amasado de manos limpias?

— No sé yo eso — le dije —; mas a mí no me pone asco el sabor dello.

— Así plega a Dios — dijo el pobre de mi amo.

Y, llevándolo a la boca, comenzó a dar en él tan fieros bocados como yo en lo otro.

—¡Sabrosísimo pan está— dijo —, por Dios!

Y como le sentí de qué pie cojeaba, dime priesa, porque le vi en disposición, si acababa antes que yo, se comediría a ayudarme a lo que me quedase. Y con esto acabamos casi a una. Y mi amo comenzó a sacudir con las manos unas pocas de migajas, y bien menudas, que en los pechos se le habían quedado. Y entró en una camareta que allí estaba, y sacó un jarro desbocado y no muy nuevo, y desque hubo bebido, convidóme con él. Yo, por hacer del continente, dije:

— Señor, no bebo vino.

— Agua es — me respondió—. Bien puedes beber.

Entonces tomé el jarro y bebí, no mucho, porque de sed no era mi congoja.

Así estuvimos hasta la noche, hablando en cosas que me preguntaba, a las cuales yo le respondí lo mejor que supe. En este tiempo metióme en la cámara donde estaba el jarro de que bebimos y díjome:

— Mozo, párate allí y verás cómo hacemos esta cama, para que la sepas hacer de aquí adelante.

Púseme de un cabo y él de otro, e hicimos la negra cama, en la cual no había mucho que hacer, porque ella tenía sobre unos bancos un cañizo, sobre el cual estaba tendida la ropa, que por no estar muy continuada a lavarse, no parescía colchón, aunque servía dél, con harta menos lana que era menester. Aquél tendimos, haciendo cuenta de ablandalle, lo cual era imposible, porque de lo duro mal se puede hacer blando. El diablo del enjalma maldita la cosa tenía dentro de sí, que, puesto sobre el cañizo, todas las cañas se señalaban y parecían a lo proprio entrecuesto de flaquísimo puerco. Y sobre aquel hambriento colchón, un alfamar del mismo jaez, del cual el color yo no pude alcanzar.

Hecha la cama, y la noche venida, díjome:

—Lázaro, ya es tarde, y de aquí a la plaza hay gran trecho. También en esta ciudad andan muchos ladrones, que, siendo de noche, capean. Pasemos como podamos, y mañana, venido el día, Dios hará merced; porque yo, por estar solo, no estoy proveído, antes he comido estos días por allá fuera. Mas agora hacerlo hemos de otra manera.

—Señor, de mí—dije yo—ninguna pena tenga Vuestra Merced, que bien sé pasar una noche y aún más, si es menester, sin comer.

—Vivirás más y más sano—me respondió—, porque, como decíamos hoy, no hay tal cosa en el mundo para vivir mucho que comer poco.

"Si por esa vía es—dije entre mí—, nunca yo moriré, que siempre he guardado esa regla por fuerza, y aún espero, en mi desdicha, tenella toda mi vida".

Y acostóse en la cama, poniendo por cabecera las calzas y el jubón, y mandóme echar a sus pies, lo cual yo hice; mas maldito el sueño que yo dormí, porque las cañas y mis salidos huesos en toda la noche dejaron de rifar y encenderse; que con mis trabajos, males y hambre, pienso que en mi cuerpo no había libra de carne, y también, como aquel día no había comido casi nada, rabiaba de hambre, la cual con el sueño no tenía amistad. Maldíjeme mil veces (Dios me lo perdone), y a mi ruin fortuna, allí lo más de la noche, y lo peor, no osándome revolver por no despertalle, pedí a Dios muchas veces la muerte.

La mañana venida, levantámonos, y comienza a limpiar y sacudir sus calzas y jubón y sayo y capa. ¡Y yo que le servía de pelillo! Y vísteseme muy a su placer de espacio. Echéle aguamanos, peinóse y púsose su espada en el talabarte, y al tiempo que la ponía, díjome:

—¡Oh, si supieses, mozo, qué pieza es ésta! No hay marco de oro en el mundo por que yo la diese; mas así, ninguna de cuantas Antonio hizo no acertó a ponelle los aceros tan prestos como ésta los tiene.

Y sacóla de la vaina y tentóla con los dedos, diciendo:

—¿La ves aquí? Yo me obligo con ella cercenar un copo de lana.

Y yo dije entre mí: "Y yo con mis dientes, aunque no son de acero, un pan de cuatro libras".

Tornóla a meter y ciñósela, y un sartal de cuentas gruesas del talabarte. Y con un paso sosegado y el cuerpo derecho, haciendo con él y con la cabeza muy gentiles meneos, echando el cabo de la capa sobre el hombro y a veces so el brazo, y poniendo la mano derecha en el costado, salió por la puerta, diciendo:

—Lázaro, mira por la casa en tanto que voy a oír misa, y haz la cama y ve por la vasija de agua al río, que aquí bajo está, y cierra la puerta con llave, no nos hurten algo, y ponla aquí al quicio porque, si yo viniere en tanto, pueda entrar.

Y súbese por la calle arriba con tan gentil semblante y continente, que quien no le conociera pensara ser muy cercano pariente al conde de Arcos, o, al menos, camarero que le daba de vestir.

"¡Bendito seáis Vos, Señor—quedé yo diciendo—que dais la enfermedad y ponéis el remedio! ¿Quién encontrará a aquel mi señor que no piense, según el contento de sí lleva, haber anoche bien cenado y dormido en buena cama, y aunque agora es de mañana, no le cuenten por muy bien almorzado? ¡Grandes secretos son, Señor, los que Vos hacéis y las gentes ignoran! ¿A quién no engañará aquella buena disposición y razonable capa y sayo? ¿Y quién pensará que aquel gentil hombre se pasó ayer todo el día sin comer con aquel mendrugo de pan que su criado Lázaro trajo un día y una noche en el arca de su seno, do no se le podía pegar mucha limpieza, y hoy, lavándose las manos y cara, a falta de paño de manos, se hacía servir de la halda del sayo? Nadie por cierto lo sospechará. ¡Oh Señor, y cuántos de aquéstos debéis Vos tener por el mundo derramados, que padecen por la negra que llaman honra, lo que por Vos no sufrirán!"

Así estaba yo a la puerta, mirando y considerando estas cosas y otras muchas, hasta que el señor mi amo traspuso la larga y angosta calle. Y como lo vi trasponer, tornéme a entrar en casa y en un credo la anduve toda, alto y bajo, sin hacer represa ni hallar en qué. Hago la negra dura cama y tomo el jarro y doy conmigo en el río, donde en una huerta vi a mi amo en gran recuesta con dos rebozadas mujeres, al parecer de las que en aquel lugar no hacen falta, antes muchas tienen por estilo de irse a las mañanicas del verano a refrescar y almorzar sin llevar qué, por aquellas frescas riberas, con confianza que no ha de faltar quién se lo dé, según las tienen puestas en esta costumbre aquellos hidalgos del lugar.

Y como digo, él estaba entre ellas hecho un Macías, diciéndoles más dulzuras que Ovidio escribió. Pero, como sintieron de él que estaba bien enternecido, no se les hizo de vergüenza pedirle de almorzar con el acostumbrado pago.

Él, sintiéndose tan frío de bolsa cuanto caliente del estómago, tomóle tal calofrío que le robó la color del gesto, y comenzó a turbarse en la plática y a poner excusas no válidas. Ellas, que debían ser bien instituidas, como le sintieron la enfermedad, dejáronle para el que era.

Yo, que estaba comiendo ciertos tronchos de berzas, con los cuales me desayuné, con mucha diligencia, como mozo nuevo, sin ser visto de mi amo, torné a casa. De la cual pensé barrer alguna parte, que era bien menester; mas no hallé con qué. Púseme a pensar qué haría, y parecióme esperar a mi amo hasta que el día demediase, y si viniese y por ventura trajese algo que comiésemos; mas en vano fue mi experiencia.

Desque vi ser las dos y no venía y la hambre me aquejaba, cierro mi puerta y pongo la llave do mandó, y tórnome a mi menester. Con baja y enferma voz e inclinadas mis manos en los senos, puesto Dios ante mis ojos y la lengua en su nombre, comienzo a pedir pan por las puertas y casas más grandes que me parecía. Mas como yo este oficio le hubiese mamado en la leche (quiero decir que con el gran maestro, el ciego, lo aprendí), tan suficiente discípulo salí, que aunque en este pueblo no había caridad, ni el año fuese muy abundante, tan buena maña me di, que antes que el reloj diese las cuatro ya yo tenía otras tantas libras de pan ensiladas en el cuerpo, y más de otras dos en las mangas y senos. Volvíme a la posada, y al pasar por la tripería pedí a una de aquellas mujeres, y dióme un pedazo de uña de vaca con otras pocas de tripas cocidas.

Cuando llegué a casa, ya el bueno de mi amo estaba en ella, doblada su capa y puesta en el poyo, y él paseándose por el patio. Como entré, vínose para mí. Pensé que me quería reñir por la tardanza; mas mejor lo hizo Dios. Preguntóme dó venía. Yo le dije:

—Señor, hasta que dio las dos estuve aquí, y de que vi que Vuestra Merced no venía, fuime por esa ciudad a encomendarme a las buenas gentes, y hanme dado esto que veis.

Mostréle el pan y las tripas, que en un cabo de la halda traía, a lo cual él mostró buen semblante, y dijo:

—Pues, esperado te he a comer, y de que vi que no viniste, comí. Mas tú haces como hombre de bien en eso, que más vale pedillo por Dios que no hurtallo. Y así Él me ayude, como ello me parece bien, y solamente te encomiendo no sepan que vives conmigo por lo que toca a mi honra; aunque bien creo que será secreto, según lo poco que en este pueblo soy conocido. ¡Nunca a él yo hubiera de venir!

—De eso pierda, señor, cuidado—le dije yo—, que maldito aquel que ninguno tiene de pedirme esa cuenta ni yo de dalla.

—Agora, pues, come, pecador, que si a Dios place, presto nos veremos sin necesidad; aunque te digo que, después que en esta casa entré, nunca bien me ha ido. Debe ser de mal suelo, que hay casas desdichadas y de mal pie, que a los que viven en ellas pegan la desdicha. Ésta debe de ser, sin duda, de ellas; mas yo te prometo, acabado el mes, no quede en ella, aunque me la den por mía.

Sentéme al cabo del poyo, y porque no me tuviese por glotón, callé la merienda. Y comienzo a cenar y morder en mis tripas y pan, y, disimuladamente, miraba al desventurado señor mío, que no partía sus ojos de mis faldas, que aquella sazón servían de plato. Tanta lástima haya Dios de mí como yo había de él, porque sentí lo que sentía, y muchas veces había por ello pasado y pasaba cada día. Pensaba si sería bien comedirme a convidalle; mas, por haberme dicho que había comido, temíame no aceptaría el convite. Finalmente yo deseaba que el pecador ayudase a su trabajo del mío, y se desayunase como el día antes hizo, pues había mejor aparejo, por ser mejor la vianda y menos mi hambre.

Quiso Dios cumplir mi deseo, y aun pienso que el suyo, porque como comencé a comer y él se andaba paseando, llegóse a mí y díjome:

—Dígote, Lázaro, que tienes en comer la mejor gracia que en mi vida vi a hombre, y que nadie te lo verá hacer que no le pongas gana, aunque no la tenga.

"La muy buena que tú tienes—dije yo entre mí—te hace parecer la mía hermosa". Con todo, parecióme ayudarle, pues se ayudaba y me abría camino para ello, y díjele:

—Señor, el buen aparejo hace buen artífice. Este pan está sabrosísimo, y esta uña de vaca tan bien cocida y sazonada que no habrá a quien no convide con su sabor.

—¿Uña de vaca es?

—Sí, señor.

—Dígote que es el mejor bocado del mundo, y que no hay faisán que así me sepa.

—Pues pruebe, señor, y verá qué tal está.

Póngole en las uñas la otra, y tres o cuatro raciones de pan de lo más blanco. Y asentóseme al lado y comienza a comer como aquél que lo había gana, royendo cada huesecillo de aquéllos mejor que un galgo suyo lo hiciera.

—Con almodrote—decía—es este singular manjar.

"¡Con mejor salsa lo comes tú!"—respondí yo paso.

—Por Dios, que me ha sabido como si hoy no hubiera comido bocado.

"¡Así me vengan los buenos años como es ello!"—dije yo entre mí.

Pidióme el jarro del agua y díselo como lo había traído. Es señal que, pues no le faltaba el agua, que no le había a mi amo sobrado la comida. Bebimos, y muy contentos nos fuimos a dormir, como la noche pasada.

Y por evitar prolijidad, de esta manera estuvimos ocho o diez días, yéndose el pecador en la mañana con aquel contento y paso contado a papar aire por las calles, teniendo en el pobre Lázaro una cabeza de lobo.

Contemplaba yo muchas veces mi desastre, que, escapando de los amos ruines que había tenido y buscando mejoría, viniese a topar con quien no sólo no me mantuviese, mas a quien yo había de mantener. Con todo, le quería bien, con ver que no tenía ni podía más, y antes le había lástima que enemistad. Y muchas veces, por llevar a la posada con que él lo pasase, yo lo pasaba mal. Porque una mañana, levantándose el triste en camisa, subió a lo alto de la casa a hacer sus menesteres, y en tanto yo, por salir de sospecha, desenvolvíle el jubón y las calzas que a la cabecera dejó, y hallé una bolsilla de terciopelo raso, hecha cien dobleces y sin maldita la blanca ni señal que la hubiese tenido mucho tiempo.

"Éste — decía yo — es pobre, y nadie da lo que no tiene; mas el avariento ciego y el malaventurado mezquino clérigo, que, con dárselo Dios a ambos, al uno de mano besada y al otro de lengua suelta, me mataban de hambre, aquéllos es justo desamar, y aquéste de haber mancilla".

Dios es testigo que hoy día, cuando topo con alguno de su hábito con aquel paso y pompa, le he lástima con pensar si padece lo que aquél le vi sufrir; al cual, con toda su pobreza, holgaría de servir más que a los otros por lo que he dicho. Sólo tenía dél un poco de descontento: que quisiera yo que no tuviera tanta presunción; mas que abajara un poco su fantasía con lo mucho que subía su necesidad. Mas, según me parece, es regla ya entre ellos usada y guardada: aunque no haya cornado de trueco ha de andar el birrete en su lugar. El Señor lo remedie, que ya con este mal han de morir.

Pues, estando yo en tal estado, pasando la vida que digo, quiso mi mala fortuna, que de perseguirme no era satisfecha, que en aquella trabajada y vergonzosa vivienda no durase. Y fue, como el año en esta tierra fuese estéril de pan, acordaron el Ayuntamiento que todos los pobres extranjeros se fuesen de la ciudad, con pregón que el que de allí adelante topasen fuese punido con azotes. Y así, ejecutando la ley, desde a cuatro días que el pregón se dio, vi llevar una procesión de pobres azotando por las Cuatro Calles. Lo cual me puso tan gran espanto que nunca osé desmandarme a demandar.

Aquí viera, quien vello pudiera, la abstinencia de mi casa y la tristeza y silencio de los moradores, tanto que nos acaeció estar dos o tres días sin comer bocado ni hablar palabra. A mí diéronme la vida unas mujercillas hilanderas de algodón, que hacían bonetes y vivían par de nosotros, con las cuales yo tuve vecindad y conocimiento. Que, de la laceria que les traían, me daban alguna cosilla, con la cual muy pasado me pasaba.

Y no tenía tanta lástima de mí como del lastimado de mi amo, que en ocho días maldito el bocado que comió. A lo menos en casa bien lo estuvimos sin comer. No sé yo cómo o dónde andaba y qué comía. ¡Y velle venir a mediodía la calle abajo con estirado cuerpo, más largo que galgo de buena casta! Y por lo que toca a su negra que dicen honra, tomaba una paja, de las que aun asaz no había en casa, y salía a la puerta escarbando los que nada entre sí tenían, quejándose todavía de aquel mal solar, diciendo:

—Malo está de ver, que la desdicha de esta vivienda lo hace. Como ves, es lóbrega, triste, oscura. Mientras aquí estuviéremos, hemos de padecer. Ya deseo se acabe este mes por salir della.

Pues estando en esta afligida y hambrienta persecución, un día, no sé por cuál dicha o ventura, en el pobre poder de mi amo entró un real, con el cual él vino a casa tan ufano como si tuviera el tesoro de Venecia, y con gesto muy alegre y risueño me lo dio, diciendo:

—Toma, Lázaro, que Dios ya va abriendo su mano. Ve a la plaza y merca pan y vino y carne: ¡quebremos el ojo al diablo! Y más te hago saber, porque te huelgues: que he alquilado otra casa y en ésta desastrada no hemos de estar más de en cumpliendo el mes. ¡Maldita sea ella y el que en ella puso la primera teja, que con mal en ella entré! Por Nuestro Señor, cuanto ha que en ella vivo, gota de vino ni bocado de carne no he comido, ni he habido descanso ninguno; mas ¡tal vista tiene y tal oscuridad y tristeza! Ve y ven presto y comamos hoy como condes.

Tomo mi real y jarro, y a los pies dándoles prisa, comienzo a subir mi calle encaminando mis pasos para la plaza, muy contento y alegre. Mas ¿qué me aprovecha, si está constituido en mi triste fortuna que ningún gozo me venga sin zozobra? Y así fue éste, porque yendo la calle arriba, echando mi cuenta en lo que le emplearía que fuese mejor y más provechosamente gastado, dando infinitas gracias a Dios que a mi amo había hecho con dinero, a deshora me vino al encuentro un muerto, que por la calle abajo muchos clérigos y gente en unas andas traían. Arriméme a la pared por darles lugar y, desque el cuerpo pasó, venía luego a par del lecho una que debía ser su mujer del difunto, cargada de luto, y con ella otras muchas mujeres, la cual iba llorando a grandes voces y diciendo:

—Marido y señor mío, ¿adónde os me llevan? ¡A la casa triste y desdichada, a la casa lóbrega y oscura, a la casa donde nunca comen ni beben!

Yo, que aquello oí, juntóseme el cielo con la tierra y dije:

"¡Oh desdichado de mí, para mi casa llevan este muerto!"

Dejo el camino que llevaba y hendí por medio de la gente, y vuelvo por la calle abajo a todo el más correr que pude para mi casa. Y entrando en ella, cierro a grande priesa, invocando el auxilio y favor de mi amo, abrazándome de él, que me venga a ayudar y a defender la entrada. El cual, algo alterado, pensando que fuese otra cosa, me dijo:

—¿Qué es eso, mozo? ¿Qué voces das? ¿Qué has? ¿Por qué cierras la puerta con tal furia?

—¡Oh señor —dije yo—, acuda aquí, que nos traen acá un muerto!

—¿Cómo así?— respondió él.

—Aquí arriba lo encontré y venía diciendo su mujer: "Marido y señor mío, ¿adónde os llevan? ¡A la casa lóbrega y oscura, a la casa triste y desdichada, a la casa donde nunca comen ni beben!". Acá, señor, nos le traen.

Y ciertamente, cuando mi amo esto oyó, aunque no tenía por qué estar muy risueño, rió tanto que muy gran rato estuvo sin poder hablar. En este tiempo tenía ya yo echada el aldaba a la puerta y puesto el hombro en ella por más defensa. Pasó la gente con su muerto, y yo todavía me recelaba que nos le habían de meter en casa. Y desque fue ya más harto de reír que de comer, el bueno de mi amo díjome:

—Verdad es, Lázaro, según la viuda lo va diciendo, tú tuviste razón de pensar lo que pensaste; mas, pues Dios lo ha hecho mejor y pasan adelante, abre, abre y ve por de comer.

—Dejálos, señor, acaben de pasar la calle —dije yo.

Al fin vino mi amo a la puerta de la calle, y ábrela esforzándome, que bien era menester, según el miedo y alteración, y me torno a encaminar. Mas, aunque comimos bien aquel día, maldito el gusto yo tomaba en ello. Ni en aquellos tres días torné en mi color. Y mi amo, muy risueño todas las veces que se le acordaba aquella mi consideración.

De esta manera estuve con mi tercero y pobre amo, que fue este escudero, algunos días, y en todos deseando saber la intención de su venida y estada en esta tierra; porque, desde el primer día que con él asenté, le conoscí ser extranjero, por el poco conocimiento y trato que con los naturales della tenía.

Al fin se cumplió mi deseo y supe lo que deseaba, porque, un día que habíamos comido razonablemente y estaba algo contento, contóme su hacienda y díjome ser de Castilla la Vieja, y que había dejado su tierra no más de por no quitar el bonete a un caballero, su vecino.

—Señor—dije yo—, si él era lo que decía y tenía más que vos, ¿no errábades en no quitárselo primero, pues decís que él también os lo quitaba?

—Sí es y sí tiene, y también me lo quitaba él a mí; mas, de cuantas veces yo se le quitaba primero, no fuera malo comedirse él alguna y ganarme por la mano.

—Parésceme, señor—le dije yo—, que en eso no mirara, mayormente con mis mayores que yo y que tienen más.

—Eres mochacho—me respondió—y no sientes las cosas de la honra, en que el día de hoy está todo el caudal de los hombres de bien. Pues te hago saber que yo soy, como ves, un escudero; mas ¡vótote a Dios!, si al Conde topo en la calle y no me quita muy bien quitado del todo el bonete, que otra vez que venga, me sepa yo entrar en una casa, fingiendo yo en ella algún negocio, o atravesar otra calle, si la hay, antes que llegue a mí, por no quitárselo. Que un hidalgo no debe a otro que a Dios y al rey nada, ni es justo, siendo hombre de bien, se descuide un punto de tener en mucho su persona. Acuérdome que un día deshonré en mi tierra a un oficial y quise poner en él las manos, porque cada vez que le topaba, me decía: "Mantenga Dios a Vuestra Merced". "Vos, don villano ruin—le dije yo—, ¿por qué no sois bien criado? ¿Manténgaos Dios, me habéis de decir, como si fuese quienquiera?" De allí adelante, de aquí acullá, me quitaba el bonete y hablaba como debía.

—¿Y no es buena manera de saludar un hombre a otro—dije yo—decirle que le mantenga Dios?

—¡Mira, mucho de enhoramala!—dijo él—. A los hombres de poca arte dicen eso; mas a los más altos, como yo, no les han de hablar menos de: "Beso las manos de Vuestra Merced", o por lo menos: "Bésoos, señor, las manos", si el que me habla es caballero. Y así, de aquél de mi tierra que me atestaba de mantenimiento, nunca más le quise sufrir, ni sufriría ni sufriré a hombre del mundo, del rey abajo, que: "Manténgaos Dios", me diga.

"Pecador de mí—dije yo—, por eso tiene tan poco cuidado de mantenerte, pues no sufres que nadie se lo ruegue".

—Mayormente—dijo—que no soy tan pobre que no tengo en mi tierra un solar de casas, que a estar ellas en pie y bien labradas, dieciséis leguas de donde nací, en aquella Costanilla de Valladolid, valdrían más de doscientas veces mil maravedís, según se podrían hacer grandes y buenas. Y tengo un palomar que, a no estar derribado como está, daría cada año más de doscientos palominos. Y otras cosas que me callo, que dejé por lo que tocaba a mi honra; y vine a esta ciudad pensando que hallaría un buen asiento, mas no me ha sucedido como pensé. Canónigos y señores de la iglesia muchos hallo; mas es gente tan limitada que no los sacarán de su paso todo el mundo. Caballeros de media talla también me ruegan; mas servir a éstos es gran trabajo, porque de hombre os habéis de convertir en malilla, y, si no, "andad con Dios" os dicen. Y las más veces son los pagamentos a largos plazos, y las más y las más ciertas, comido por servido. Ya, cuando quieren reformar consciencia y satisfaceros vuestros sudores, sois librado en la recámara, en un sudado jubón o raída capa o sayo. Ya, cuando asienta un hombre con un señor de título, todavía pasa su laceria. Pues, por ventura, ¿no hay en mí habilidad para servir y contentar a éstos? Por Dios, si con él topase, muy gran su privado pienso que fuese, y que mil servicios le hiciese, porque yo sabría mentille tan bien como otro y agradalle a las mil maravillas. Reílle ya mucho sus donaires y costumbres, aunque no fuesen las mejores del mundo; nunca decille cosa con que le pesase, aunque mucho le cumpliese; ser muy diligente en su persona, en dicho y hecho; no me matar por no hacer bien las cosas que él no había de ver, y ponerme a reñir, donde él lo oyese, con la gente de servicio, porque pareciese tener gran cuidado de lo que a él tocaba.

Si riñese con algún su criado, dar unos puntillos agudos para encenderle la ira y que pareciesen en favor del culpado; decirle bien de lo que bien le estuviese y, por el contrario, ser malicioso, mofador, malsinar a los de casa, y a los de fuera pesquisar y procurar de saber vidas ajenas para contárselas, y otras muchas galas de esta calidad que hoy día se usan en palacio y a los señores dél parecen bien; y no quieren ver en sus casas hombres virtuosos, antes los aborrecen y tienen en poco y llaman necios y que no son personas de negocios, ni con quien el señor se puede descuidar. Y con éstos los astutos usan, como digo, el día de hoy, de lo que yo usaría; mas no quiere mi ventura que le halle.

De esta manera lamentaba tanbién su adversa fortuna mi amo, dándome relación de su persona valerosa.

Pues estando en esto, entró por la puerta un hombre y una vieja. El hombre le pide el alquiler de la casa y la vieja el de la cama. Hacen cuenta, y de dos en dos meses le alcanzaron lo que él en un año no alcanzara. Pienso que fueron doce o trece reales. Y él les dio muy buena respuesta: que saldría a la plaza a trocar una pieza de a dos y que a la tarde volviesen; mas su salida fue sin vuelta.

Por manera que a la tarde ellos volvieron; mas fue tarde. Yo les dije que aún no era venido. Venida la noche y él no, yo hube miedo de quedar en casa solo, y fuime a las vecinas y contéles el caso, y allí dormí.

Venida la mañana, los acreedores vuelven y preguntan por el vecino; mas a esta otra puerta. Las mujeres le responden:

—Veis aquí su mozo y la llave de la puerta.

Ellos me preguntaron por él, y díjele que no sabía adónde estaba, y que tampoco había vuelto a casa desque salió a trocar la pieza, y que pensaba que de mí y de ellos se había ido con el trueco.

De que esto me oyeron, van por un alguacil y un escribano. Y helos do vuelven luego con ellos, y toman la llave, y llámanme, y llaman testigos, y abren la puerta y entran a embargar la hacienda de mi amo hasta ser pagados de su deuda. Anduvieron toda la casa y halláronla desembarazada, como he contado, y dícenme:

—¿Qué es de la hacienda de tu amo, sus arcas y paños de pared y alhajas de casa?

—No sé yo eso—le respondí.

—Sin duda—dicen ellos—esta noche lo deben de haber alzado y llevado a alguna parte. Señor alguacil, prended a este mozo, que él sabe dónde está.

En esto vino el alguacil y echóme mano por el collar del jubón, diciendo:

—Mochacho, tú eres preso, si no descubres los bienes de este tu amo.

Yo, como en otra tal no me hubiese visto (porque asido del collar sí había sido muchas e infinitas veces, mas era mansamente dél trabado, para que mostrase el camino al que no veía), yo hube mucho miedo y, llorando, prometíle de decir lo que me preguntaban.

—Bien está—dicen ellos—. Pues di todo lo que sabes y no hayas temor.

Sentóse el escribano en un poyo para escribir el inventario, preguntándome qué tenía.

—Señores—dije yo—, lo que este mi amo tiene, según él me dijo, es un muy buen solar de casas y un palomar derribado.

—Bien está—dicen ellos—; por poco que eso valga, hay para nos entregar de la deuda. ¿Y a qué parte de la ciudad tiene eso?—me preguntaron.

—En su tierra—les respondí.

—Por Dios, que está bueno el negocio—dijeron ellos—. ¿Y adónde es su tierra?

—De Castilla la Vieja me dijo él que era—le dije.

Riéronse mucho el alguacil y el escribano, diciendo:

—Bastante relación es ésta para cobrar vuestra deuda, aunque mejor fuese.

Las vecinas, que estaban presentes, dijeron:

—Señores, éste es un niño inocente y ha pocos días que está con ese escudero y no sabe dél más que vuestras mercedes; sino cuanto el pecadorcico se llega aquí a nuestra casa, y le damos de comer lo que podemos por amor de Dios, y a las noches se iba a dormir con él.

Vista mi inocencia, dejáronme, dándome por libre. Y el alguacil y el escribano piden al hombre y a la mujer sus derechos. Sobre lo cual tuvieron gran contienda y ruido, porque ellos alegaron no ser obligados a pagar, pues no había de qué ni se hacía el embargo. Los otros decían que habían dejado de ir a otro negocio, que les importaba más, por venir a aquél.

Finalmente, después de dadas muchas voces, al cabo carga un porquerón con el viejo alfamar de la vieja, aunque no iba muy cargado, allá van todos cinco dando voces. No sé en qué paró. Creo yo que el pecador alfamar pagara por todos. Y bien se empleaba, pues el tiempo que había de reposar y descansar de los trabajos pasados, se andaba alquilando.

Así, como he contado, me dejó mi pobre tercero amo, do acabé de conocer mi ruin dicha, pues, señalándose todo lo que podía contra mí, hacía mis negocios tan al revés, que los amos, que suelen ser dejados de los mozos, en mí no fuese así, mas que mi amo me dejase y huyese de mí.

Tratado Cuarto

Cómo Lázaro se asentó con un fraile de la Merced, y de lo que le acaeció con él.

Hube de buscar el cuarto, y éste fue un fraile de la Merced, que las mujercillas que digo me encaminaron, al cual ellas le llamaban pariente. Gran enemigo del coro y de comer en el convento, perdido por andar fuera, amicísimo de negocios seglares y visitar, tanto que pienso que rompía él más zapatos que todo el convento. Éste me dio los primeros zapatos que rompí en mi vida; mas no me duraron ocho días, ni yo pude con su trote durar más. Y por esto, y por otras cosillas que no digo, salí dél.

Tratado Quinto

Cómo Lázaro se asentó con un buldero, y de las cosas que con él pasó.

En el quinto por mi ventura di, que fue un buldero, el más desenvuelto y desvergonzado, y el mayor echador dellas que jamás yo vi ni ver espero, ni pienso nadie vio, porque tenía y buscaba modos y maneras y muy sutiles invenciones.

En entrando en los lugares do habían de presentar la bula, primero presentaba a los clérigos o curas algunas cosillas, no tampoco de mucho valor ni sustancia: una lechuga murciana, si era por el tiempo, un par de limas o naranjas, un melocotón, un par de duraznos, cada sendas peras verdiñales. Así procuraba tenerlos propicios, porque favoresciesen su negocio y llamasen sus feligreses a tomar la bula. Ofreciéndosele a él las gracias, informábase de la suficiencia de ellos. Si decían que entendían, no hablaba palabra en latín por no dar tropezón; mas aprovechábase de un gentil y bien cortado romance y desenvoltísima lengua. Y si sabía que los dichos clérigos eran de los reverendos, digo que más con dineros que con letras y con reverendas se ordenan, hacíase entre ellos un santo Tomás, y hablaba dos horas en latín, a lo menos que lo parecía, aunque no lo era.

Cuando por bien no le tomaban las bulas, buscaba cómo por mal se las tomasen. Y para aquello hacía molestias al pueblo, y otras veces con mañosos artificios. Y porque todos los que le veía hacer sería largo de contar, diré uno muy sutil y donoso, con el cual probaré bien su suficiencia.

En un lugar de la Sagra de Toledo había predicado dos o tres días, haciendo sus acostumbradas diligencias, y no le habían tomado bula ni, a mi ver, tenían intención de tomársela. Estaba dado al diablo con aquello, y pensando qué hacer, se acordó de convidar al pueblo para otro día de mañana despedir la bula.

Y esa noche, después de cenar, pusiéronse a jugar la colación él y el alguacil. Y sobre el juego vinieron a reñir y a haber malas palabras. Él llamó al alguacil ladrón y el otro a él falsario. Sobre esto, el señor comisario, mi señor, tomó un lanzón que en el portal do jugaban estaba. El alguacil puso mano a su espada, que en la cinta tenía. Al ruido y voces que todos dimos, acuden los huéspedes y vecinos y métense en medio. Y ellos, muy enojados, procurándose de desembarazar de los que en medio estaban, para matarse. Mas, como la gente al gran ruido cargase, y la casa estuviese llena de ella, viendo que no podían afrentarse con las armas, decíanse palabras injuriosas, entre las cuales el alguacil dijo a mi amo que era falsario y las bulas que predicaba eran falsas.

Finalmente, que los del pueblo, viendo que no bastaban a ponellos en paz, acordaron de llevar al alguacil de la posada a otra parte. Y así quedó mi amo muy enojado. Y después que los huéspedes y vecinos le hubieron rogado que perdiese el enojo y se fuese a dormir, se fue y así nos echamos todos.

La mañana venida, mi amo se fue a la iglesia y mandó tañer a misa y al sermón para despedir la bula. Y el pueblo se juntó, el cual andaba murmurando de las bulas, diciendo cómo eran falsas y que el mismo alguacil, riñendo, lo había descubierto. De manera que, atrás que tenían mala gana de tomalla, con aquello del todo la aborrecieron.

El señor comisario se subió al púlpito, y comienza su sermón y a animar la gente que no quedasen sin tanto bien y indulgencia como la santa bula traía.

Estando en lo mejor del sermón, entra por la puerta de la iglesia el alguacil, y desque hizo oración, levantóse, y con voz alta y pausada, cuerdamente comenzó a decir:

— Buenos hombres, oídme una palabra, que después oiréis a quien quisiéredes. Yo vine aquí con este echacuervo que os predica, el cual me engañó, y dijo que le favoreciese en este negocio, y que partiríamos la ganancia. Y agora, visto el daño que haría a mi conciencia y a vuestras haciendas, arrepentido de lo hecho, os declaro claramente que las bulas que predica son falsas, y que no le creáis ni las toméis y que yo, directe ni indirecte, no soy parte en ellas, y que desde agora dejo la vara y doy con ella en el suelo. Y si en algún tiempo éste fuere castigado por la falsedad, que vosotros me seáis testigos cómo yo no soy con él ni le doy a ello ayuda; antes os desengaño y declaro su maldad.

Y acabó su razonamiento.

Algunos hombres honrados que allí estaban se quisieron levantar y echar al alguacil fuera de la iglesia, por evitar escándalo; mas mi amo les fue a la mano y mandó a todos que, so pena de excomunión, no le estorbasen, mas que le dejasen decir todo lo que quisiese. Y así él también tuvo silencio mientras el alguacil dijo todo lo que he dicho. Como calló, mi amo le preguntó si quería decir más que lo dijese. El alguacil dijo:

—Harto hay más que decir de vos y de vuestra falsedad; mas por agora basta.

El señor comisario se hincó de rodillas en el púlpito, y puestas las manos y mirando al cielo, dijo así:

—Señor Dios, a quien ninguna cosa es escondida, antes todas manifiestas, y a quien nada es imposible, antes todo posible: Tú sabes la verdad y cuán injustamente yo soy afrentado. En lo que a mí toca, yo le perdono, porque Tú, Señor, me perdones. No mires a aquél, que no sabe lo que hace ni dice; mas la injuria a ti hecha te suplico, y por justicia te pido no disimules. Porque alguno que está aquí, que por ventura pensó tomar aquesta santa bula, y dando crédito a las falsas palabras de aquel hombre, lo dejará de hacer. Y pues es tanto perjuicio del prójimo, te suplico yo, Señor, no lo disimules; mas luego muestra aquí milagro, y sea de esta manera: que si es verdad lo que aquél dice y que yo traigo maldad y falsedad, este púlpito se hunda conmigo y meta siete estados debajo de tierra, do él ni yo jamás parezcamos; y si es verdad lo que yo digo y aquél, persuadido del demonio, por quitar y privar a los que están presentes de tan gran bien, dice maldad, también sea castigado y de todos conocida su malicia.

Apenas había acabado su oración el devoto señor mío, cuando el negro alguacil cae de su estado y da tan gran golpe en el suelo que la iglesia toda hizo resonar, y comenzó a bramar y echar espumajos por la boca y torcella, y hacer visajes con el gesto, dando de pie y de mano, revolviéndose por aquel suelo a una parte y a otra.

El estruendo y voces de la gente era tan grande, que no se oían unos a otros. Algunos estaban espantados y temerosos. Unos decían: "El Señor le socorra y valga". Otros: "Bien se le emplea, pues levantaba tan falso testimonio".

Finalmente, algunos que allí estaban, y a mi parecer no sin harto temor, se llegaron y le trabaron de los brazos, con los cuales daba fuertes puñadas a los que cerca dél estaban. Otros le tiraban por las piernas y tuvieron reciamente, porque no había mula falsa en el mundo que tan recias coces tirase. Y así le tuvieron un gran rato. Porque más de quince hombres estaban sobre él y a todos daba las manos llenas, y, si se descuidaban, en los hocicos.

A todo esto el señor mi amo estaba en el púlpito de rodillas, las manos y los ojos puestos en el cielo, transportado en la divina esencia, que el planto y ruido y voces, que en la iglesia había, no eran parte para apartalle de su divina contemplación.

Aquellos buenos hombres llegaron a él, y dando voces le despertaron y le suplicaron quisiese socorrer a aquel pobre que estaba muriendo y que no mirase a las cosas pasadas ni a sus dichos malos, pues ya dellos tenía el pago; mas, si en algo podría aprovechar para libralle del peligro y pasión que padecía, por amor de Dios lo hiciese, pues ellos veían clara la culpa del culpado y la verdad y bondad suya, pues a su petición y venganza el Señor no alargó el castigo.

El señor comisario, como quien despierta de un dulce sueño, los miró y miró al delincuente y a todos los que alrededor estaban, y muy pausadamente les dijo:

— Buenos hombres, vosotros nunca habíades de rogar por un hombre en quien Dios tan señaladamente se ha señalado; mas, pues Él nos manda que no volvamos mal por mal y perdonemos las injurias, con confianza podremos suplicalle que cumpla lo que nos manda, y Su Majestad perdone a éste que le ofendió poniendo en su santa fe obstáculo. Vamos todos a suplicalle.

Y así, bajó del púlpito y encomendó a que muy devotamente suplicasen a Nuestro Señor tuviese por bien de perdonar a aquel pecador y volverle en su salud y sano juicio y lanzar dél el demonio, si Su Majestad había permitido que por su gran pecado en él entrase.

Todos se hincaron de rodillas y delante del altar, con los clérigos, comenzaban a cantar con voz baja una letanía; y viniendo él con la cruz y agua bendita, después de haber sobre él cantado, el señor mi amo, puestas las manos al cielo y los ojos que casi nada se le parescía sino un poco de blanco, comienza una oración no menos larga que devota, con la cual hizo llorar a toda la gente, como suelen hacer en los sermones de Pasión, de predicador y auditorio devoto, suplicando a Nuestro Señor, pues no quería la muerte del pecador, sino su vida y arrepentimiento, que aquél, encaminado por el demonio y persuadido de la muerte y pecado, le quisiese perdonar y dar vida y salud para que se arrepintiese y confesase sus pecados.

Y esto hecho, mandó traer la bula y púsosela en la cabeza. Y luego el pecador del alguacil comenzó poco a poco a estar mejor y tornar en sí. Y desque fue bien vuelto en su acuerdo, echóse a los pies del señor comisario y, demandándole perdón, confesó haber dicho aquello por la boca y mandamiento del demonio; lo uno, por hacer a él daño y vengarse del enojo; lo otro, y más principal, porque el demonio recibía mucha pena del bien que allí se hiciera en tomar la bula.

El señor mi amo le perdonó, y fueron hechas las amistades entre ellos. Y a tomar la bula hubo tanta prisa, que casi ánima viviente en el lugar no quedó sin ella: marido y mujer, y hijos y hijas, mozos y mozas.

Divulgóse la nueva de lo acaescido por los lugares comarcanos, y cuando a ellos llegábamos, no era menester sermón ni ir a la iglesia, que a la posada la venían a tomar como si fueran peras que se dieran de balde. De manera que, en diez o doce lugares de aquellos alrededores donde fuimos, echó el señor mi amo otras tantas mil bulas sin predicar sermón.

Cuando él hizo el ensayo, confieso mi pecado que también fui dello espantado, y creí que así era, como otros muchos; mas con ver después la risa y burla que mi amo y el alguacil llevaban y hacían del negocio, conocí cómo había sido industriado por el industrioso y inventivo de mi amo.

Acaeciónos en otro lugar, el cual no quiero nombrar por su honra, lo siguiente, y fue que mi amo predicó dos o tres sermones, y dó a Dios la bula tomaban. Visto por el astuto de mi amo lo que pasaba, y que aunque decía se fiaban por un año no aprovechaba, y que estaban tan rebeldes en tomarla, y que su trabajo era perdido, hizo tocar las campanas para despedirse, y hecho su sermón y despedido desde el púlpito, ya que se quería abajar, llamó al escribano y a mí, que iba cargado con unas alforjas, y hízonos llegar al primer escalón, y tomó al alguacil las que en las manos llevaba, y las que yo tenía en las alforjas púsolas junto a sus pies, y tornóse a poner en el púlpito con cara alegre, y arrojar desde allí de diez en diez y de veinte en veinte de sus bulas hacia todas partes diciendo:

—Hermanos míos, tomad, tomad de las gracias que Dios os envía hasta vuestras casas, y no os duela, pues es obra tan pía la redención de los cautivos cristianos que están en tierra de moros, porque no renieguen nues-

tra santa fe y vayan a las penas del infierno, siquiera ayudalles con vuestra limosna y con cinco Pater Nostres y cinco Ave Marías, para que salgan de cautiverio. Y aun también aprovechan para los padres y hermanos y deudos que tenéis en el Purgatorio, como lo veréis en esta santa bula.

Como el pueblo las vio así arrojar, como cosa que la daba de balde y ser venida de la mano de Dios, tomaban a más tomar, aun para los niños de la cuna y para todos sus difuntos, contando desde los hijos hasta el menor criado que tenían, contándolos por los dedos. Vímonos en tanta priesa, que a mí aínas me acabaron de romper un pobre y viejo sayo que traía, de manera que certifico a Vuestra Merced que en poco más de una hora no quedó bula en las alforjas y fue necesario ir a la posada por más.

Acabados de tomar todos, dijo mi amo desde el púlpito a su escribano y al del Concejo que se levantasen, y para que se supiese quién eran los que habían de gozar de la santa indulgencia y perdones de la santa bula y para que él diese buena cuenta a quien le había enviado, se escribiesen.

Y así, luego todos de muy buena voluntad decían las que habían tomado, contando por orden los hijos y criados y difuntos.

Hecho su inventario, pidió a los alcaldes que, por caridad, porque él tenía que hacer en otra parte, mandasen al escribano le diese autoridad del inventario y memoria de las que allí quedaban, que según decía el escribano eran más de dos mil.

Hecho esto, él se despidió con mucha paz y amor, y así nos partimos de este lugar. Y aun antes que nos partiésemos, fue preguntado él por el teniente cura del lugar y por los regidores si la bula aprovechaba para las criaturas que estaban en el vientre de sus madres. A lo cual él respondió, según las letras que él había estudiado, que no, que lo fuesen a preguntar a los doctores más antiguos que él, y que esto era lo que sentía en este negocio.

Y así nos partimos, yendo todos muy alegres del buen negocio. Decía mi amo al alguacil y escribano:

—¿Qué os parece, cómo a estos villanos, que con sólo decir cristianos viejos somos, sin hacer obras de caridad, se piensan salvar sin poner nada de su hacienda? Pues, por vida del licenciado Pascasio Gómez, que a su costa se saquen más de diez cautivos.

Y así nos fuimos hasta otro lugar de aquel cabo de Toledo, hacia la Mancha que se dice, adonde topamos otros más obstinados en tomar bulas.

Hechas mi amo y los demás que íbamos nuestras diligencias, en dos fiestas que allí estuvimos no se habían echado treinta bulas. Visto por mi amo la gran perdición y la mucha costa que traía, y el ardideza que el sutil de mi amo tuvo para hacer despender sus bulas fue que este día dijo la misa mayor, y después de acabado el sermón y vuelto al altar, tomó una cruz que traía de poco más de un palmo, y en un brasero de lumbre que encima del altar había, el cual habían traído para calentarse las manos, porque hacía gran frío, púsole detrás del misal, sin que nadie mirase en ello. Y allí, sin decir nada, puso la cruz encima la lumbre, y ya que hubo acabado la misa y echada la bendición, tomóla con un pañizuelo bien envuelta la cruz en la mano derecha y en la otra la bula, y así se bajó hasta la postrera grada del altar, adonde hizo que besaba la cruz. E hizo señal que viniesen adorar la cruz. Y así vinieron los alcaldes los primeros y los más ancianos del lugar, viniendo uno a uno, como se usa. Y el primero que llegó, que era un alcalde viejo, aunque él le dio a besar la cruz bien delicadamente, se abrasó los rostros y se quitó presto afuera. Lo cual visto por mi amo, le dijo:

—¡Paso, quedo, señor alcalde! ¡Milagro!

Y así hicieron otros siete u ocho, y a todos les decía:

—¡Paso, señores! ¡Milagro!

Cuando él vio que los rostriquemados bastaban para testigos del milagro, no la quiso dar más a besar. Subióse al pie del altar y de allí decía cosas maravillosas, diciendo que por la poca caridad que había en ellos había Dios permitido aquel milagro, y que aquella cruz había de ser llevada a la santa iglesia mayor de su obispado, que por la poca caridad que en el pueblo había, la cruz ardía.

Fue tanta la prisa que hubo en el tomar de la bula, que no bastaban dos escribanos ni los clérigos ni sacristanes a escribir. Creo de cierto que se tomaron más de tres mil bulas, como tengo dicho a Vuestra Merced.

Después, al partir, él fue con gran reverencia, como es razón, a tomar la santa cruz, diciendo que la había de hacer engastonar en oro, como era razón. Fue rogado mucho del Concejo y clérigos del lugar les dejase allí aquella santa cruz, por memoria del milagro allí acaescido. Él en ninguna manera lo quería hacer, y al fin, rogado de tantos, se la dejó; con que le dieron otra cruz vieja que tenían, antigua, de plata, que podrá pesar dos o tres libras, según decían.

Y así nos partimos alegres con el buen trueque y con haber negociado bien. En todo no vio nadie lo susodicho, sino yo, porque me subía par del altar para ver si había quedado algo en las ampollas, para ponello en cobro, como otras veces yo lo tenía de costumbre, y como allí me vio, púsose el dedo en la boca, haciéndome señal que callase. Yo así lo hice, porque me cumplía, aunque después que vi el milagro, no cabía en mí por echallo fuera, sino que el temor de mi astuto amo no me lo dejaba comunicar con nadie, ni nunca de mí salió, porque me tomó juramento que no descubriese el milagro, y así lo hice hasta agora.

Y aunque mochacho, cayóme mucho en gracia, y dije entre mí: "¡Cuántas de éstas deben hacer estos burladores entre la inocente gente!".

Finalmente, estuve con este mi quinto amo cerca de cuatro meses, en los cuales pasé también hartas fatigas, aunque me daba bien de comer, a costa de los curas y otros clérigos do iba a predicar.

TRATADO SEXTO
Cómo Lázaro se asentó con un capellán, y lo que con él pasó.

Después desto, asenté con un maestro de pintar panderos, para molelle los colores, y también sufrí mil males.

Siendo ya en este tiempo buen mozuelo, entrando un día en la iglesia mayor, un capellán de ella me recibió por suyo, y púsome en poder un asno y cuatro cántaros y un azote, y comencé a echar agua por la ciudad. Éste fue el primer escalón que yo subí para venir a alcanzar buena vida, porque mi boca era medida. Daba cada día a mi amo treinta maravedís ganados, y los sábados ganaba para mí, y todo lo demás, entre semana, de treinta maravedís.

Fueme tan bien en el oficio, que al cabo de cuatro años que lo usé, con poner en la ganancia buen recaudo, ahorré para vestirme muy honradamente de la ropa vieja, de la cual compré un jubón de fustán viejo, y un sayo raído de manga trenzada y puerta, y una capa que había sido frisada, y una espada de las viejas primeras de Cuéllar.

Desque me vi en hábito de hombre de bien, dije a mi amo se tomase su asno, que no quería más seguir aquel oficio.

Tratado Séptimo
Cómo Lázaro se asentó con un alguacil, y de lo que le acaeció con él.

Despedido del capellán, asenté por hombre de justicia con un alguacil; mas muy poco viví con él, por parecerme oficio peligroso. Mayormente que una noche nos corrieron a mí y a mi amo a pedradas y a palos unos retraídos. Y a mi amo, que esperó, trataron mal; mas a mí no me alcanzaron. Con esto renegué del trato.

Y pensando en qué modo de vivir haría mi asiento, por tener descanso y ganar algo para la vejez, quiso Dios alumbrarme y ponerme en camino y manera provechosa. Y con favor que tuve de amigos y señores, todos mis trabajos y fatigas hasta entonces pasados fueron pagados con alcanzar lo que procuré, que fue un oficio real, viendo que no hay nadie que medre, sino los que le tienen.

En el cual el día de hoy vivo y resido a servicio de Dios y de Vuestra Merced. Y es que tengo cargo de pregonar los vinos que en esta ciudad se venden, y en almonedas y cosas perdidas, acompañar los que padecen persecuciones por justicia y declarar a voces sus delitos: pregonero, hablando en buen romance.

En el cual oficio, un día que ahorcábamos un apañador en Toledo, y llevaba una buena soga de esparto, conocí y caí en la cuenta de la sentencia que aquel mi ciego amo había dicho en Escalona, y me arrepentí del mal pago que le di, por lo mucho que me enseñó, que, después de Dios, él me dio industria para llegar al estado que ahora estó.

Hame sucedido tan bien, y yo le he usado tan fácilmente, que casi todas las cosas al oficio tocantes pasan por mi mano, tanto que, en toda la ciudad, el que ha de echar vino a vender, o algo, si Lázaro de Tormes no entiende en ello, hacen cuenta de no sacar provecho.

En este tiempo, viendo mi habilidad y buen vivir, teniendo noticia de mi persona el señor arcipreste de San Salvador, mi señor, y servidor y amigo de Vuestra Merced, porque le pregonaba sus vinos, procuró casarme con una criada suya. Y visto por mí que de tal persona no podía venir sino bien y favor, acordé de hacerlo. Y así, me casé con ella, y hasta agora no estoy arrepentido, porque, allende de ser buena hija y diligente servicial, tengo en mi señor arcipreste todo favor y ayuda. Y siempre en el año le da, en veces, al pie de una carga de trigo; por las Pascuas, su carne; y cuando el par de los bodigos, las calzas viejas que deja. E hízonos alquilar una casilla par de la suya; los domingos y fiestas casi todas las comíamos en su casa.

Mas malas lenguas, que nunca faltaron ni faltarán, no nos dejan vivir, diciendo no sé qué y sí sé qué, de que ven a mi mujer irle a hacer la cama y guisalle de comer. Y mejor les ayude Dios que ellos dicen la verdad.

Aunque en este tiempo siempre he tenido alguna sospechuela, y habido algunas malas cenas por esperalla algunas noches hasta las laudes, y aún más; y se me ha venido a la memoria lo que a mi amo el ciego me dijo en Escalona, estando asido del cuerno. Aunque, de verdad, siempre pienso que el diablo me lo trae a la memoria por hacerme malcasado, y no le aprovecha.

Porque, allende de no ser ella mujer que se pague destas burlas, mi señor me ha prometido lo que pienso cumplirá; que él me habló un día muy largo delante della y me dijo:

—Lázaro de Tormes, quien ha de mirar a dichos de malas lenguas nunca medrará. Digo esto, porque no me maravillaría alguno, viendo entrar en mi casa a tu mujer y salir della. Ella entra muy a tu honra y suya. Y esto te lo prometo. Por tanto, no mires a lo que pueden decir, sino a lo que te toca, digo, a tu provecho.

—Señor—le dije—, yo determiné de arrimarme a los buenos. Verdad es que algunos de mis amigos me han dicho algo deso, y aun por más de tres veces me han certificado que, antes que conmigo casase, había parido tres veces, hablando con reverencia de Vuestra Merced, porque está ella delante.

Entonces mi mujer echó juramentos sobre sí, que yo pensé la casa se hundiera con nosotros. Y después tomóse a llorar y a echar maldiciones sobre quien conmigo la había casado, en tal manera que quisiera ser muerto antes que se me hubiera soltado aquella palabra de la boca. Mas yo de un cabo y mi señor de otro, tanto le dijimos y otorgamos que cesó su llanto, con juramento que le hice de nunca más en mi vida mentalle nada de aquello, y que yo holgaba y había por bien de que ella entrase y saliese de noche y de día, pues estaba bien seguro de su bondad. Y así quedamos todos tres bien conformes.

Hasta el día de hoy nunca nadie nos oyó sobre el caso; antes, cuando alguno siento que quiere decir algo della, le atajo y le digo:

—Mirá, si sois amigo, no me digáis cosa con que me pese, que no tengo por amigo al que me hace pesar, mayormente si me quieren meter mal con mi mujer, que es la cosa del mundo que yo más quiero, y la amo más que a mí, y me hace Dios con ella mil mercedes y más bien que yo merezco. Que yo juraré sobre la hostia consagrada que es tan buena mujer como vive dentro de las puertas de Toledo. Quien otra cosa me dijere, yo me mataré con él.

Desta manera no me dicen nada, y yo tengo paz en mi casa.

Esto fue el mismo año que nuestro victorioso Emperador en esta insigne ciudad de Toledo entró y tuvo en ella Cortes, y se hicieron grandes regocijos, como Vuestra Merced habrá oído. Pues en este tiempo estaba en mi prosperidad y en la cumbre de toda buena fortuna.

De lo que de aquí adelante me suscediere, avisaré a Vuestra Merced.

Notes

Preface

1. Alberto Blecua, ed., *Lazarillo de Tormes* (Madrid: Castalia, 1972), pp. 49–70.
2. See A. Rumeau, "Notes au *Lazarillo*: Des editions d'Anvers, 1554–1555, à celles de Milan, 1587–1615," in *Bulletin Hispanique* LXVI (1964), pp. 272–293.
3. José de Sigüenza, *Historia de la Orden de San Jerónimo*, Nueva Biblioteca de Autores Españoles, vol. 12 (Madrid: 1909), II, p. 145 *b*.
4. *Recherches sur Lazarillo de Tormes*, Études sur l'Espagne, Première série (Paris: Bouillon et Viewege, 1888, 2 ed., 1895).
5. *Vida y obras de Don Diego Hurtado de Mendoza*, (Madrid: 1943), vol. III, pp. 206–222. Luis Jaime Cisneros adds his opinion in favor of the Hurtado de Mendoza theory in his *Lazarillo* edition (Buenos Aires: Kier, 1946), pp. 38–43.
6. *An Outline on the History of the Novela Picaresca in Spain* (The Hague and New York: 1903).
7. Julio Cejador y Frauca, Introduction to his edition of *La vida de Lazarillo de Tormes*, in Clásicos Castellanos de "La Lectura" (Madrid: 1914), vol. 25, pp. 45 and 65.
8. Alfred Morel-Fatio, Preface to his French translation of the *Lazarillo de Tormes*, Paris, 1886; also his Études sur l'Espagne, Première série (Paris: Bouillon et Viewege, 1888), p. 156.
9. Marcel Bataillon, *Erasmo y España* (Mexico, D.F.: Fondo de Cultura Económica, 1982, 2nd Spanish ed.), p. 610.
10. Américo Castro, *España en su historia* (Buenos Aires: 1948), p. 569, and *Realidad histórica de España* (Mexico: Porrúa, 1954), p. 572.
11. For a possible first edition of the *Lazarillo* (Antwerp, 1553) see J. E. Gillet's edition of the *Propalladia*, vol. III, Bryn Mawr, 1951, p. 468.
12. Marcel Bataillon, *Novedad y fecundidad del Lazarillo de Tormes* (New York: Las Américas, 1968), p. 23, and cfr. Baudrier, *Bibliographie Lyonnaise* (Lyon: 1899), vol. IV, pp. 326–327

Introduction

1. Joseph Pérez, "Pour une nouvelle interpretátion des 'Comunidades de Castille,'" In *Bulletin Hispanique*, LXV, 1963, pp. 238–283.

The Life of Lazarillo de Tormes

1. Psalm 87 (88), 13 Numquid cognoscentur in tenebris mirabilia tua et iustitia tua in terra oblivionis. "Shall thy wonders be known in the dark; and thy justice in the land of forgetfulness?" This was a well-established exordium.

2. Pliny the Younger referring to his uncle Pliny the Elder in an *Epistle* (III, 5, to Marcus): "He was accustomed to say, no book was so ill penned, but it might to some degree be serviceable."

3. An idea that is found in Horace, *Epistles* II, 2, 58–63. See Alberto Blecua's edition of *Lazarillo de Tormes* (Madrid: Castalia, 1972) p. 87, n. 5.

4. Actually Cicero in Tusc. 1.2.4: Honos alit artes omnesque incenduntur ad studia gloria, iacentque ea semper, quae apud quosque inprobantur. Also in the *Aurea Gemma (Gallica)* 1.1: Gloria, que ex preclare gestis rebus nascitur, animos hominum ad virtutis gymnasium exhortatur. Ipsa enim virtus in se marcesceret, si nullam sui memoriam posteris relinqueret. Letatur quippe mens a natura instituta multis prodesse multorumque gratiam inire. Beautudo est summorum virorum vestigia factis vel dictis imitari. "Glory, which is born of righteous deeds, drives the intellect of men to the pursuit of virtue. Virtue would silently fade away if it should bequeath no memorial of itself to posterity. Indeed the mind, a child of nature, rejoices in its usefulness to the many and in the obtainment of their favor. It is a blessing to pursue by deeds or words the paradigm left by the greatest men." The *Aurea Gemma (Gallica)* was collated in the XII and XIII centuries; it contains models for style of address, diplomatic protocol, many types of contracts and legally binding arrangements, etc. Also see Seneca, *Epistulae morales*, 79.13: Gloria umbra virtutis est, etiam invitam comitabitur.

5. Of all the machines exploited in XVI century Spain, the mill was the most pervasive. It turned wind or waterpower into cost-effective energy for grinding flour, as in the *Lazarillo*, tanning leather, processing cloth and a sundry array of other tasks. The mills had a crucial economic function in medieval and Renaissance societies. Although the initial investment in mill mechanisms and plant was costly, the long-term earnings were exceptional. Consequently, it is not surprising to discover that important institutions such as the Church and orders of Knights owned mills on rivers in or close to the towns. These mills had a large, round, horizontal stone as the essential piece of the grinding mechanism, and rivers such as the Tormes provided a fairly consistent flow of water ideal for driving it. For these mills in eastern Spain, see F. Palanca, et. al., *La memòria d'abans: del grà al pà, els molins.* (Valencia: Ed. Museu d'Etnologia. Diputació de València, 1986.)

6. Parody of the Gospel according to John (1:20): Et confessus est, et non negavit: et confessus est: Quia non sum ego Christus. "And he confessed, and denied not; but confessed, I am not the Christ." See Blecua, p. 92, n.

7. Parody of the Gospel according to Matthew (5:10): beati qui persecutionem patiuntur propter iustitiam. quoniam ipsorum est regnum caelorum. "Blessed [are] they which are persecuted for righteousness' sake: for theirs is the kingdom of heaven." See Blecua, p. 92, n.

8. The church of the Magdalena belonged to the military order of Alcántara, founded in 1156 by knights from Salamanca under the command of Don Suero Fernández Barrientos. See Blecua, p. 93, n.

9. As the boy apparently accepts and "loves" his stepfather because he is responsible for the general improvement in his standard of living, it could be surmised that

Lázaro here parodies the well-known Christian tenet, which charges the believer to "love thy neighbor as thyself." Yet the manner in which he speaks of his relationship with his little brother leads the reader to believe that he's not only accepted his mother's association with Zaide, but has developed some positive feelings towards him. See Leviticus 19:18; specially Leviticus 19:34: "But the stranger that dwelleth with you shall be unto you as one born among you, and thou shalt love him as thyself; for ye were strangers in the land of Egypt: I am the Lord your God"; also Matthew 7:12, 19:19 and 22:39; Mark 12:31 and 12:33; Luke 6:31 and 10:27; Romans 13:9 and 13:10; Galatians 5:14 and James 2:8.

10. The stable master initiates the query because he obviously does not believe that a groom in the stables can actually support a family. The name Zaide has commonly been associated with Moors. The *Romancero* is full of Moorish characters that bear that name, as the first verses of the following romances indicate: "Merienda del moro Zaide," "Mira, Zaide, que te aviso," "Zaide ha prometido fiestas," "Fijó, pues, Zaide los ojos," "No faltó, Zaide, quien trujo," "Gallardo pasea Zaide," "Zaide esparce por el viento," "Mora Zaida, hija de Zaide," "No piques, Zaide, el caballo," "Cristiana me vuelvo, Zaide," and "Aben Zaide, moro ilustre." Zaide ben Kesadi was a Moorish general under the command of Tariq; in 711 his forces occupied southern Andalucía, the area around Fuengirola. Félix Lope de Vega Carpio (1562–1635) began his career as a writer penning Moorish romances in many of which a lady calls her suitor "Zaide." The "Romance de Zaide" is a famous example of this cycle in Lope's poetry. For further study of Lazarillo's stepfather, see Baltasar Fra-Molinero, "El negro Zaide: marginación social y textual en el Lazarillo." *Hispania* 76.1 (1993): 20–29, and "La identidad de Zaide y la parodia del amor cortés en el Lazarillo de Tormes." *Romance Quarterly* 40.1 (Winter 1993): 23–34.

11. The building that is presently the Salamanca Town Hall. See Blecua, p. 95, n.

12. Conducted in 1510 by Spanish emperor Charles I against the Turks in the Tunisian island today known as Djerba, located in the gulf of Gabes 513 kilometers south of Tunis. In Antiquity it was known to the Phoenicians as Meninx.

13. Acts of the Apostles, 3:6. "Then Peter said, Silver and gold have I none; but such as I have give I thee: In the name of Jesus Christ of Nazareth rise up and walk."

14. See Colossians 1:13 "For He rescued us from the domain of darkness, and transferred us to the kingdom of His beloved Son." Also 1 John 1:6 "If we say that we have fellowship with Him and yet walk in the darkness, we lie and do not practice the truth." Lázaro has been rescued from the domain of darkness (i.e. ignorance of the world around him) and has been transferred to the truth of life as it really is. Right after the stone bull episode, event that "enlightens" Lázaro, the boy begins to sing the praises of his master, bringing to mind Matthew 5:16 "Let your light shine before men in such a way that they may see your good works, and glorify your Father who is in heaven."

15. The biblical precedent for using prayer as a cure for barrenness is in 1 Sm 1: 11, where Hannah, barren and distraught, prays to God for a child: "Oh Lord of hosts, if you will indeed look on the affliction of your maidservant, and remember me, and not forget your maidservant, but will give to your maidservant a son, then I will give him to the Lord all the days of his life." She, of course, gets her wish.

16. Access to professional medical treatment, especially for the poor, was consistently difficult in Spain, as in the rest of Europe. In 1352, for example, the Lord of Nules, Valencia, sent an urgent plea to King Pedro IV stating that "In the town of

Nules and in your other towns and villages there is no physician or surgeon or other skilled person from whom you and the inhabitants of these towns and villages could get help and assistance and medicines for sickness and other afflictions." See Luis García-Balleste, Michael McVaughn, and Agustín Rubio-Vela, *Medical Licensing and Learning in Fourteenth-century Valencia.* Philadelphia: Transactions of the American Philosophical Society, 1989, vol. 79, no. 6, p. 20. In the XIV and XV centuries there is an abundance of compilations of herbal remedies, usually illustrated with woodcuts and full of detailed descriptions of plants and their properties. These illustrations and minute descriptions are ostensibly intended to assist the reader in collecting and using these herbs. Most of these compilations are derived from Pliny and Discorides, yet one can point to Apuleius Platonicus' *Herbarium* (c. 1481); a Latin *Herbarius* (1484); a German *Herbarius* (1485); the *Hortus Sanitatis* (1491); Richard Blancke's *Herball* (1525), and many more in the mid and late XVI century. See *The Book of Secrets of Albertus Magnus, of the Virtues of Herbs, Stones and Certain Beasts. Also a Book of the Marvels of the World.* Ed. Michael Best and Frank H. Brightman, Oxford: Clarendon, 1973, pp. xxxiii and xxxiv. Spain and Portugal were especially poised to make a contribution to botany in the sixteenth century, as their expansion in the Americas, Asia and Africa brought them into contact with new plants and remedies. Spanish versions of Discorides and of the commentaries of Amatus Lusitanus appeared this century, and traveling Iberian botanists published works such as *Coloquios dos simples, e drogas he cousas mediçinais da India* (García de Orta, 1563); its Spanish version *Tractado de las drogas y medicinas de las Indias Orientales con sus plantas* (Cristóbal Acosta, 1578); *Dos libros, el uno que trata de todas las cosas que traen de nuestras Indias Occidentales, que sirven al uso de la medicina, y el otro que trata de la piedra Bezaar y de la yerba …* (Nicolás Monardes, 1569). Moreover, two Mexican Indians, Martín de la Cruz and Juanes Badiano published the *Badianus Herbal* in 1552. See Agnes Arber, *Herbals*, Cambridge: Cambridge University Press, 1912 (1986 ed., pp. 104–110).

17. The Spanish expression "rehacer la chaza" refers to hitting a ball back to the player that has played it to your court. The following expression "rehacer la falta" is a play on the meanings of "falta," which is fault, grief, or an error in a ball game. See Blecua, p. 99, n.

18. Deuteronomy 32:39 "See now that I myself am He! There is no god besides me. I put to death and I bring to life, I have wounded and I will heal, and no one can deliver out of my hand." and 1 Sam. 2:6 "The Lord puts to death and gives life; he casts down to the nether world; he raises up again."

19. The complete reverse of Isa 42:16 "And I will bring the blind by a way [that] they knew not; I will lead them in paths [that] they have not known: I will make darkness light before them, and crooked things straight. These things will I do unto them, and not forsake them."

20. The same general idea is in Aesop's *The Bald Man and the Fly.* A Fly bit the bare head of a Bald Man who, endeavoring to destroy it, gave himself a heavy slap. Escaping, the Fly said mockingly, "You who have wished to revenge, even with death, the prick of a tiny insect, see what you have done to yourself to add insult to injury?" The bald man replied, "I can easily make peace with myself, because I know there was no intention to hurt. But you, an ill-favored and contemptible insect who delights in sucking human blood, I wish that I could have killed you even if I had incurred a heavier penalty." See also Mat 5:38 "Ye have heard that it hath been said, an eye for an eye, and a tooth for a tooth."

21. Blecua (op. cit., p. 103, n) believes this is a reference to the large community of Jewish "conversos" that made their home in Toledo.

22. The expression used by Lázaro here is "hacíamos Sant Juan," referring to the Spanish custom of renewing old contracts, changing jobs, friends, etc. on the day of Saint John, 24 June. See Blecua, p. 104, n.

23. A village in the district of Escalona, 7 kilometers north of the town of Escalona in the northwest of the province of Toledo. Rodrigo Méndez Silva, in his book *Población general de España, sus trofeos, blasones* ... published in Madrid in 1675, states that "Yaze la Villa de Almorox una legua de Escalona, puesta en tierra quebrada, fértil para vino, aceite y frutas, con trescientos vecinos, una parroquia, seis Ermitas. Pobláronla Hebreos de Nabucodonosor, y domináronla Sarracenos." "The village of Almorox lies one league from Escalona, on hilly terrain. It is fertile for wine, olive oil and fruit; it has 300 inhabitants, a parish and six hermitages. It was populated by the Hebrews of Nebuchadnezzar, and was dominated by the Sarracens." The village has several prehistoric dolmens in its vicinity and was very important during Alfonso VI's march on Toledo in 1085. The founding of Toledo and several of its neighboring towns by Jews after the destruction of the first temple in 587 B.C. is legendary. The word Almorox comes from the Arabic for "the fields."

24. The Alcalá edition of 1554 adds the approximately one page of text that I include in Italics below.

25. Escalona, on the northwest corner of the province of Toledo, is famous for having been the birthplace in 1282 of Don Juan Manuel, author of *El libro del conde Lucanor*, nephew of King Alfonso X the Sage and grandson of King Fernando III the Saint.

26. A common way for the young to address their elders.

27. This conversation refers to the common practice in the Spanish-speaking world of depicting cuckolded men wearing horns.

28. This insert feels absolutely alien to the novel. It is highly improbable that it comes from the same hand that penned the rest of the novel.

29. A probable reference to Don Diego López Pacheco, Marquis of Villena and Count of Santisteban. See Blecua p. 106, n., and Manuel J. Asensio, "La intención religiosa del Lazarillo de Tormes y Juan de Valdés." *Hispanic Review*, XXVII (1959), p. 79.

30. Probably inspired by the Bible. See Exd 22:12 "And if it be stolen from him, he shall make restitution unto the owner thereof." As for the condition of the goods, see Exd 22:13 "If it be torn in pieces, [then] let him bring it [for] witness, [and] he shall not make good that which was torn."

31. His throat (where his appetite and his lying originate) is the cause of this and sundry other problems for Lázaro. He therefore feels this is appropriate punishment for this part of his body. The idea of punishing that particular part of the anatomy where a sin is thought to have originated is biblical. See Pro 23:2 "And put a knife to thy throat, if thou [be] a man given to appetite," and Rom 3:13 "Their throat [is] an open sepulchre; with their tongues they have used deceit; the poison of asps [is] under their lips." Compare with Mat 18:8 "Wherefore if thy hand or thy foot offend thee, cut them off, and cast [them] from thee: it is better for thee to enter into life halt or maimed, rather than having two hands or two feet to be cast into everlasting fire," and Mar 9:43 "And if thy hand offend thee, cut it off: it is better for thee to enter into life maimed, than having two hands to go into hell, into the fire that never shall be quenched."

32. The Council of Trent (1545–1563) officially designed the terminology of transubstantiation as dogma of the Catholic Church. According to it, the bread and wine used in the Eucharist become the flesh and blood of Christ. The blind man's quip about life-giving wine may be an attempt at a witticism regarding this controversial concept.

33. The idea that God has granted Lázaro an opportunity to avenge himself is contrary to biblical teaching: 1Sa 24:12 "The Lord judge between me and thee, and the Lord avenge me of thee: but mine hand shall not be upon thee," Rom 12:19 "Dearly beloved, avenge not yourselves, but [rather] give place unto wrath: for it is written, Vengeance [is] mine; I will repay, saith the Lord," Rom 12:20 "Therefore if thine enemy hunger, feed him; if he thirst, give him drink: for in so doing thou shalt heap coals of fire on his head," and Rom 12:21 "Be not overcome of evil, but overcome evil with good."

34. Village on the road form Escalona to Toledo. Occupied by Celts, Romans (who gave it the name Turris), Visigoths and Moors, in 1214 it was given by King Alfonso VIII to don Rodrigo Jiménez de Rada, Archbishop of Toledo, as a prize for his role in the Christian victory at the Battle of Las Navas de Tolosa (1212). Rada subsequently gave it to the Toledo Cathedral. King Alfonso XI built a palace in Torrijos to commemorate the Christian victory over the Moors at the Battle of Salado (1340), and this palace became a residence for the kings of Castile. Pedro I the Cruel's (1334–1369) daughter Beatriz, a product of his affair with doña María Padilla, had her birth commemorated at this palace with a lavish celebration. Owing to its large population of Jews, Torrijos had two synagogues, no longer in existence. Juan II of Castile (1405–1454) was a frequent resident of the village.

35. Maqueda is a village halfway between Almorox and Torrijos. Also heavily populated by Jews, legend has it that they founded it, giving it the name "Magda." The name may have its roots in the Biblical Makkedah, a city in the territory of the tribe of Judah. Jos 10:10 has it that when the five kings of the Amorites made war on Gibeon, Joshua, its defender, got very special help: "And the Lord discomfited them before Israel, and slew them with a great slaughter at Gibeon, and chased them along the way that goeth up to Bethhoron, and smote them to Azekah, and unto Makkedah." Makkedah occurs in several places in Joshua: 10:16, 10:17, 10:21, 10:28, 10:29, 12:16 and 15:41. One of the five royal cities of the Canaanites, it is the place where Joshua slew the five Amorite kings who hid in a cave after their defeat, and hung their heads from five trees. It has been identified alternately as the modern village of Sumeil, built on a small hill approximately 7 miles northwest of Eleutheropolis (Beit Jibrin), site of a large cave, and as el-Mughar (literally "the caves"), a little over three miles from modern Jabneh, less than three miles southwest of modern Ekron, and 25 miles northwest of Jerusalem, a place — as its name states — where one can still find a number of caves. The name Makkedah means "the herdman's place." Although it is not known how long Lázaro stayed in Torrijos, his itinerary is unusual indeed. He has left Escalona in the evening and traveled 28 kilometers to Torrijos overnight, and "not feeling safe" there, he retraces his steps and returns to Maqueda, a village he must have crossed on the way from Escalona to Torrijos. Lázaro is traveling on the path that today is National Road 403, which from Ávila leads in a southeasterly direction to Almorox, Escalona, Maqueda, Torrijos and, eventually, to Toledo. The silence attending the places and villages in Salamanca and Ávila that the duo must have traversed to arrive at Almorox is a bit puzzling. The most logical route taken by the pair is what today is National Road 501, which covers the 96 kilometers from Salamanca to Ávila, where it links up

with 403. From there it's another 80 kilometers to Almorox, all in total silence as to the places where their adventures take place. One is tempted to conclude from this that the author knew the area of northern Toledo province quite well, and that he is probably a Toledano who studied in Salamanca.

36. Lázaro literally says that he escaped the thunder but was hit by the lightning.

37. Spanish coin that began its currency in medieval times and was copied from a Moorish coin associated with the Almorávides (Al murabiti), a tribe from the Atlas Mountains of North Africa that dominated Moslem Spain from 1093 to 1148. They were known as the men of the "rabita," Arabic word meaning hermitage or convent and given in Spanish as "rábida." The convent of Santa María de la Rábida, made famous by Columbus, derives its name from this Arabic word.

38. The "Face of God" (Cara de Dios) is what you call bread that has fallen on the ground as you pick it up. See *Lazarillo de Tormes*, ed Alberto Blecua, p. 118, footnote 149. Also, in *Genesis* 33:10: "And Jacob said [to Esau], Nay, I pray thee, if now I have found grace in thy sight, then receive my present at my hand: for therefore I have seen thy face, as though I had seen the face of God, and thou wast pleased with me." More specifically, as the sight of the bread (God's face) is preserving Lázaro's life, the author may have been thinking of *Genesis* 32:30: "And Jacob called the name of the place Peniel: for I have seen God face to face, and my life is preserved." The sense of contemporary Spain as a world turned upside down is skillfully conveyed by the author in this "death is life; life is death" wordplay.

39. Type of fever, like malaria, that recurs every other day, every third day when figured inclusively. Interestingly, the author is here playing with the idea that Jesus, after being alive for 33 years, dies for three days, after which He comes back to life. In a perfect reversal of this, Lázaro portrays his sojourn with the cleric as a form of death; he finds life in the bread for three days, and then returns to his previous condition. See *Matthew* 27:63 "... After three days I will rise again," and *Marc 8:31* "And he began to teach them, that the Son of man must suffer many things, and be rejected of the elders, and [of] the chief priests, and scribes, and be killed, and after three days rise again." This can also be interpreted as a reversal of *Revelation* 11:11 "And after three days and an half the Spirit of life from God entered into them, and they stood upon their feet; and great fear fell upon them which saw them." The author is at pains to convey the idea that the Spirit of God entered Lázaro only during those three days in which he had access to the bread in the chest.

40. Blecua found in a treatise by Manuel Rodríguez (*Suma de casos de conciencia*, Salamanca, 1603, I, p. 203) the following account: "Confessors observe that some very devout Christians, being clean of heart and fearful of God, upon reaching this divine Sacrament humiliate themselves and do not dare receive the Host, [believing themselves to be unworthy.] Op cit., p. 119, note 153. [English translation is mine.]

41. Lázaro is taking Communion.

42. A good fencing master will only touch his opponent slightly when scoring, thus avoiding injury.

43. Already in Plato, "Necessitas facit industriam paradi victus," and many others. See Andrea Eborense, *Sententia et exempla*, Venice, 1585, I, p. 206.

44. Some critics take this to be a reference to Francis I, who was imprisoned in Madrid from February 1525 to February 1526 after the Spanish victory over the French at the Battle of Pavía. See Blecua, op. cit., pp. 9 and 22.

45. The currency denomination to which the priest refers here is the "real." Bear-

ing the royal seal from which its name derives, it was the first coin to be used by the Catholic Monarchs Isabel and Fernando in the newly unified kingdom of Spain. The coin was also known as the "excelente" and the "ducado."

46. The idea of a trap laid out at one's table is already in the *Bible*. See Psalms 69:22 "Let their table become a snare before them: and [that which should have been] for [their] welfare, [let it become] a trap," and Romans 11:9 "And David saith, Let their table be made a snare, and a trap, and a stumbling block, and a recompense unto them."

47. This popular belief has its origins in folktales. See Blecua, op. cit., p. 125, n. 168, and María Rosa de Malkiel, "Función del cuento popular en el *Lazarillo de Tormes*" in *APCICH* (1964) p. 355.

48. Matthew 12:40 "For as Jonah was three days and three nights in the whale's belly; so shall the Son of man be three days and three nights in the heart of the earth," and Jonah 1:17 "Now the Lord had prepared a great fish to swallow up Jonah. And Jonah was in the belly of the fish three days and three nights"; 2:1 "Then Jonah prayed unto the Lord his God out of the fish's belly"; 2:2 And said, I cried by reason of mine affliction unto the Lord, and he heard me; out of the belly of hell cried I, [and] thou heardest my voice."

49. The blind were considered to have unusual abilities that, if put at the service of iniquity, could prove very destructive. The priest obviously believes that Lázaro is so cunning because he's learned his mischief from his previous master. Juan Luis Vives touches upon the subject in his *Tratado del alma*, chapter IX, "De los sentidos en general." (1538): "Es increíble hasta qué punto se mostró cuidadosa la Naturaleza para compensar a quienes privó de algún sentido, bien aumentando el vigor de los restantes, bien por el conocimiento interno. Así, dio a los ciegos y a los sordos sutilidad de tacto, una memoria rápida y firme y agudeza de entendimiento; agrégase a esto la necesidad, con cuyo estímulo se despierta el ingenio." "It amazes one to think of how Nature deemed it necessary to compensate those to whom it denied any of the senses, either by enhancing the vitality of the rest or by augmenting the person's innate intelligence. Thus, it gave the blind and the deaf a fine tact, a quick and solid memory and sharp wit and understanding. If you add necessity to the mix, their resourcefulness is awakened."

http://www.cervantesvirtual.com/servlet/SirveObras/00369400886881318510046/p0000001.htm#3 (6 April 2004). English version is my own.

50. This ill treatment of Lázaro in a large and important town, presumably exposed to humanist thought, might seem odd at first glance. But some critics see humanism as unkind to the poor, considering them a shame to enlightened society and as the agents of their own adversity. The social malfunction of poverty conflicted with the humanist promotion of personal self-fulfillment, and in many ways, the praise for the virtues of poverty gave way to admiration of wealth. For a study of this phenomenon see Mollat, Michel and Arthur Goldhammer, *The Poor in the Middle Ages, an Essay in Social History* (Yale Univ. Press, 1986), especially p. 55. Some humanist writers deemed poverty to be an unnecessary handicap to human prosperity. They placed emphasis on the merits of hard work and on God's mandate that one should earn one's bread by the sweat of one's brow. The perils of idleness were also habitually condemned, calling on the State to promote employment and endorse tough measures against the indolent. For a study on humanist attitudes on the poor, see Gutton, Jean-Pierre, *La société et les pauvres en Europe, XVIe-XVIIIe siecles.* (Paris: Presses Universitaires de France), especially pp. 99–101. This idea of government involvement to eradicate poverty is

echoed by Vives in 1526, when he states: "moreover, it is not the part of a wise magistrate, and one that studies the public welfare, to allow so large a section of the citizens to be not only useless but actively harmful to itself and to others. ... The young children of the poor are villainously brought up, they and their sons lying outside the churches or wandering round begging; they do not attend the Sacraments or hear the sermon; nothing is known as to their manner of life, or as to their religious or moral opinions. Vives, Juan Luis, *De subventione pauperum*, Book II, Chapter 1, in *Some Early Tracts on Poor Relief*, edited by F. R. Salter (London: Methuen, 1926), pp. 6–9. Also, in 1531 Emperor Charles V issued forth a decree in which he prohibited begging in every part of the Empire. Local regulations in its cities reiterated the ideas proposed by Vives. The Spain of Lazarillo had its royal decree of 1540 that regulated begging, limiting it to the "truly poor." And even these could only beg within a limited distance from their dwelling. See Flynn, Maureen, *Sacred Charity. Confraternities and Social Welfare in Spain, 1400–1700* (Ithaca: Cornell Univ. Press, 1989), pp. 88–93.

A good idea of how significant the issue of poverty was in Lázaro's Spain can be obtained by looking at one of the philosophical controversies it spawned. Juan de Medina (also known as Juan de Robles) maintained that begging was not an individual's inherent right, but was more accurately an undesirable aspect of contemporary life. Accordingly, he supported laws barring private almsgiving in favor of centralized charity management, which he believed would appropriately curtail individual liberties for the sake of the common good. Moreover, he felt it proper to try to limit almsgiving to those who are truly poor, in spite of the fact that Christianity exhorts people to give to all who beg in the name of God –"por Dios," whence "pordioseros-". The common good of society and the state, he asserted, necessitates such limitations. See Flynn, Maureen, *Sacred Charity. Confraternities and Social Welfare in Spain, 1400–1700* (Ithaca: Cornell Univ. Press, 1989), 96–97. De Medina's book, *De la orden que en algunos pueblos de España se ha puesto en la limosna para remedio de los verdaderos pobres* (Salamanca 1545) had succeeding editions in Valladolid (1757) and Madrid (1766) with the title *La caridad discreta, practicada con los mendigos, y utilidades que logra la república en su recogimiento*.

On the other side of the issue was Domingo de Soto, who originally backed the introduction of aid to the poor edicts in Zamora (1540). De Soto changed his mind and by 1544 was involved in a public debate with de Medina. De Soto was adamant that begging was a basic human right, that any restriction on beggars" movements could place them in mortal jeopardy. It was a law of nature that man go wherever his survival needs were met. Even worse than that was the attempt to allocate contributions on the basis of the individual beggar's supposed moral virtues. He was particularly opposed to use poverty edicts as a form of social control, and disputed the plan to have those people categorized as "truly poor" confess their sins and receive Holy Communion before being licensed and given assistance. The rich, he concluded, didn't have to confess in order to eat. De Soto's position won the day in Spain. See Flynn, Maureen, *Sacred Charity. Confraternities and Social Welfare in Spain, 1400–1700* (Ithaca: Cornell Univ. Press, 1989), 94–95. De Soto's book was published in Salamanca in 1545 in both Latin (*In causa pauperum deliberatio*) and Spanish (*Deliberación en la causa de los pobres*).

With regard to this controversy, it must be remembered that before the humanist reforms benevolence was not intended essentially to assist the poor, but rather to obtain the benefactor's own personal salvation. Charity was relatively plentiful in specific situations and funds were established, usually with the cooperation of the Church. But as the controversy and its outcome illustrate, the effort to rationalize the whole through a regimented system met with philosophical as well as practical problems. The outcome was the chaotic, generalized mendicancy that is replicated in Lázaro's world. In a way, the little novel gives a disparaging analytical description of the results of this lack of regimentation and state control, which would lead one to believe that the author was in Juan de Medina's camp and was trying to promote his point of view. The fact that in Toledo Lázaro is told to get a job and stop begging emphasizes the fact that there is no other option available to him. The unpleasant circumstances under which he finally procures a job at the end of the novel underscores the senselessness of abandoning the poor to fend for themselves. This would suggest that the author was at the very least unsympathetic to De Soto's *laissez faire* stance.

51. Lázaro commits the un–Christian act of despairing: Luke 6:21 "Blessed [are ye] that hunger now: for ye shall be filled. Blessed [are ye] that weep now: for ye shall laugh." Hunger does not allow him to respond to his situation in the conformist or gallant manner a contemporary reader would expect from a conventional hero. Hope is a luxury he can't give himself.

52. The reference to "clean hands" may be an allusion to the probable religion of the baker. Non Christian bakers would not have the "clean hands" or cleanliness of blood (limpieza de sangre) to which the squire is referring. For further scrutiny of this passage see Blecua, p. 133, n. 190. Toledo was renowned for its population of "new" Christians who had not altogether given up their former religion. The "sentencia-Estatuto de Toledo" (5 June 1449) gives an idea of this ongoing situation and the way authorities dealt with it: "..Among the privileges and liberties granted by the kings to the city of Toledo is that given by King Alfonso of Castile of glorious memory, in which following canon law he orders and rules that no convert of Jewish lineage may possess or hold any office or benefice in the city of Toledo or its lands and jurisdiction, being suspect in their Christian faith. [...]

We, Pedro Sarmiento, royal governor and commander of the most noble and loyal city of Toledo, and all the councilors and officers, nobles, citizens and people of the city, order and declare that inasmuch as it is notorious by canon law as by civil law, that the converses of Jewish lineage, being suspect in their Christian faith which they frequently abuse and make light of by their Judaizing, may hold neither public or private offices nor benefices in which they may do injury, harm and other abuses to Old Christians of pure blood [lindos], nor may they bear witness against them. This by reason of the said privileges granted to the city by King Alfonso. And against the very great majority of converts in this city, descendents of the lineage of Jews, it is proven that they be persons very suspect in the holy Catholic faith who hold and commit the greatest errors against its articles, for they preserve the rites and ceremonies of their former law, describing our Redeemer Christ as a hanged man whom the Christians adore as God, and asserting that we believe there are a God and Goddess in heaven. [...]

That we must decree and order, that all the said converses, descendents of the perverse lineage of the Jews, in whichever guise they may be, by virtue of both canon and civil law, and the aforesaid Privileges of King Alfonso as also by reason of the heresies and other crimes, insults and seditions in which they are entrenched ... are held to be incapable and unsuitable and unworthy to hold any office or benefice, public or private, whereby they may exercise power over Old Christians.... And we name as converses of Jewish lineage the following: López Fernández Cota – Gonzalo Rodríguez de San Pedro...

And we prohibit the said converses from acting as notaries and witnesses under pain of death and confiscation of all their property.... These are descendents of the lineage and race [linaje y ralea] of the Jews.... And this sentence against the converses in favor of the Old Christians of pure stock is to apply and extend against past conversos, and present conversos, and future conversos...." These statutes have their origin in a million-maravedí loan that King Juan II's minister Álvaro de Luna requested from the city of Toledo. Castile was at war with Aragón and the king sorely needed the funds for the war effort. The trouble started when it became known that Rodrigo Cota, a wealthy converso merchant, was behind the loan initiative. The "old Christians" of Toledo assembled and went on a rampage, burning down Cota's house and sacking the converso neighborhood of La Magdalena. Led by Pedro Sarmiento, they prepared to defend the city against reprisals by the royal army commanded by Luna. The arguments used against the conversos must have seemed familiar to them: the "Jews" were collecting money from old Christians to be used to fight other Christians and enrich Jews. The issue was not resolved militarily: several influential individuals defended the conversos, among them Alonso Díaz de Montalvo, who argued that disputes like this only served to divide Christendom, and by Burgos bishop Alonso de Cartagena, of converso stock himself, who wrote his famous *Defensorium Unitatis Christianae*, which appeared in 1450. Pope Nicholas V joined in the defense of the conversos, expressly condemning the Estatutos on 24 September 1449. But the issue was not resolved, and in the following centuries and leading up to the publication of *Lazarillo de Tormes* there were many influential voices still condemning the conversos, among them Alonso de Espina (*Fortalitiom Fidei*, 1459). The conversos' situation was not helped when a number of Jeronimite priests were discovered practicing the Jewish faith in hiding and were burned at the stake (1485) in Toledo by the Inquisition. For further information see Gerber, Jane S. *The Jews of Spain: A History of the Sephardic Experience*. New York: The Free Press, 1994; Kamen, Henry. *The Spanish Inquisition: A Historical Revision*. New Haven: Yale University Press, 1997; Peters, Edward. *Inquisition*. Berkley: University of California Press, 1988, and Tejada, Luis Coronas, *Conversos and Inquisition in Jaen*. Jerusalem: The Magnes Press of Hebrew University, 1988. For the ideological foundations of Spanish anti–Semitism, see Álvarez-Chillida, Gonzalo. *El antisemitismo en España. La imagen del judío (1812–2002)*. (Madrid: Marcial Pons, 2003), especially pages 22–23 and 43–44.

53. Renowned swordsmith that forged Fernando the Catholic's sword. Blecua, p. 136, n. 206.

54. Title created by Juan II of Castile on 8 December 1429 and bestowed upon Pedro Ponce de León (1360–1448), first Count of Arcos.

55. Deuteronomy 32:39 "see now that I, [even] I, [am] he, and [there is] no god with me: I kill, and I make alive; I wound, and I heal: neither [is there any] that can deliver out of my hand."; Jeremiah 33:6 "Behold, I will bring it health and cure, and I will cure them, and will reveal unto them the abundance of peace and truth," and Job 5:18 "For he maketh sore, and bindeth up: he woundeth, and his hands make whole."

56. Job 5:9 "Which doeth great things and unsearchable; marvelous things without number." But the author might be suggesting that folks around Toledo find the ways of the Lord mysterious because of their own shortcomings. Lázaro's forthcom-

ing comment on the supremacy of honor over God's ways makes one believe that the remark is facetious. See Hosea 14:9 "Who [is] wise, and he shall understand these [things]? prudent, and he shall know them? for the ways of the LORD [are] right, and the just shall walk in them: but the transgressors shall fall therein," and Acts 13:10 "And said, O full of all subtlety and all mischief, [thou] child of the devil, [thou] enemy of all righteousness, wilt thou not cease to pervert the right ways of the Lord?"

57. Galician poet Macías was born in Padrón, Galicia, and died in Arjonilla, Andalucía, in 1434. He is considered to be the last great Galician poet of the Middle Ages, and the famous *Cancionero de Baena* brings together 21 of his "Cantigas." He is commonly called "Macías el enamorado" because, as the tale is told, when he was at the service of the Marquis de Villena he fell madly in love with Doña Elvira, a lady in the entourage of Villena's wife. She also fell for him. At a time when Macías was away from Villena's court, the marquis married Elvira to Hernán Pérez, a rich hidalgo. But Macías and Elvira were so enamored that they maintained an adulterous relationship. Learning of it, the marquis had Macías imprisoned in a tower in the ancient castle of Arjonilla, but the poet kept divulging his love for Elvira through his poetry. The enraged husband traveled to Arjonilla, entered Macías" cell and killed him with a spear (some say that he was escaping with Elvira when the husband caught up with them). As Lázaro shows, he became a symbol of intense and tragic love. Macías inspired works by Lope de Vega and Larra and praise by Juan de Mena in his *Laberinto de fortuna.*

58. *Ars Amatoria*; *Remedia Amoria*; *Amores.*

59. Lázaro, the most downtrodden, wretched of beings has the first and only act of Christian piety here. See Proverbs 28:8 "He that hath pity upon the poor lendeth unto the LORD; and that which he hath given will He pay him again." The concept is turned on its head, though, as it is a poor boy pitying an individual who, ostensibly, is a member of the privileged class.

60. The hidalgo has always been the image of Spanish quality and worth, symbolizing values such as honor, courage, faith and virility. Lázaro's squire/hidalgo has become a caricature of the hidalgo, serving to display these attributes as false and fabricated. Honor, which should be an intimate attribute of the human being, has become a social role to be played to the audience of public opinion. Thus, in the Spain of *Lazarillo* honor has become a perversion of the real thing. As a result, the pícaro's social "dishonor" seems exalted in comparison to the hidalgo's "honor."

61. This is probably a reference to the drought that began in 1542 and lasted several years. See Blecua, pp. 12–13.

62. Area of Toledo between the Cathedral and Zocodover Plaza inhabited mostly by conversos. See Francisco Rico, *La novela picaresca española,* (Barcelona: Clásicos Planeta, 1971), p. 61, n. 89.

63. In 1497 the basic monetary system of the unified kingdom of Spain was fixed upon the "excelente" (made of gold and called "ducado" beginning in 1504), the "real" (made of silver) and the "blanca" (also called "vellón"). The basic Castilian monetary unit, the "maravedí," established the relationship among these coins: The "ducado" was worth 375 maravedís, the "real" 34 and the "blanca" 2.5.

64. If, in fact, the writer of the novel is no stranger to the pulpit, the damnation or curse upon the house to which the squire constantly refers might be associated with the deceit and pretense with which he (and most of Spain) lives his daily existence. See *Jeremiah* 9:6 "thine habitation [is] in the midst of deceit; through deceit they refuse to know me, saith the Lord."

65. These are professional wailers called "endecheras" or "plañideras." They were restricted by the Inquisition, which deemed the practice a thing of Jews and pagans. "Las judías endecheras cantaban por dinero en los entierros de cristianos...." Alejo Carpentier, *El camino de Santiago*. It was common practice among Jews. See *Jeremiah* 9:20 "Yet hear the word of the Lord, O ye women, and let your ear receive the word of his mouth, and teach your daughters wailing, and every one her neighbor lamentation." Also *Jeremiah* 9:17, 9:18 and 9:19.

66. A main thoroughfare in Valladolid, today it is called "Platerías." Saint Peter Regalado, Patron Saint of Valladolid, was born on that street in 1390. The famous fire that ravaged Valladolid beginning on 21 September, 1561, started in a house on the corner of Costanilla and Cantarranas Streets.

67. Two gold castellanos were worth about 30 reales.

68. For a good background on the Order of Mercy, see Brodman, James W. *L'Ordre de la Merce: El rescat de captius a l'Espanya de les croades.* (Barcelona: Edicions dels Quaderns Crema, 1990); *Ransoming Captives in Crusader Spain: The Order of Merced on the Christian-Islamic Frontier.* (The Middle Ages Series. Philadelphia: University of Pennsylvania Press, 1986), and "The Origins of the Mercedarian Order: A Reassessment," *Studia monastica*, 19 (1977): 353–360. Also see Taylor, Bruce, *Structures of Reform: The Mercedarian Order in the Spanish Golden Age* (Boston: Brill, 2000). Founded on August 10, 1218 by Catalonian priest Saint Pedro Nolasco, one of its main missions was to ransom Christians enslaved in Moslem lands, a task for which Spain was especially fertile ground. Its Santa Catalina monastery in Toledo was substantially transformed in 1450. Pedro de Alcocer (*Historia o descripción de la imperial cibdad de Toledo*, Toledo, 1554, f. 113 *b*) states that after 1450 the friars considerably altered their previous, impeccably spiritual behavior. In Spanish America they were not known to be very earnest in their evangelizing, preferring the more secular pursuits. Their conduct noticeably displeased other churchmen, to the point where the Bishop of Guatemala once stated he'd like them expelled from the New World. In this regard see Bataillon, Marcel, *Novedad y fecundidad del Lazarillo de Tormes* (Salamanca: Anaya, 1968), p. 20. Considering their reputation, it would be unwise to overlook the homosexual connotations insinuated in this condensed and enigmatic chapter.

69. It was common practice for priests to refer to women with whom they had intimate relationships as "niece" and the like, using expressions denoting kinship.

70. "Bulderos," or sellers of bulls or indulgences, were among the lowest forms of life in Lázaro's Spain. Also called "echacuervos" and "embaucadores," they not only retailed bulls to repentant sinners, but also dealt in ointments, oils, herbs, stones and sundry other objects that they claimed had supernatural powers. In Cervantes we come across a buldero: "My name is Pedro Rincón. My father is a person of quality, as he is a minister of the Holy Crusade, that is to say, he is a bulero, like common people call them (although others call them echacuervos)" (*Rinconete y Cortadillo*, Porras ms., Avalle-Arce, I, 277. English translation is mine).

These indulgences for the remission of sin were delivered through the sale of the Papal Bull. This consisted of a paper document that was sealed with the "Bulla," the round wax seal that was supposed to certify it as legitimate. Dealers like the one portrayed here worked on commission, so it was to their advantage to sell as many as possible. Part of the proceeds also went to the king's coffers, and sheriffs or constables with their scribes went along with the dealers to ensure that the king and the Church got all that was coming to them.

Notes

The sale of indulgences was one of the most controversial and divisive issues in the XVI century. The practice effectively meant that for a certain amount of money you could buy forgiveness for your sins, a custom deemed so abominable by so many Christians that it was one of the main causes of the split of Western Christendom between Catholics and Protestants. An indulgence was the remission of all or a portion of the works of satisfaction demanded by the priest in the sacrament of penance. The Roman Catholic Church understands it as such even today. From contemporary sources, it appears that in Spain and much of western Europe it came to be considered as a remission of the penalty of sin itself, here and in purgatory; as a dismissal from the guilt of sin and from its penalty. But the exploitation of indulgences was a problem from earlier times. Innocent III (1160–1216) issued a decree intended to curb their abuse by limiting the time for which bishops could bestow indulgence to 40 days, periods of time called the quarantines. Thomas Aquinas (alluded to earlier by Lázaro) taught that souls in purgatory are covered by the jurisdiction of the Church here on earth, so indulgences may be granted not only to the living, but also to souls deemed to be in Purgatory, over which the earthly Church also has authority.

Indulgences came to be interpreted as a panacea, a quick and relatively painless way to get rid of your many sins and open the doors to paradise. Thus, the expression, "full remission of sins," (plena [or] plenissima remissio peccatorum,) is found continuously in papal bulls from the famous Portiuncula indulgence, granted by Honorius III to Saint Francis in 1216, to well into the 1600's.

Erasmus was a declared enemy of indulgences, a fact from which many have inferred that the author of the *Lazarillo* was a fervent Erasmist. In his *Praise of Folly,* he writes clearly about the deception of pardons and indulgences: "Or what should I say of them that hug themselves with their counterfeit pardons; that have measured purgatory by an hourglass, and can without the least mistake demonstrate its ages, years, months, days, hours, minutes, and seconds, as it were in a mathematical table? Or what of those who, having confidence in certain magical charms and short prayers invented by some pious impostor, either for his soul's health or profit's sake, promise to themselves everything: wealth, honor, pleasure, plenty, good health, long life, lively old age, and the next place to Christ in the other world, which yet they desire may not happen too soon, that is to say before the pleasures of this life have left them?" The type of mentality derided by Erasmus allowed priests to calculate the time of every soul's residence in purgatory and to allot them a longer or shorter stay according to the number of indulgences their family members bought. By this easy way of buying dismissal of sins any evildoer could lawfully come into God's good graces: "And now suppose some merchant, soldier, or judge, out of so many rapines, parts with some small piece of money. He straight conceives all that sink of his whole life quite cleansed; so many perjuries, so many lusts, so many debaucheries, so many contentions, so many murders, so many deceits, so many breaches of trusts, so many treacheries bought off, as it were by compact; and so bought off that they may begin upon a new score. But what is more foolish than those, or rather more happy, who daily reciting those seven verses of the Psalms promise to themselves more than the top of felicity? Which magical verses some devil or other, a merry one without doubt but more a blab of his tongue than crafty, is believed to have discovered to St. Bernard, but not without a trick. And these are so foolish that I am half ashamed of them myself, and yet they are approved, and that not only by the common people but even the professors of religion. And what, are not they also almost the same where several countries avouch to themselves their peculiar saint, and as everyone of them has his particular gift, so also his particular form of worship? As, one is good for the toothache; another for groaning women; a third, for stolen goods; a fourth, for making a voyage prosperous; and a fifth, to cure sheep of the rot; and so of the rest, for it would be too tedious to run over all. And some there are that are good for more things than one; but chiefly, the Virgin Mother, to whom the common people do in a manner attribute more than to the Son." It is apparent that the author of the *Lazarillo* has his characters act out many of the abuses and wrongs being perpetrated in the name of God by the Church and its servants, just as they are detailed by Erasmus in his *Praise of Folly* and other works.

Tyndale in answering a letter sent him by Sir Thomas More, wrote that "men might quench almost the terrible fire of hell for three halfpence." (In Gasquet, Francis Aidan, *The Eve of the Reformation,* 1899, p. 384). It is fair to say that indulgences had ill repute everywhere in Europe, although the extant copies of papal indulgences always attached the stipulation that to be truly pardoned, the purchaser of an indulgence must be "truly penitent and confessing their sins" (vere poenitentibus et confessio.) It is to be believed that indulgence sellers customarily claimed that their products had qualities with which they were not really endowed by Rome. James of Jüterbock in his *Tract. de indulg.* (ca. 1451) says he does not remember seeing or reading a single papal brief promising indulgence "a poena et culpa." (See W. Köhler: *Dokumente zum Ablassstreit,* Tubingen., 1902, p. 48.)

The *Lazarillo de Tormes* is a treasury of the many grievances held against contemporary Church practices and customs. The practice of prayer for profit, in which at least a couple of Lázaro's masters are proficient, is a case in point. Prayers had extraordinary offers of grace connected to them. As stated in the penitential book *The Soul's Joy,* the believer that offered its prayers to Mary would be the lucky recipient of 11,000 years' indulgence. Some other prayers liberated 15 souls from purgatory and pardoned 15 earthly sinners of their sins. One prayer made three times to St. Anna obtained for the sinner 5,000 years' indulgence for mortal sins and 20,000 for venial sins. Another text, *The Soul's Garden,* declared that one of Julius II's indulgences granted 80,000 years to anyone that offered a prayer to the Virgin that was, of course, included in the book, the same amount of time as one indulgence by Boniface VIII. (See *Hore Beatissime virginis Marie ad legitimum Sarisburiensis...,* Paris: F. Regnault, 1526, reprinted by Hoskins, London, 1901, especially 124–125)

71. Lázaro's statement that he will only recount one of his master's many transgressions demonstrates that the Alcalá addition, given at the end of this chapter in italics, is alien to the original text. The Alcalá addition recounts the pardoner's further exploits.

Many sources have been proposed for the story that follows, from Boccaccio to Sercambi di Luca, and from the *Till Eulenspiegel* to the Flemish (1547) version of the *Liber Vagatorum.* The most probable source, one proposed by Morel-Fatio and more recently by J.V. Ricapito, is the fourth novel of Masuccio's *Novellino.* Tommaso Guardati (Masuccio) was a member of a noble Italian family born in Sorrento or Salerno c. 1410, dying in Salerno in 1475. The *Novellino* is his only known work and consists of fifty tales divided into five parts (novels). It was published posthumously by Neapolitan writer and printer Francesco del Truppo in 1476. The fourth novel's introduction gives its synopsis: " Fra Girolamo of Spoleto makes the people of Sorrento believe that the bone of a certain dead body which he has gotten is the arm of St. Luke. His accomplice contradicts this statement, whereupon Fra Girolamo prays to God that he will demonstrate the truth of his words by the working of a miracle. Then the accomplice feigns to fall down dead, and Fra Girolamo by prayer restores him to life. Having by the fame of this double miracle collected a great sum of money, Fra Girolamo becomes a prelate, and hereafter lives a lazy life with his comrade." See J.V. Ricapito, "*Lazarillo de Tormes* (Chapter 5) and Masuccio's Fourth Novella," *Romance Philology*, XXIII [1970], pages 305–311.

72. A region in the northeastern part of the province of Toledo.

73. Luke 23:34 "Then said Jesus, Father, forgive them; for they know not what they do. And they parted his raiment, and cast lots." Also see Mark 11:25 "And when ye stand praying, forgive, if ye have ought against any: that your Father also which is in heaven may forgive you your trespasses." And Mark 11:26 "But if ye do not forgive, neither will your Father which is in heaven forgive your trespasses."

74. 1Peter 3:16 "Having a good conscience; that, whereas they speak evil of you, as of evildoers, they may be ashamed that falsely accuse your good conversation in Christ."

75. Ezekiel 33:11 "Say unto them, [As] I live, saith the Lord God, I have no pleasure in the death of the wicked; but that the wicked turn from his way and live: turn ye, turn ye from your evil ways; for why will ye die, O house of Israel?" See also Ezekiel 33:15 "[If] the wicked restore the pledge, give again that he had robbed, walk in the statutes of life, without committing iniquity; he shall surely live, he shall not die." Also 2Peter 3:9 "The Lord is not slack concerning his promise, as some men count slackness; but is longsuffering to us-ward, not willing that any should perish, but that all should come to repentance."

76. What follows in italics only appears in the Alcalá edition. This final part of chapter five, in style and substance, appears disjointed and inconsistent with the rest of the story; new characters show up out of nowhere and even Lázaro's role changes from that of a poor child following his master to that of an assistant that has an important role in his master's transactions.

77. Again we see the principal vocation of the Mercedarian Order being alluded to: the rescue of Christian captives from Moslem lands.

78. That is to say, not descended from Jewish or Moslem converts.

79. The type of roguery and general approach to the subject of priestly misconduct reminds the reader of Masuccio's *Novellino*. Each of the *Novellino's* tales commences with a dedication to an upper-class individual that is followed by a didactic "Exordium." In the Exordium the author enlightens the reader as to the features of the particular form of roguery or mischief being depicted, loosely mirrored by what Lázaro does with the enigmatic "Vuesa Merced." Tale 10, for example, narrates the misadventures of Fra Antonio de San Marcello, who through trickery sells the gift of Paradise to dim-witted parishioners for considerable amounts of money. Tale 18 has a friar of Saint Anthony obtain a piece of linen from a woman by pretending to cure two pigs who were not ill in the first place. Much like the cross incident in this chapter of the *Lazarillo*, the bad priest puts a lighted brand into the linen when he spots the woman's irate husband coming to retrieve it. As the man leaves with his linen, it experiences what seems like spontaneous combustion, which all take to be a miracle that proclaims the priest's innocence and benevolence. All the people in the village shower the priest with gifts, which he turns into cash at his earliest convenience. See W. G. Waters' two-volume translation, (London: Lawrence and Butler, 1895), vol. 1, pages 145–160 and 263–269.

80. The rogue in *Till Ulenspiegel* passed himself off as a painter in order to swin-

dle people. But, as Blecua points out, (p. 170, n. 320) there are old Spanish proverbs that point to a possible source in a Spanish story dealing with tambourine painters.

81. Town in the province of Segovia that was famous for its swords. The celebrated swordsmith Antonio, already mentioned in the text, had his workshop there. See Blecua, p. 171, n. 325.

82. These crooks are "retraídos," those who take refuge in a church after committing a crime. The long arm of justice did not extend into church grounds, and authorities could not follow lawbreakers into them.

83. What follows in italics is yet another addition in the Alcalá edition.

84. The mysterious "Vuesa Merced," or "Your Worship" to whom Lázaro tells his story is apparently his employer's superior, who may have asked Lázaro for particulars concerning his relationship with the Archpriest.

85. The spectacle of the town crier wearing the very recognizable pants of an archpriest must have been great fodder for gossips in their relentless assault on his wife.

86. What follows in italics is added to the Alcalá edition.

87. Lázaro literally says until Lauds. This is an office of solemn praise to God, the first of the canonical hours.

88. Again, a reference to cuckoldry.

89. Toledo was known for its prostitutes. Spain was perhaps the first nation in the world to try to control prostitution. Recared, King (586–601) of the Visigothic Kingdom of Spain, prohibited the practice and established tough penalties for everyone involved in it. By the beginning of the XVI century the *Ordenanzas de Sevilla*, a text containing rules and regulations for the practice of prostitution, was reprinted in one volume in Toledo, a city famous for its practitioners of the oldest profession. It was finished in 1527, in one volume with 37 chapters. One chapter reads: "Todas las concubinas en general, y en particular las de los eclesiásticos y las mujeres de costumbres sospechosas o escandalosas, no podrán llevar vestidos largos, ni velos, ni prenda alguna que las asemeje a las mujeres honestas. La misma prohibición alcanza a las mujeres públicas que corren el mundo." In other words: "All concubines in general, and in particular those of clerics and other women of suspicious or scandalous inclinations, will be prohibited from wearing long dresses, veils, or any article of clothing that might make them look like decent women. The same prohibition is in effect for public women who travel freely." Alfonso X's *Códice* prescribes the wearing of a saffron-colored ornament and a glittery headpiece in the "indecent" woman's hair as a sign of shame. Those who did not faced a fine of fifty maravedís and confiscation of their clothes. These women were also prohibited from using gold jewelry, pearls, silk clothing or any other article that might make them pass for "decent" women. See *De la prostitución en España. Compendio higiénico, estadístico y administrativo*, by. J. M. Guardia, printed as an annex to Parent-Duchâtelet. *De la prostitution dans la ville de Paris*, p. 774, 1857.

90. 1538

91. This last sentence, which I've written in italics, is an addition to the Alcalá edition.

Bibliography of Recent *Lazarillo* Studies

Albrecht, Jane W. "Linguistic Style and Point of View in Lazarillo de Tormes." Neophilologus, 77:2 (1993 Apr), pp. 223–28.

Allatson, Paul. "Policing the Picaresque: Lazarillo de Tormes and El buscón on Trial." Journal of Iberian and Latin American Studies, 1:1–2 (1995 Dec), pp. 119–27.

Archer, Robert. "Lazarillo de Tormes como carta de amenazas: Revaloración de una hipótesis de lectura." pp. 95–114. Núñez García-Saúco, Antonio (pref.). La enseñanza de la lengua y cultura españolas en Australia y Nueva Zelanda. Camberra — Madrid: Consejería de Educación de la Embajada de España — Iberediciones, 1993. 222 pp.

Asencio, Manuel J. "El Lazarillo en su circunstancia histórica." Revista de Literatura, 54:107 (1992 Jan–June), pp. 101–28.

Beckman, Pierina E. "Fantastic Elements within the Picaresque Genre: Lazarillo de Tormes (1555)." RLA: Romance Languages Annual, 3 (1991), pp. 354–56.

_____. "El valor literario del Lázaro de 1555: Género, evolución y metamorfosis." American University Studies II: Romance Languages and Literature. 153. New York: Peter Lang, 1991. xiii, 171 pp.

Blecua, Alberto. "La edición del Lazarillo de Medina del Campo (1554) y los problemas metodológicos de su filiación." Salina: Revista de Lletres, 17 (2003 Nov), pp. 59–70.

Boelcskevy, Mary Anne Stewart. "Narrating Cultural Transition: Lazarillo's Picaresque in the Twentieth Century." Dissertation Abstracts International, Section A: The Humanities and Social Sciences, 59:5 (1998 Nov), 1569. (Dissertation abstract).

Borowski de Llanos, Haydée; Ferrari de Zink, Silvia; García Saraví de Miranda, Mercedes. "'Lázaro,' 'Gardelito' y 'Eva': Tres nombres y una tradición." pp. 340–47. Martínez Cuitiño, Luis (ed.); Lois, Elida (ed.) and Barrenechea, Ana María (introd.). Actas del III Congreso Argentino de Hispanistas "España en América y América en España". Buenos Aires: Inst. de Filol. & Lits. Hispánicas, Facultad de Filosofía y Letras, Univ. de Buenos Aires, 1993. 1031 pp.

Bourret, Michel. "Trajets et trajectoires dans le Lazarillo de Tormes." Sociocriticism, 6:1–2 (11–12) (1990), pp. 19–31.

Bozzetto-Ditto, Lucienne. "L'Enfant et le vieillard dans La Vie de Lazarillo de Tormès, Kim, et Sans famille." pp. 149–69. Chauvin, Danièle (ed. & introd.) and Durand, Gilbert (postface). L'Imaginaire des âges de la vie. Grenoble: ELLUG, 1996. 322 pp. (1865–1936); Kim (1901).]

Brenes Carrillo, Dalai. "¿Quién es V. M. en Lazarillo de Tormes?." Boletin de la Biblioteca de Menendez Pelayo, 68 (1992), pp. 73–88.

Broncano, Manuel. "Del Tormes al Mississipi [Misisipí]: La tradición picaresca en España y los Estados Unidos." pp. 55–65. Álvarez Maurin, María José (ed. and foreword); Broncano, Manuel (ed. and foreword) and Chamosa, José Luis (ed. and foreword). Letras en el espejo: Ensayos de literatura americana comparada. León, Spain: Universidad de León, 1997. 213 pp.

Cabo Aseguinolaza, Fernando. "El caso admirable de Lázaro de Tormes: Otra vez sobre el prólogo del Lazarillo." Salina: Revista de Lletres, 8 (1994 Dec), pp. 29–32.

Carrasco, Félix. "'Esto fue el mesmo año que,' ¿anáfora de 'el caso' o del acto de escritura? (Lazarillo tract. VII)." Bulletin Hispanique, 93:2 (1991 July–Dec), pp. 343–52.

_____. "Hacia un nuevo estema de Lazarillo de Tormes: I. La relación de los Lazarillos de Alcalá y Medina. II. La relación de los Lazarillos de Burgos, Amberes y Medina." Voz y Letra: Revista de Literatura, 9:1 (1998), pp. 97–122.

_____. "La transmisión textual del Lazarillo a la luz de la edición de Medina del Campo (1554)." Edad de Oro, 18 (1999 Spring), pp. 47–70.

_____. "La vida de Lazarillo de Tormes, y de sus fortunas y adversidades." Ibérica. 23. New York, NY: Peter Lang, 1997. clv, 108 pp.

Casa, Frank P. "In Defense of Lázaro de Tormes." Crítica Hispánica, 19:1–2 (1997), pp. 87–98.

Castañedo Arriandiaga, Fernando. "La focalización en el relato autobiográfico." pp. 147–52. Romera Castillo, José (ed.). Escritura autobiográfica: Actas del II seminario internacional del instituto de semiótica literaria y teatral. Biblioteca Filológica Hispana. 14. Madrid: Visor, 1993. 505 pp.

Castillo, David; Spadaccini, Nicholas. "Lazarillo de Tormes and The Picaresque in Light of Current Political Culture." Crítica Hispánica, 19:1–2 (1997), pp. 128–40.

Charron, Marc. "Pour une critique interliminale des traductions du 'Lazarillo de Tormes'." Dissertation Abstracts International, Section A: The Humanities and Social Sciences, 62:10 (2002 Apr), 3365. (Dissertation abstract).

Colahan, Clark. "Epicurean vs. Stoic Debate and Lazarillo's Character." Neophilologus, 85:4 (2001 Oct), pp. 555–64.

Colahan, Clark and Rodríguez, Alfred. "De vuelta sobre la alusividad sexual del tratado IV del Lazarillo." Revista de Literatura, 61:121 (1999 Jan–June), pp. 215–23.

_____, and _____. Rodríguez, Alfred. "Juan Maldonado and Lazarillo de Tormes." Bulletin of Hispanic Studies, 72:3 (1995 July), pp. 289–311.

Colahan, Clark. "Imágenes hagiográficas de Cabeza en el Lazarillo." Hispanic Journal, 20:1 (1999 Spring), pp. 49–56.

_____, and _____. Rodríguez, Alfred. "¿Por qué se llaman 'tratados' los capítulos del Lazarillo?." Hispanófila, 130 (2000 Sept), pp. 21–25.
Coll-Tellechea, Reyes; Zahareas, Anthony N. "On the Historical Function of Narrative Forms: Lazarillo de Tormes." Crítica Hispánica, 19:1–2 (1997), pp. 110–27.
Colomer, José Luis. "Traducción y recepción: La lectura europea de la picaresca en Il picariglio castigliano de Barezzo Barezzi (1622)." Revista de Literatura, 53:106 (1991 July–Dec), pp. 391–443.
Cruz, Anne J. "The Abjected Feminine in the Lazarillo de Tormes." Crítica Hispánica, 19:1–2 (1997), pp. 99–109.
Cruz-Cámara, Nuria; Kaplan, Gregory. "Una revisitación franquista del Lazarillo de Tormes." pp. 27–42. Mínguez Arranz, Norberto (ed.). Literatura española y cine. Madrid, Spain: Complutense, 2002. ix, 214 pp.
Davies, Gareth Alban. "Lazarillo de Tormes and Don Quixote: The Role of Audience." pp. 9–27. Macklin, John (ed.). After Cervantes: A Celebration of 75 Years of Iberian Studies at Leeds. Leeds: Trinity and All Saints, 1993. 276 pp.
Dehennin, Elsa. "La Structure en abyme dans Lazarillo de Tormes." pp. 83–97. Maier-Troxler, Katharina (ed.); Maeder, Costantino (ed.) and Geninasca, Jacques (introd.). Fictio poetica. Florence, Italy: Cesati, 1998. 321 pp.
Díaz Balsera, Viviana. "Un diálogo cervantino con la picaresca: Intertextualidad, desplazamiento y apropiación en el Coloquio de los perros." Crítica Hispánica, 17:2 (1995), pp. 185–202.
El Saffar, Ruth. "The 'I' of the Beholder: Self and Other in Some Golden Age Texts." pp. 178–205.Brownlee, Marina S. (ed. & introd.) and Gumbrecht, Hans Ulrich (ed. & introd.). Cultural Authority in Golden Age Spain. Baltimore, MD: Johns Hopkins UP, 1995. xvii, 325 pp.
Febres, Eleodoro J. "Life of Lazarillo de Tormes: Evil Tongues, Unity and Success." Torre de Papel, 8:1 (1998 Spring), pp. 63–104.
Fernández, James D. "The Last Word, The First Stone: Lázaro's Legacy." Journal of Interdisciplinary Literary Studies, 5:1 (1993), pp. 23–37.
Ferro, Margarita. "Perversión del aprendizaje violento en el Tratado 1o de Lazarillo de Tormes: La violencia como construcción-destrucción de un sujeto (Un ejemplo renacentista: El lazarillo de Tormes — Tratado I)." Espéculo: Revista de Estudios Literarios, 23 (2003 Mar–June), (no pagination).
Ferver-Chivite, Manuel. "El de Lázaro de Tormes: ¿Caso o casos?." pp. I: 425–31. Vilanova, Antonio (ed.); Bricall, Josep Ma (fwd.) and Rivers, Elías L. (pref.). Actas del X Congreso de la Asociación de Hispanistas, I–IV. Barcelona: Promociones y Publicaciones Universitarias, 1992. xxxiv, 1851 + xiii, 1428 pp.
Fiore, Robert L. "Lazarillo de Tormes." Crítica Hispánica, 19:1–2 (1997).
_____. "Lazarillo de Tormes: The Sceptic Histor and the Poetics of Silence." Crítica Hispánica, 19:1–2 (1997), pp. 11–23.
Forcadas, Alberto M. "El entretejido de la Propalladia de Torres Naharro en el prólogo y tratado I del Lazarillo de Tormes." Revista de Literatura, 56:112 (1994 July–Dec), pp. 307–48.
_____. "El negro Zaide: Marginación social y textual en el Lazarillo." Hispania: A Jour-

nal Devoted to the Interests of the Teaching of Spanish and Portuguese, 76:1 (1993 Mar), pp. 20–29.
Fra-Molinero, Baltasar. "La identidad de Zaide y la parodia del amor cortés en el Lazarillo de Tormes." Romance Quarterly, 40:1 (1993 Winter), pp. 23–34.
Freire, Jesús. "La verdad dialógica en el 'Lazarillo de Tormes' según la filosofía de Martín Buber." Dissertation Abstracts International, Section A: The Humanities and Social Sciences, 57:1 (1996 July), 249. (Dissertation abstract).
Friedman, Edward H. "Coming to Terms with Lázaro's Prosperity: Framing Success in Lazarillo de Tormes." Crítica Hispánica, 19:1–2 (1997), pp. 41–56.
_____. "'Cómo se hace un autor': Lazarillo de Tormes and the Rigors of Anonymity." pp. 33–48. Galván, Delia V. (ed.); Stoll, Anita K. (ed.) and Brown Yin, Philippa (ed.). Studies in Honor of Donald W. Bleznick. Homenajes. 11. Newark, DE: Juan de la Cuesta, 1995. 218 pp.
Gabilondo, Angel. "El Eros como conversación." Edad de Oro, 9 (1990), pp. 69–80.
García-Gómez, Jorge. "Type and Concept in Lazarillo de Tormes: Self-Knowledge and the Spanish Picaresque Narrative." pp. 145–78. Tymieniecka, Anna-Teresa (ed.). Allegory Revisited: Ideals of Mankind. Analecta Husserliana. 41. Dordrecht: Kluwer Acad. under Auspices of World Inst. for Advanced Phenomenological Research and Learning, 1994. xv, 410 pp.
Gitlitz, David. "Inquisition Confessions and Lazarillo de Tormes." Hispanic Review, 68:1 (2000 Winter), pp. 53–74.
Gómez-Moriana, Antonio. "Du texte au discours: Le Concept d'interdiscursitivité." Versus: Quaderni di Studi Semiotici, 77–78 (1997 May–Dec), pp. 57–73.
González Echevarría, Roberto. "García Márquez y la voz de Bolívar." pp. 23–40. Engelbert, JoAnne (ed. and introd.) and Bono, Dianne (ed.). Hacia un nuevo canon literario. Inca Garcilaso Series. 603. Montclair, NJ — Hanover, NH: Montclair State University — Ediciones del Norte, 1995. xi, 176 pp.
Gornall, John. "Where Does the Prologue of Lazarillo End?." Neophilologus, 86:3 (2002 July), pp. 387–90.
Guerra Bosch, Teresa. "Los héroes cómicos del 'Lazarillo'." pp. 557–69. Quintana, R. M. (ed.) and Arencibia, Yolanda (ed. and foreword). Homenaje a Alfonso Armas Ayala. Las Palmas de Gran Canaria, Spain: Cabildo de Gran Canaria, 2000. 1600 pp.
Guevara-Geer, Geoffrey W. "Lazarillo de Tormes and the Little Tramp of Modern Times: Two Modern Pícaros Find Their Ways." Canadian Review of Comparative Literature/Revue Canadienne de Littérature Comparée, 24:2 (1997 June), pp. 235–45.
Halvonik, Brent Norman. "The Rhetoric of Picaresque Irony: A Study of the 'Satyricon' and 'Lazarillo de Tormes'." Dissertation Abstracts International, Section A: The Humanities and Social Sciences, 61:5 (2000 Nov), 1827. (Dissertation abstract).
Hart, Thomas R. "Renaissance Dialogue and Narrative Fiction: The Viaje de Turquía." Modern Language Review, 95:1 (2000 Jan), pp. 107–13.
Herráiz de Tresca, Teresa. "La casa lóbrega y triste y la imagen del mundo en el Lazarillo." pp. II: 192–95. Vanbiesem de Burbridge, Martha (ed. and presentation).

II Coloquio Internacional de Literatura Comparada: 'El cuento,' I–II. Buenos Aires, Argentina: Fundación María Teresa Maiorana, 1995. 133, 319 pp.
Hoffmeister, Gerhart. "Adaptation as Acculturation: The Picaro's Birth as Schelm in German Literature." Prism(s): Essays in Romanticism, 7 (1999), pp. 105–14.
Iarocci, Michael P. "Alegoría, parodia, y teatro en el Lazarillo de Tormes." Revista Canadiense de Estudios Hispanicos, 19:2 (1995 Winter), pp. 327–40.
_____. "Lázaro and Oedipus: Notes on the Structural Unity of Lazarillo de Tormes." RLA: Romance Languages Annual, 2 (1990), pp. 459–61.
Incledon, John. "Textual Subversion in Lazarillo de Tormes and Don Quixote." Indiana Journal of Hispanic Literatures, 5 (1994 Fall), pp. 161–80.
Jones, R. O. "La vida de Lazarillo de Tormes y de sus fortunas y adversidades." Manchester, England: Manchester Univ. Press, 1993. 89 pp.
Jungman, Robert E.; Lewis, Tom J. "Some Unnoticed Classical Allusions and Topoi in the Last Paragraph of the Preface to Lazarillo de Tormes." Classical and Modern Literature: A Quarterly, 12:4 (1992 Summer), pp. 327–32.
Kennedy, Joan Marlene. "The Philosophical Picaresque from 'Lazarillo de Tormes' to Camus' 'The Plague.'" Dissertation Abstracts International, 54:11 (1994 May), 4083A. (Dissertation abstract)
Laurenti, Joseph L. "La imagen de las mujeres en la Segunda parte de la vida de Lazarillo de Tormes ... (1620), de Juan de Luna." La Torre: Revista de la Universidad de Puerto Rico, 4:14 (1990 Apr–June), pp. 181–95.
Lefkowitz, Linda S. "The Squire Goes to Mass: Retrieving Festive Meaning in Lazarillo de Tormes." Hispanic Journal, 12:2 (1991 Fall), pp. 211–21.
Lepetit, Jean-Claude. "La recepción del 'Lazarillo de Tormes' en las traducciones al francés e inglés del siglo XVI." Dissertation Abstracts International, Section A: The Humanities and Social Sciences, 61:3 (2000 Sept), 976. (Dissertation abstract).
López, Victoriano Roncero. "Lazarillo, Guzmán, and Buffoon Literature." MLN, 116:2 (2001 Mar), pp. 235–49.
Lozano Yagüe, Salvador. "La función semio-literaria de los recursos proxémicos en el Lazarillo de Tormes." Signa: Revista de la Asociación Española de Semiótica, 7 (1998), pp. 217–31.
Maorino, Giancarlo. "Picaresque Econopoetics: At the Watershed of Living Standards." pp. 1–39. Maiorino, Giancarlo (ed. and introd.). The Picaresque: Tradition and Displacement. Hispanic Issues. 12. Minneapolis, MN: U of Minnesota P, 1996. xxviii, 318 pp.
Maroto Camino, Mercedes. "Practising Places: Saint Teresa, Lazarillo and the Early Modern City." Portada Hispanica. 10. Amsterdam, Netherlands: Rodopi, 2001. 189 pp.
Martino, Alberto. "Die Rezeption des Lazarillo de Tormes im deutschen Sprachraum (1555/62-1750)." Daphnis: Zeitschrift für Mittlere Deutsche Literatur, 26:2–3 (1997), pp. 301–99.
Merino, Eloy E. "El nuevo Lazarillo de Camilo J. Cela: Política y cultura en su palimpsesto." Lewiston, NY: Mellen, 2000. vii, 372 pp.
Merino, Eloy Eduardo. "'Nuevas andanzas y desventuras de Lazarillo de Tormes':

Política y cultura en el palimpsesto de Camilo José Cela." Dissertation Abstracts International, Section A: The Humanities and Social Sciences, 59:9 (1999 Mar), 3483. (Dissertation abstract).
Moore, Roger Gerald. "Post-Influence, Proto-Intertextuality: Pablos's Rewrite of Lazarillo's House of Death." RLA: Romance Languages Annual, 7 (1995), pp. 555–61.
Morrow, J. A. "El protestantismo de Juan de Luna." Lemir: Revista Electrónica sobre Literatura Española Medieval y del Renacimiento, 5 (2001), (no pagination).
_____. "De cómo Lázaro de Tormes tal vez no escribió el prólogo a su obra." Insula: Revista de Letras y Ciencias Humanas, 661–662 (2002 Jan–Feb), pp. 10–12.
_____. "Sobre la fecha y el autor de La vida de Lazarillo de Tormes." Insula: Revista de Letras y Ciencias Humanas, 666 (2002 June), pp. 7–13.
Nowak, Stanley J., Jr. "The Blindman's New Function: An Exemplum of the Capital Sin of Anger in Lazarillo de Tormes." Hispania: A Journal Devoted to the Teaching of Spanish and Portuguese, 73:4 (1990 Dec), pp. 900–05.
_____. "The 'cerrar/puerta' Imagery and the Theme of Hopelessness in Tractado segundo of Lazarillo." Hispanic Journal, 11:2 (1990 Fall), pp. 47–55.
_____. "A New Perspective on Tractado primero of Lazarillo de Tormes: The Structural Prophecy." Hispania: A Journal Devoted to the Teaching of Spanish and Portuguese, 73:2 (1990 May), pp. 324–31.
Parr, James A. "Rhetoric and Referentiality: Historical Allusiveness and Artful Innuendo." Crítica Hispánica, 19:1–2 (1997), pp. 75–86.
_____, and Mayer, María Eugenia. "El apartamiento y la herida voceada: Jesuitas, místicos, pícaros." pp. 65–80. Tibbitts, Mercedes Vidal (ed. and introd.) and Paolini, Claire J. (biography). Studies in Honor of Gilberto Paolini. Homenajes. 12. Newark, DE: Cuesta, 1996. xxxi, 496 pp.
Paterson, Alan K. G. "The Englishing of Lazarillo de Tormes." pp. 129–54, in Friedman, Edward H. (ed. and introd.) and Sturm, Harlan (ed.). "Never-Ending Adventure": Studies in Medieval and Early Modern Spanish Literature in Honor of Peter N. Dunn. Homenajes. 19. Newark, DE: Cuesta, 2002. 439 pp.
Pereira Zazo, Oscar. "La perspectiva del Lazarillo de Tormes." Torre de Papel, 5:2 (1995 Summer), pp. 55–79.
Piñero Ramírez, Pedro M. "Lázaro de Tormes (el original y el de los atunes), caballero en clave paródica." Bulletin Hispanique, 96:1 (1994), pp. 133–51.
_____. "Lázaro entre los doctores o la sátira de los saberes universitarios." Romanistisches Jahrbuch, 41 (1990), pp. 326–39.
Piskunova, S. I. "Roman. Rech'. Pis'mo: 'Don Kikhot' i Lasaril'o de Tormes'." Vestnik Moskovskogo Universiteta. Seriia 9, Filologiia, 3 (1998 May–June), pp. 30–40.
Rabell, Carmen R. "La confesión en jerigonza del Lazarillo de Tormes." Bulletin of Hispanic Studies, 73:1 (1996 Jan), pp. 19–32.
Redondo, Augustin. "Censura, literatura y transgresión en época de Felipe II: El Lazarillo castigado de 1573." Edad de Oro, 18 (1999 Spring), pp. 135–49.
Reed, Helen H. "Dining with Lazarillo: The Discourse of Pleasure in Lazarillo de Tormes." Crítica Hispánica, 19:1–2 (1997), pp. 57–74.

Rey Poveda, Juan José del. "El Tratado primero del Lazarillo de Tormes." Espéculo: Revista de Estudios Literarios, 17 (2001 Mar–June), (no pagination).

Ricapito, Joseph V. "Commonality of Thought: Juan Luis Vives and Lazarillo de Tormes." Crítica Hispánica, 19:1–2 (1997), pp. 24–40.

Rico, Francisco. "Lazarillo de Tormes." pp. 95–98. Reichenberger, Kurt (ed.) and Reichenberger, Theo (ed.). Siete siglos de autores españoles. Kassel: Reichenberger, 1991. 362 pp.

Ridley, Alison Jane. "Variations on the Use of Silence in Four Spanish Picaresque Novels: The Picaros' Quest for a Voice." Dissertation Abstracts International, 53:1 (1992 July), 171A. (Dissertation abstract).

Rodríguez, Alfred and Aleixandre, Eduardo. "Sobre la intensidad irónica del comienzo del Lazarillo." Quaderni Ibero-Americani: Attualita Culturale della Penisola Iberica e America Latina, 75 (1994 June), pp. 65–69.

Rodríguez, Alfred and Billat, Astrid. "Algo más sobre el tratado VI del Lazarillo." Hispanófila, 113 (1995 Jan), pp. 11–17.

Rodríguez, Alfred and Cornejo-Patterson, Deanna. "Una nota sobre el 'padrastro' de Lazarillo." Revista de Literatura, 54:108 (1992 July–Dec), pp. 641–44.

Rodríguez, Alfred and McLoughlin, Betsy W. "Algo más sobre el 'arrimarse a los buenos' del Lazarillo." Hispanic Journal, 16:2 (1995 Fall), pp. 417–20.

Rodríguez, Alfredo and Pernia, José Rafael. "La 'casa encantada' del escudero del Lazarillo." Neuphilologische Mitteilungen: Bulletin de la Societe Neophilologique/ Bulletin of the Modern Language Society, 95:4 (1994), pp. 389–91.

Rodríguez, Alfred and Romero, Yolanda. "La posibilidad anti-judaizante del tratado segundo del Lazarillo." Bulletin Hispanique, 96:1 (1994), pp. 227–34.

Rodríguez Gallardo, Angel. "Complementos preposicionales argumentales con verbos de dirección en español clásico." pp. I: 735–46. García Turza, Claudio (ed. and preface); González Bachiller, Fabián (ed.) and Mangado Martínez, Javier (ed.). Actas del IV Congreso Internacional de Historia de la Lengua Española, I-II. Logroño, Spain: Universidad de la Rioja, 1998. 910 + 973 pp.

Rosario-Angleró, Margarita del. "La influencia de las teorías sobre la educación en Quintiliano en La vida de Lázaro de Tormes y Guzmán de Alfarache." pp. 1129–37. Albaladejo, Tomás (ed. and foreword); Del Río, Emilio (ed. and foreword); Caballero, José Antonio (ed. and foreword); Fernández López, Jorge (index) and Gómez Alonso, Juan Carlos (index). Quintiliano: Historia y actualidad de la retórica, I-III. Colección Quintiliano de Retórica y Comunicación. 2 (1–3). Logroño, Spain — Calahorra, Spain: Instituto de Estudios Riojanos — Ayuntamiento de Calahorra, 1998. 1563 pp.

Rovatti, Loreta. "Interrelaciones entre tiempo y espacio en el Nuevo Lazarillo de Cela." Insula: Revista de Letras y Ciencias Humanas, 45:518–519 (1990 Feb.–Mar.), pp. 61–63.

Ruffinato, Aldo. "Notas sobre el Lazarillo de Medina del Campo, 1554." Incipit, 16 (1996), pp. 189–204.

_____. "La princeps del Lazarillo, toda problemas." Revista de Filología Española, 70:3–4 (1990 July–Dec), pp. 249–96.

Ruffinatto, Aldo. "Medina y las nuevas fronteras textuales del Lazarillo." Voz y Letra: Revista de Literatura, 9:2 (1998), pp. 87–121.

Sackett, Theodore Alan. "Juan Criollo de Carlos Loveira: De la picaresca a la revolución." Monographic Review/Revista Monográfica, 15 (1999), pp. 161–69.

Sáinz, José Angel. "Lazarillo de Tormes o la conciencia de una nueva normativa." República de las Letras, 61 (1999 Mar), pp. 41–54.

Sánchez, Angel. "Lázaro y su alternativa a la pobreza." Crítica Hispánica, 19:1–2 (1997), pp. 141–50.

_____. "Tres espacios temporales en el Lazarillo." Hispanic Journal, 16:1 (1995 Spring), pp. 161–67.

Santos, Teresa de. "La picaresca y las formas didácticas." Analecta Malacitana: Revista de la Sección de Filología de la Facultad de Filosofía y Letras, 13:1 (1990), pp. 35–37.

Santoyo y Mediavilla, Julio-César. "La vida de Lazarillo de Tormes y de sus fortunas y aduersidades, Burgos, Amberes y Alcalá de Henares, 1554/The Plesaunt Historie of Lazarillo de Tormes a Spaniarde, wherein is conteined his marueilous deedes and life, London, 1568." pp. 11–24. Sánchez Escribano, F. Javier (ed. and introd.). Picaresca española en traducción inglesa (ss. XVI y XVII): Antología y estudios. Zaragoza, Spain: Universidad de Zaragoza, 1998. 206 pp.

Sears, Theresa Ann. "Sight Unseen: Blindness, Form, and Reform in the Spanish Picaresque Novel." Bulletin of Spanish Studies: Hispanic Studies and Researches on Spain, Portugal, and Latin America, 80:5 (2003 Sept), pp. 531–43.

Selig, Karl-Ludwig. "Lazarillo de Tormes, tratado 3, and the Mediating Inter-Text." pp. 92–94. Baasner, Frank (ed.). Spanische Literatur-Literatur Europas: Wido Hempel zum 65. Geburtstag. Tübingen: Niemeyer, 1996. viii, 551 pp.

_____. "Observations on Some 'Supporting' Characters in Lazarillo de Tormes: A Matter of Perspective." pp. 26–27. Hölz, Karl (ed.); Jüttner, Siegfried (ed.); Stillers, Rainer (ed.) and Strosetzki, Christoph (ed.). Sinn und Sinnverständnis: Festschrift für Ludwig Schrader zum 65. Geburtstag. Berlin, Germany: Schmidt, 1997. 302 pp.

Severin, Dorothy S. "Pármeno, Lazarillo y las novelas ejemplares." Insula: Revista de Letras y Ciencias Humanas, 633 (1999 Sept), p. 26.

Shipley, George A. "'Otras cosillas que no digo': Lazarillo's Dirty Sex." pp. 40–65. Maiorino, Giancarlo (ed. and introd.). The Picaresque: Tradition and Displacement. Hispanic Issues. 12. Minneapolis, MN: U of Minnesota P, 1996. xxviii, 318 pp.

Sifuentes, Jáuregui B. "The Swishing of Gender: Homographetic Marks in Lazarillo de Tormes." pp. 123–40. Molloy, Sylvia (ed. and introd.) and Irwin, Robert McKee (ed. and introd.). Hispanisms and Homosexualities. Durham, NC: Duke UP, 1998. xvi, 319 pp.

Silverman, Joseph H. "The Meaning of Hunger in Lazarillo de Tormes." pp. 283–90. Gerli, E. Michael (ed.) and Sharrer, Harvey L. (ed.). Hispanic Medieval Studies in Honor of Samuel G. Armistead. Madison: Hispanic Seminary of Medieval Studies, 1992. 301 pp.

Sitler, Robert. "The Presence of Jesus Christ in Lazarillo de Tormes." Dactylus, 12 (1993), pp. 85–97.

Suárez-Galbán Guerra, Eugenio. "De la Vida de Torres a la de Lázaro de Tormes: Burguesía y picaresca." pp. 141–54. Pérez López, Manuel María (ed.) and Martínez Mata, Emilio (ed.). Revisión de Torres Villarroel. Acta Salmanticensia Estudios Filológicos. 270. Salamanca, Spain: Universidad de Salamanca, 1998. 216 pp.

_____. "Parody in the 'Lazarillo de Tormes'." Dissertation Abstracts International, 54:10 (1994 Apr), 3770A. (Dissertation abstract).

Tirado, Pilar del Carmen. "Parody, Poverty and the Lazarillo de Tormes." Hispanófila, 115 (1995 Sept), pp. 1–10.

Tomita, Ikuko. "La Celestina, La Lozana y el Lazarillo: El germen del género picaresco español." Dissertation Abstracts International, Section A: The Humanities and Social Sciences, 58:9 (1998 Mar), 3555–56. (Dissertation abstract).

Tomlinson, Janis A.; Welles, Marcia L. "Picturing the Picaresque: Lazarillo and Murillo's Four Figures on a Step." pp. 66–85. Maiorino, Giancarlo (ed. and introd.). The Picaresque: Tradition and Displacement. Hispanic Issues. 12. Minneapolis, MN: U of Minnesota P, 1996. xxviii, 318 pp.

Torrijos de Fides, Alicia. "'Beso las manos de Vuestra Merced': Alegoría, decodificación y la figura del 'beau semblant' en Lazarillo de Tormes." Bulletin of Hispanic Studies, 75:1 (1998 Jan), pp. 45–63.

Torris-Horwitt, C. Aída. "Lazarillo en su historia." Dissertation Abstracts International, Section A: The Humanities and Social Sciences, 61:12 (2001 June), 4799. (Dissertation abstract).

Vallarino, Jesús María. "Leer el Lazarillo de Tormes hoy." Razón y Fe: Revista Hispanoamericana de Cultura, 238:1199–1200 (1998 Sept–Oct), pp. 224–32.

Vaquero Serrano, María del Carmen. "Una posible clave para el Lazarillo de Tormes: Bernardino de Alcaraz, ¿El arcipreste de San Salvador?." Lemir: Revista Electrónica sobre Literatura Española Medieval y del Renacimiento, 5 (2001), (no pagination).

Whitenack, Judith A. "'Cronista y no autor': Juan de Luna's Lazarillo." Hispanic Journal, 15:1 (1994 Spring), pp. 45–62.

Wolff, Maria Tai. "The Telling Situation." Dissertation Abstracts International, 51:1 (1990 July), 158A.

Ynduráin, Domingo. "El renacimiento de Lázaro." Hispania: A Journal Devoted to the Teaching of Spanish and Portuguese, 75:3 (1992 Sept), pp. 474–83.

_____. "Play and Laughter in Lazarillo de Tormes." Hispanófila, 127 (1999 Sept), pp. 1–17.

Yovanovich, Gordana. "Play and the Picaresque: Lazarillo de Tormes, Libro de Manuel, and Match Ball." Toronto, ON: Univ. of Toronto Press, 1999. x, 152 pp.

Index

Index